Winds of Change
Mary Metcalfe

ALSO BY MARY METCALFE:

"NEW BEGINNINGS"
"ROAD TO TOMORROW"

Acknowledgements

Over the course of writing Winds of Change, many people were wonderfully supportive. I am particularly grateful to an editor at The Wild Rose Press who recommended I join the Romance Writers of America Women's Fiction chapter. Joining RWA opened up a whole new world of online learning and contacts, including my wonderful critique partner Anne Crowder, a Texan who lives and writes in France. Anne's advice along the way saw me through a major re-write of whole sections of the book and was instrumental in making it a much better product. Thank you Anne.

And to all the others who provided support and advice: Pat Hunter, Lauren Evans, Ruth Edgett, Greg Ioannou and Ellen Henderson. I took all your words to heart.

Finally, to my husband Jacques Chenail and our daughter and a fellow author, Danielle Metcalfe-Chenail – we have always encouraged each other to chase our dreams. Thank you for your love and support while I chased mine. This book is for you.

Dedicated to the memory of
Shirley Theresa Barrett

You have a strong voice through your children,
grandchildren and great-grandson

Chapter 1

Jennifer Barrett was almost sprinting down the long hallway when she heard her name being called out. "Jennifer. Hold up a second." She was so focused on getting to her father's room she found it difficult to slow down. Her pulse was racing as she slowed her steps and finally turned around. "I'm pretty sure your dad is okay." A petite young nurse caught up to her. "Dr. Anderson is checking him over now."

"Hi Lana. Got here as fast as I could." She willed her breathing and heart rate to slow down as she absorbed the news. "What happened this time?"

"It looks like he went back to his room after breakfast and tripped. He went down between the bed and the window. Sprained his wrist as he tried to break the fall." Lana Fitzpatrick looked up into Jennifer's worried face. "He refuses to use a walker. We've all been concerned this might happen."

"The nurse who called was talking about calling an ambulance. The traffic was so sluggish. It took me forever to get here."

"Judging by his complaining, I'd say he's fine. He really hates anyone fussing over him."

"My father is such a curmudgeon." Jennifer was feeling more reassured. She smiled and sighed. "I don't know how my mother put up with him for over fifty years. It's only gotten worse with the Alzheimer's. He gets frustrated so easily."

"Dr. Anderson'll page me when it's clear for you to come up. I examined him. There are no broken bones as far as I could tell but his right wrist will be sore for awhile. He's got a nasty gash on his right temple, which I sutured." Lana was the charge nurse for Art Severn's floor. Jennifer patted down some silver hairs that were beginning to salt her auburn bob. The movement helped her loosen up, if only slightly.

"I can't help it. I won't be able to relax until I see him for myself."

"Won't be long. I expect a page in a few minutes. I brought Danny with me today. He has a dentist appointment after lunch. Let's check up on him while we're waiting." Lana guided Jennifer along the brightly lit hall towards a sun-drenched solarium. As they walked arm in arm along the long corridor, Jennifer smiled at residents she recognized and said hello. "I remember the day he moved in permanently. He was so confused and upset. He couldn't really remember you or Brentwood from his respite stays." Jennifer waved to an elderly resident in a wheelchair. "He demanded I take him home. It almost broke my heart to have to tell him no."

"He wanted to go back home in no uncertain terms. I haven't been lectured like that since nursing school and never as sternly." Lana chuckled at the memory. "You managed to calm him down and stop threatening to leave. I was impressed." Jennifer remembered being surprised the young nurse had handled her father so adroitly. She was young enough to be his granddaughter.

"I overpowered him with sweetness and charm." Lana's slight Irish lilt carried the humor in her voice. "He just couldn't resist the Fitzpatrick magic. But really, I think it was when we took him out to the gardens. As soon as he started to talk gardening with Fred, I knew he'd be fine."

"I wasn't so sure. I had to really cajole him into going for that ride. Told him we were going to visit the place with the pretty gardens. But he'd seen me put the suitcases in the trunk. Somehow he knew he wouldn't be going back home."

"You didn't have a choice."

"I know." Jennifer shook her head slowly. "I think every child wants their parents to live forever and be strong and healthy."

"Doesn't work that way. It's called life."

"True enough. True enough." Jennifer shook her head again and looked at Lana. "Would you and Danny like to come over for dinner this Sunday?" She and Lana had forged a strong friendship over the past few years. She was even honorary aunt to her son. "Sure. My turn to make dessert."

"You're on. Just make it a diet dessert."

"No such thing in my cookbook." They laughed. No-one could resist one of Lana's confections. There always seemed to be a plate of something enticing at the nursing station. Banana bread, muffins or oatmeal cookies. Cheesecake was a specialty.

Rounding a corner, they strolled into a large, airy room scattered with groupings of couches, tables, chairs, a piano and bookcases. Some tables held fresh flower arrangements and magazines. At one end, Ellen Degeneres was rocking her daily dance on a large television screen. At first glance, it seemed the room was full of seniors. Then they heard the sound of a child's laughter. "Mom! Come see this. Ever cool!" The pint-sized caller waved his arms energetically, drawing them to a corner of the room with a small television. Lana could feel his vibrating excitement from several feet away.

"What's up Danny?" Lana looked on as her son waved a game controller and pointed at the screen. Looking closer, she realized her little guy was in the midst of a spelling lesson with his favorite superhero. "It's the first time I've seen it." Danny turned back to the screen. "The bad guys have messed up the spelling of all the street signs. Spider-Man needs my help to get them right again. Isn't it neat? Wish I had one. Maybe for my birthday? Hi Aunt Jennifer. When can I come see Charlie?" Danny's questions stopped abruptly as he turned back to the game.

"You're coming over for Sunday dinner." Jennifer sat on the arm of the chair and peered down at the screen.

"Charlie told me this morning you need to come and play."

"Charlie's a dog. He can't talk."

"All animals can talk to us if we know how to listen. Charlie keeps running to the back gate. That tells me he needs time with a friend like you." Danny was focused intently on the spelling game.

"Your birthday is coming up pretty soon, right?"

"I'll be five years old on June twenty-sixth," he bragged, without taking his eyes off the screen.

"Starting school come September?"

"Yeah, I'm gonna be too old for that day care thing." Danny was arranging and rearranging letters on the screen. Jennifer smiled and stood up as Lana reached out to tousle his hair.

Lana's pager had gone off.

"I'm going to take Aunt Jennifer to see her father. You good to stay here and help Spider-Man?" Danny nodded vigorously. He didn't look up as they left; his eyes were glued to the game. A few minutes later the two women walked into Art Severn's sun-bathed room. A young doctor standing by the window turned as they came in. "Jennifer, hi. Art here decided to do some dancing after breakfast and collided with his bedside table." They avoided calling him Jennifer's father. It upset him.

"How are you feeling?" Jennifer winced at her father's bruised face and bandaged forehead. He was tenderly cradling his right wrist. "That was a pretty bad fall I hear."

"Hello miss. I am doing just fine thank you. Had a little spill is all. Why are you here?" Her father was reclining on his bed but Jennifer could see he wasn't comfortable.

"I thought if you feel up to it we could go outside and see how the flower beds are doing." She looked over at the doctor, who nodded. Her father didn't seem any the worse for his accident. No sign of concussion. He was bright and alert. "I need to get going Jennifer." The doctor's pager sounded. "Lana, please be sure he's monitored every hour for the next twenty-four hours. And, Mr. Severn, please use your walker. If you'd been using it this probably wouldn't have happened." Art looked at bit sheepish but stubbornly held his ground.

"I can walk perfectly fine without one of those contraptions."

"No, you can't." The doctor was firm. "Lana, he's to use a wheelchair until the wrist is healed. Please post it on his chart. After that, walker at all times." He left the room before there was any further argument from his cantankerous patient. Lana went to find a spare wheelchair. "I'd like to go outside miss." Art Severn had been an avid gardener and knew the names of all the flowering shrubs and perennials that graced the garden beds around Jennifer's childhood home. For over fifty-five years he wouldn't hear of missing the New England Spring Flower Show.

"It's very kind of you to offer to go with me. I want to see if they have any coreopsis. Every garden should have some coreopsis. My particular favorite is Crème Brulée, although you can't go wrong with Zagreb or Moonbeam."

He refused Jennifer's offer of help, getting off the bed stiffly as Lana returned and positioned a wheelchair in front of him. "And hostas. In my garden beds I have eight varieties of hostas.

Not everyone knows there are over a dozen varieties of hostas." As Lana helped Jennifer's father transfer from his chair into the wheelchair, he continued to lecture them about gardens and proper varieties for Boston's temperate climate. Jennifer accepted that her father didn't know her today. It was enough, she supposed, that she still had her father and that there were still rare days when he remembered her.

"Lana, thanks for everything. I'm so glad you were on shift when this happened." Jennifer took her father out into the bright sunny gardens as Lana went back to her other duties. "I can't stay very long today. I have a meeting at two and the traffic is always bad." He never asked what she did or why she was visiting unless he was having a really good day. "You really should use your walker you know. You could walk further and sit down on it when you want to stop to look at the flowers."

"Those azaleas over there need pruning. They're overgrown and crowding their neighbours." Her father ignored the suggestion. "I'll speak to someone about it." There was no point in belaboring a point with him. Once, logic and reasoning would have swayed him if he was in the mood. Now he rarely listened, offering complaints and observations to everyone around him. After a leisurely stroll dominated by her father's view of what needed to be done in the gardens, she wheeled him into the solarium where Danny was still engrossed in his spelling game.

"Here's a good spot. You can see the flowers from here. I'll be back tomorrow." She squeezed his shoulders and kissed his cheek. "I have to get back to the hospital now for a meeting. I love you."

"Thank you taking me to see the flowers. Please come back any time."

As she made her way across the busy core of Boston, Jennifer thought about how much her father was changing. The tall angular man of her youth was morphing before her eyes. Watching him struggle to get off the bed, she'd seen a stoop to his shoulders she hadn't noticed before. I never imagined him using a walker,

let alone a wheelchair. Today is the first time in my life I've ever seen him in a wheelchair. Jennifer blinked back hot tears.

Turning into the hospital entrance she drove into the employee parking lot, circling it a couple of times before finding a spot. Later, as she listened to a colleague wrapping up yet another Alzheimer's patient update, she thought of her father. She could easily imagine how the family felt.

When it was her turn, Jennifer was ready. "The patient is eighty-four years old, has advanced Alzheimer's and is diabetic. He has no family in Massachusetts. He's been screened for MassHealth and will need to be discharged to long-term care. I've sent the forms through but it could be a week or more before a bed opens up. He needs assisted living with full services including security. We can't keep him here now that he's stabilized. He can no longer live alone."

Jennifer wearily massaged her temple with one hand as she used the other to close the final file for the day. Her colleagues were all gathering up their files as the meeting ended. The hospital's psychiatric caseload was growing quickly with dementias among seniors. Many had multiple health issues, making their care complex and challenging for the entire system. She sprinted to catch up with her boss.

"John, I'm going to put a priority on seeing what we can do for Mr. Ellis to ensure he doesn't slip through any cracks. He was not in good shape when he was brought in. His daughter is arranging to come in from Ohio. She'll be here within the next two days. We need to find a bed as soon as possible. She said she can stay for a week to ten days but then she has to get back to family and work. She'd like to be here to help him get settled wherever we can get a placement."

Jennifer thought of the conversation she'd had with the distraught daughter, who believed she had a network of supports for her widowed father. She didn't realize her father had been refusing to allow health care workers in to care for him.

"Does she have a durable medical power of attorney?" Jennifer's director was equal parts business and compassion. The durable medical power of attorney would ensure all arrangements could be made for this patient through the daughter without going to court for a guardianship hearing.

"Yes, thank goodness. One less thing to worry about." Thinking of her father, Jennifer was relieved they had reached the same agreement years earlier, long before dementia robbed him of his competence.

As she walked back into her office she thought, I definitely need my exercise class today, She shut down her computer and prepared to leave.

"Let's go girls." The sounds of Shania Twain feeling like a woman blared out of the speakers as twenty women of various sizes and shapes shifted into a last burst of high speed spinning. They were almost finished. Jennifer could feel her tension evaporating along with a good round of sweat.

"I'm getting too old for this," her friend Carol finished a long catlike stretch to wind down the session. "I'm forty-three and single. I have a great job, making great money. My kids are off to college. You'd think I'd know how to find the right kind of guy by now. But no, I fall for a schmuck years younger than me with bedroom eyes who can't hold on to a job or the money that comes with it. So what does that make me?"

Jennifer wiped a towel over her moist brow and grinned mischievously, "Well, apart from being a cougar I guess that would make you human?"

"Me? A cougar?" Carol leaned over and stretched again. "I'm going to take that as a compliment. Why not? But, seriously, I can look at a property and come within dollars of its appraised value. I can negotiate and close a sale with the best of them. Hell, I'm in the top ten in Boston. So why do the true motives of men continue to elude me? It's not like I didn't kick husband number one out to the curb when I found him cheating with a girl half his age."

Carol picked up her towel and water bottle as both headed towards the change room. "Enough about me. You need to get back into the dating scene. It's been five years since Jason and Kaylee died. You're in decent shape and you've got a good stylist.

Let's get you a couple of new outfits and introduce you back into Boston society."

"Boy, you never pull a punch. Dating? Not interested. There are days yet I still can't believe they're both gone." Jennifer shook her head and felt her throat tighten.

"They're still the two loves of my life. I talk to them. Sometimes I think they even answer." Jennifer smiled, hoping Carol could understand. "I just don't see me dating anyone I can think of."

"I still think you need to get into the social scene more." Carol pulled out a compact, checked her hair and slicked on some lip gloss. "If I were you, I'd join a Latin dance class. Find a partner with some smooth moves. Maybe do a little horizontal mambo." She raised her eyebrows suggestively.

"Carol, you're priceless." Jennifer arched her neck and laughed out loud. "You know I have two left feet. Imagine me trying to master mambo steps, vertical or horizontal. I can barely keep up with some of the moves in our class. You can't be serious."

"Okay, I'm not serious about the dance class but I am serious about you getting out. You need to care about people. You do care about people. Look at your work." Carol picked up her bag as they prepared to leave. "But deep down, you need someone to love and cherish. And you need someone who will love and cherish you too. Admit it."

As they walked into the parking lot, Jennifer shook her head. "It's a lot to think about Carol, especially with the situation with my father."

The two women chatted companionably as they walked to their cars in the warm April evening. The Boston air was bursting with the smell of fresh new growth and the soft rustling of tender young leaves.

JENNIFER OPENED HER FRONT DOOR TO FIND CHARLIE HAPPILY DANCING IN CIRCLES. "Let's get you out and get me some supper. I'm starving." Jennifer walked briskly through to her kitchen and opened the back door to let the wriggling cocker spaniel out. Stepping onto her cozy patio, she surveyed her yard and garden.

Dad would be appalled if he saw this yard, she thought, grimacing at the overgrown shrubs that were encroaching on the stone paths. I really need to get at this and tame it. It's at least two years overdue.

Stepping back into her warmly-lit kitchen, its familiarity soothed her. This is my home, she reflected as she heated up some leftovers in the microwave. I've lived here over half my life. But, it's so big for just Charlie and me.

Pouring herself a glass of Shiraz, she gazed into the dining room. The large mahogany table with its two leaves could seat twelve comfortably and had on many happy occasions. Now, the leaves were stored away in a closet, the chairs scattered around the house. All that remained were six chairs, with two of them moved to the far corners of the room.

Maybe I do need to get back into society, she thought as she her supper to the wrought iron patio table. This is a house meant for entertaining. But then again, maybe I should just sell and get into something more modest.

Jennifer ate her meal in peaceful solitude as she meditated on where her life might go next. She could hear people in their yards, the sound of children playing in the street and smelled burgers on a neighbor's barbeque. As she finished, she relaxed and sipped her wine, taking in the sounds and smells around her. Standing slowly, she carried her dishes to the sink, washed them and set them to drain. "Don't need the dishwasher just for me, do I Charlie? The spaniel looked through the patio door at her with complete adoration. "Time for your walk?"

Charlie wriggled with delight at his favorite word as Jennifer picked up his leash and some scoop bags. After locking up the house and setting her alarm, she stepped out her front door.

The neighborhood was full of activity on this warm spring evening. She waved to people mowing their lawn or working on a spring garden project. She stopped to admire the progress of one neighbor, a long-time friend of her father's.

"That's going to be a beautiful stone entryway Gerry." Jennifer walked up the new stone path to get a closer look at the verandah that was being faced in gray stone. "Nice design. It really works with the rest of the house."

Gerry wiped his brow with his arm and bent over to scratch Charlie's ear. "I have to thank my landscaper. How's your dad? I've been so busy I haven't seen him for a couple of weeks."

"He's still doing pretty well physically. He took a bad fall today because he refused to use his walker. But overall, he's healthy and still has quite a bit of long-term memory. His short-term memory has really suffered though. Did he know you the last time you visited?"

"I think he recognized me but I wouldn't say he knew me. He never spoke to me by my name. He remembered we had talked about gardening. As long as we stayed on that topic he was fine." Gerry was another passionate gardener. For over two decades they had been in friendly competition to see who would have the prettiest street view and the most intriguing back yard arrangements.

"I miss your dad. This time of year we would have been out scouting the nurseries for the latest hybrids and arguing over which fertilizer would produce the best growth for our coreopsis."

"He's still here in body and spirit but it's like a veil has dropped over his memory of us. I'll let him know we had a nice chat and tell him about your latest beautification project."

"This is nothing compared to my back yard project. He would be green with envy if he could see the Japanese garden I'm going to put in the back. Ellen thinks I'm crazy doing it at our age."

"I'll have to see it when it's finished."

"Let me know if I can help you out with anything. If there's any heavy lifting I can always ask one of my landscaper guys to go over and give you a hand." Gerry looked back at his house. "I have to excuse myself. I have to get a few things organized for the morning."

Jennifer started to turn away. "I've hired a couple of students to give me a hand with mowing the lawn and doing spring clean-up. I'm fine for now. But thanks for the offer. Appreciate it."

"Give your dad my best. Tell him I'll be over soon." Jennifer was about to walk away when Jerry put a hand on her arm. "Actually, how about I go over on Sunday afternoon and give you a break? It'll give me a break too. My back is telling me I'm not so young any more."

"That would be wonderful. I'm having company over for dinner so that would really free up some time." Jennifer smiled gratefully and gave him a warm hug. "You're such a good friend and neighbor. I know he'll be happy to tell you about the gardens at Brentwood."

"All right then. I'll bring my digital camera along and show him the progress on this porch project."

Jennifer continued her walk as the light slowly faded. Streetlights blinked on one by one. A hush began to fall over the neighborhood as children were called indoors and power tools were silenced. As she rounded the corner of her father's property, the light was almost gone.

What a lovely, peaceful evening, she thought, breathing in the soft scents wafting in the silky air.

Chapter 2

"Come in Mr. Powell. Please have a seat." Jennifer watched as her newest client quietly moved into the room and looked around her small but cheery hospital office. He was tall and slim. Not athletic looking but with a definite physical grace. With his sandy blonde hair and blue eyes, he would look right at home on one of the dozens of sailboats she'd seen out in Boston's busy harbor that morning.

His electronic file was already open on her computer. "I've been assigned your case now that Dr. Everest feels you're ready to look for full-time work. I know he's very pleased with your progress." Jennifer could see he was nervous.

"How about we get a glass of water or some tea? I've been here for a few hours." Jennifer closed his file and stood up. "I could use some tea. Let's go to the kitchen."

As they stepped into the hall, she pointed out a series of framed prints that thankful patients had donated to the hospital. "I never get tired of seeing these pictures. I find landscapes let me tell my own story. I imagine myself in the picture and what I would be doing or thinking if I were there. Sometimes I can almost feel the air and smell the trees or flowers." They walked slowly along the narrow windowless hall. "Ah, here we are. I'll just turn on the kettle and get us set up."

A few minutes later, and after establishing they were both diehard Red Sox fans, Jennifer and Mark Powell returned to her office; he with a tall glass of water and she with a hot cup of green tea. Quietly closing her office door, she went over and sat at her desk with her keyboard within reach as the tea's fragrant aroma wafted up.

"I see from your file that a lot has happened in your life in a short period of time. Your mother dying four years ago, your father overseas and you developing clinical depression." Jennifer took a cautious sip of the hot tea. "You've had a lot to cope with but Dr. Everest feels you're ready to get back into the workforce and asked me to give you any guidance you may need."

Jennifer watched him thoughtfully as she talked and sipped her tea. This young man had been thrown a major curve ball. At a critical time in his life, when his mother should have been there to guide him into adulthood, he had been forced to become a full-time caregiver. And his father seemed to have done a disappearing act. What father would abandon his wife and son at such a critical time, she wondered.

"I see you've completed all your high school credits. Where do you plan to go from here?"

Mark cleared his throat. "To be honest, I'm not sure yet."

Jennifer saw the warm sparkle in his eyes and knew the ice was melting fast between them. Talking about the Red Sox was a guaranteed ice breaker.

"My main priority right now is to find a real job, which is not easy when you have a major gap on your résumé and have worked only part-time and short-term jobs. People wonder if you've been in prison or don't know how to put in a good day's work. Mostly, I don't even get an interview."

"What kind of jobs have you done in the past?" Jennifer noted down market garden worker, tree nursery worker, greenhouse worker.

"Tell me what you can do or what you think you can do and let's work from there." Jennifer's fingers were poised over her keyboard to take more notes. She wasn't ready for what she heard next.

"Well, my mother was Heather Arlington, the concert pianist and teacher. I've been playing for as long as I can remember and singing too. Whenever she could, my mom would take me to old folk's homes and entertain for an evening. We had a great time. Once people found out I sang Sinatra they didn't want us to leave, especially in the north end." Mark was smiling as the memories rolled out.

13

"Being able to sing and play the piano are wonderful gifts. But, how have you been supporting yourself these past few years?"

"My mother had a life insurance policy that paid off all the bills. Before she died, she sold our condo in Midtown and helped me set up in a small apartment. Our private health insurance covered most of our medical costs and she had investments."

"Do you have any family in the area? Who can I contact if there is an emergency?" Jennifer looked up from her keyboard.

"My dad is on his way back from Afghanistan. I haven't spoken to him yet. We email back and forth. His name is Ben Powell."

Jennifer recognized the name from nightly newscasts and quickly saw the physical resemblance between the young man in front of her and the face she'd seen many times on television. She saw a pained look come over his face as he spoke about his father. "When was the last time you saw your dad?"

"I haven't seen him since shortly after my mother's memorial service."

Jennifer tried not to show the dismay she felt when she heard that the great Ben Powell hadn't seen his son in four years. "Does he know what you've been going through?"

"He knows some of it. He knows I was depressed but not how badly or for how long. I only contacted him when I was having a good day. The days when I was totally depressed I just stayed off his radar. No, I don't think he realizes how long it's gone on."

"Would you be interested in an outdoor job? There's a seniors' residence I visit regularly. I noticed on their job board the other day they're looking for a head groundskeeper. The pay is decent. From the jobs you've had, I'm sure you'd be qualified."

Mark sat up straighter.

"How about I see if I can get you introduced to the executive director? I don't really know her but she'll know my face and name. You interested?"

Mark smiled slowly and broadly. Jennifer noticed how it lit up his whole face.

"For sure." Mark flexed his hands. "I haven't even had a house plant since before my mom died, let alone a garden."

After Mark left, Jennifer took out the Brentwood director's business card. She keyed in the number and was pleasantly surprised to reach Kathy Hunter on her first attempt.

"Hi Kathy. Jennifer Barrett here. Art Severn's daughter."

"Oh hi Jennifer. Good to hear from you. Is your father okay? I heard he took a bad tumble this morning."

"Refused to use his walker again. His pride is bruised and he'll ache for days but he'll be fine. I'm actually calling about something else." Jennifer had another client coming to see her shortly. "I noticed on your job board you're advertising for a head groundskeeper."

"Yes and we're really up against it. Since Fred retired we haven't found a replacement. The people with good experience want about twice the salary we can offer. You know someone?"

"I met him today. He's been out of work for awhile so he's nervous about interviews but he has the experience you're looking for and he wants to work. He looked quite interested when I told him about your opening."

"What's his name? Tell him to call me. I need someone to come on board as soon as possible. There's a lot of spring cleanup and clearing to be done."

"His name's Mark Powell. I'll see if he can call you today."

"Thanks Jennifer. Appreciate it. I'll give you my cell number."

"Oh. And there's something else you should know. He's a pianist and singer. His mother was Heather Arlington."

"The Heather Arlington? Her memorial service was one of the biggest Boston has seen in years. Why is he looking for a job as a gardener?"

"He loves working outdoors with flowers and plants. He plans to keep his musical side as a personal hobby. It was pretty rough for him during his mother's illness and death. The reason I mention it is that you have that beautiful baby grand in the solarium that's rarely played. And he lives in a small apartment and probably doesn't have one."

"I like your thinking. Have Mark call me. I'd like to meet him."

Jennifer called Mark on his mobile. "She wants to meet you. Her name is Kathy Hunter. She's the executive director of Brentwood Manor. Know where that is?"

"You didn't waste any time. Can you text me her contact information? I'll call her as soon as I get off this bus."

Within half an hour Mark had made contact and was heading back to his apartment to pick up his résumé. He was going to an interview in three hours.

"Hi Mark. Please have a seat. Jennifer Barrett told me you'd like to apply for the job of head groundskeeper."

Mark felt his throat constrict. It was his first job interview in months and, after seeing the residence property with its mature trees and lush plantings, he wanted this job badly. He felt his nerves going and worried he'd go into a full-blown anxiety attack any minute. He struggled to control his breathing.

"How about if you tell me a bit about yourself and how you came to get all your experience with gardening?"

Mark's hands started shaking as he tried to make conversation. He tried to tell himself he was just meeting someone new and it would get easier in a few minutes. He told himself to just calm down.

"Well Ms. Hunter. I started working at tree farms and the market gardens when I was in high school. I, uh, ..." Mark stumbled over his words and his eyes widened. "I uh ..."

"How about we go for a walk around the residence and chat along the way? I don't think we need to be quite this formal."

Mark stood up and rubbed damp palms on his pants. Together, he and Kathy stepped into a hallway flooded with natural light and walked towards the doors. As his breathing returned to something resembling normal, Mark focused on what Kathy was telling him about the residence, its people and its history.

"We serve about one hundred residents who need assisted living plus we have a wing of bachelor, one- and two-bedroom suites for residents who are independent and need minimal support. We have nurses on staff and a full-time medical director and nursing director. Most of the residents are mobile on some level. We encourage everyone to participate as much as they can in both indoor and outdoor programs and activities," Kathy warmed to her story.

"We try to make sure all our residents feel they're part of a family who will care about them as well as care for them. We have residents who've been here for over twenty and even thirty years. As their needs change, we accommodate them so they can remain with us."

"I ask all staff, no matter what job they have, to get to know the residents and speak with them. If you become the head groundskeeper here you will find there are many residents with detailed knowledge from years of tending their own gardens. And they love to talk about it."

"Let's take a walk outside. You can give me some ideas of what needs doing in the flower beds this spring. This is actually a treat for me. Normally, the Director of Personnel would do the hiring but she's off on maternity leave, so I'm pitching in."

Almost an hour later, Kathy and a now animated Mark walked into the sun-filled solarium. With the familiarity of talking about something he really knew about, his nervousness had evaporated.

"You must have had quite a display of Oriental poppies a couple of weeks ago." They stood by one of the many windows overlooking the main garden next to a gleaming black baby grand piano.

"Our former gardener was with us from the day the residence opened. When he retired at Christmas we didn't realize just how much work is involved. We're on almost ten acres but he made it all seem so simple. We'll need a few high school students over the summer to keep up with the grass-cutting and trimming. I see on your résumé that you've supervised before."

"Yes, I have experience and yes, you would certainly need some extra help over the summer. There's a fair bit of pruning needed plus transplanting. I'd say minimum two students and probably three."

"So when can you start?" Kathy smiled at the surprised look on his face that was quickly followed by a distinct blush.

"How about tomorrow?" Mark grinned and put out his hand to shake hers and seal the deal.

JENNIFER HUNG UP THE PHONE WITH A SMILE after hearing Mark had gotten the job. She could tell by his voice he was excited and happy to have found a full-time job that would let him be outside in the coming months.

As she tidied her desk to leave for the day, the phone rang again.

"Mrs. Barrett? This is the Guildwood long-term care facility calling. You're looking for a bed for Verne Ellis I believe?" Jennifer sat back behind her desk and realized she'd be leaving late. There was going to be a pile of paperwork and e-mails over the next hour.

"You've found a bed already?" Jennifer was impressed. "That must be setting a new record." As she re-opened her computer and scrolled through the patient database she thought about Carol and their yoga class and dinner date. She'd be a bit late but she could make it if she kept her head down with no distractions. "OK, I'm ready to take the details."

Arriving late at the yoga class, Jennifer watched through the doors until there was a natural break in the routine. She slipped in quietly without speaking to anyone so as not to disrupt the flow of anyone's movements or meditations.

After the class, she and Carol walked towards the harbor to find a restaurant with a patio and a view. They settled on a seafood specialty place and were soon looking out over the Inner Harbor.

"How's your father?" Carol eyed the menu the waitress gave her while listening to the evening's specials. She liked the sound of the

Niçoise salad with grilled tuna. There was also a decadent-sounding salmon burger special. After an almost frantic day with clients throughout the city and an hour of de-stressing yoga she wanted to indulge but within reason. The tuna won.

Jennifer told her about his fall and ordered the same. "Most days he doesn't recognize me. But, he always brightens up when I come into his room or track him down in the lounge or outside. One of my young clients got a job at his residence today as head groundskeeper. He's a pleasant young man. My dad will enjoy trading gardening stories with him. It's surprising all the technical knowledge he's retained yet he doesn't know who I am or what day or year it is."

As their meals arrived, the famished friends savored the fragrant grill and tucked in hungrily. The street was quickly filling up with office workers either heading home or to one of the many restaurants and cafés that beckoned with a multitude of appetizing aromas.

"I'm thinking I need to head over to Copley Place for a little retail therapy one of these fine days. You up for it?"

"Where do you put all those clothes you buy?" Jennifer chuckled. Carol's closets were packed with more clothes and shoes than five women could wear.

"I'll give some to the Goodwill to make room. Shopping is a serious hobby that requires regular practice y'know." Carol's phone started vibrating on the table. "Just a second. It's a client."

Jennifer waited until Carol looked up. "I'll come along and carry the bags but you have to buy lunch." She could already imagine the cheering over at the Elm St. Goodwill. Within a week some lucky shopper would be trying on a little black dress that had been on a Neiman Marcus hanger in Carol's closet within the past two years, three tops. The day Carol died there would be at least three days of official mourning throughout the Boston area as clothiers, jewelers and leather goods stores revised their sales forecasts down.

"How about next Saturday?" Carol scrolled through her smart phone as Jennifer dug out a dog-eared paper appointment book.

"When are you going to get with the technology Jen?"

"Apart from the fact that I don't particularly believe in a better life through technology, there's a hospital policy that we cannot use mobile two-way communication devices to speak to or talk about patients and clients. It's a privacy issue. There are too many bad guys out there who can hack every cell phone number on the planet and others who can actually intercept conversations and data."

"Are you serious?" Carol stared at her phone. "I believe I will keep that in mind. You mean they can actually hack into a conversation?"

"Not only hack in but monitor your phone if they decide to track you."

"I did not know that." Carol's eyes were wide.

"Doesn't pay to be naïve these days, my friend."

Carol set up the shopping date on her electronic agenda. "Okay – Saturday it is then – 10 a.m. sharp at my place. I'll drive us over."

With their next date set, the two friends left the restaurant and headed towards their cars. Carol walked briskly to her electric blue BMW. Jennifer climbed into her silver sedan. Taking in the sunset spreading over the harbor she reflected that it had been a good day.

Chapter 3

I'm getting way too old for this. Ben Powell shoved a weary hand through his thick shock of silver hair. *I've been in the air or airports for easily thirty-six hours.* As tired as he was, his body was humming with either excitement or dread. He wasn't sure which.

He slowly made his way to the luggage carousel and did the math. *Oh my God,* he groaned. *I haven't been back since Heather died, which means I haven't seen Mark for over four years. No wonder his emails are so cryptic.*

At least people are leaving me alone today, he thought as yet another passenger did a double-take when she recognized the tall, lanky journalist. With his face almost a nightly fixture in millions of homes, bars and airport waiting areas, Ben was at the top of his game. His news feeds and investigative reports on war and conflict were picked up by networks around the world. They depended on journalists like him to get to hot spots, find the latest story angle and feed the news via satellite 24/7.

Today he was at Boston's Logan Airport. As his eyes swept over the milling crowd in Terminal E, he knew by the clenching muscles in his forehead, neck and stomach that his body was bracing itself as surely as if he was going into a war zone.

I'm home, he thought, *like it or not. What I really need is a long, hot shower and a big comfortable bed.* Ben rubbed the back of his neck and massaged a tight shoulder muscle.

First, I gotta get my gear back and get outta here, he thought, eyeing the endless lines at customs. Being over six feet tall definitely had its advantages. Even with dozens of people in front of him, he could see the slow-moving carrousel offloading luggage, boxes and sports bags from his British Airways flight.

"Excuse me ma'am." He easily reached around a woman guarding a stack of luggage to grab his two metal cases with their well-padded contents. His large duffel bag wasn't far behind.

Hope the border agent is in a decent mood or getting ready to go off shift. He made a futile wish. *Please don't examine all my equipment today.* But they always did. If it got really bad, they asked him to prove the equipment worked even though it was all registered with customs, right down to his laptop and satellite phone. He was a hard-working American journalist carrying the tools of his trade. But, his passport showed he had been to every terrorist hotspot in the world and some of them several times. He couldn't really blame them.

Ben was ready with his passport, customs declaration and what he hoped was a "trust me" look on his face when he reached the booth. The customs guy looked at his documents, carefully scrutinizing the equipment list and verifying it by computer.

"Thank you Mr. Powell." The agent pushed his passport across the counter without a flicker of recognition. "Please join the line to your right."

With every joint in his body groaning with fatigue, Ben realized they were going to examine all of his equipment, piece by techie-damned piece. *I'm too tired to even argue,* he thought. Let's just get 'er done.

As the next line inched forward, he guilted himself for at least the tenth time in the past few days for cutting himself off from his son and ex-wife. *Maybe,* he reasoned, *I'm like some of the soldiers I've met who became war junkies. They got it in their blood and found life back home too easy or boring.* How many military marriages had failed because they couldn't settle down to three squares a day and weekend barbeques, let alone an office. He was nearing the front of the line.

Having PTSD wasn't a good enough reason. I cut ties with Mark when he most needed me. Makes me a coward, PTSD or not. He stepped up to the counter and presented his passport, his best journalistic smile pasted in place.

Reunited at last with his equipment cases and duffel bag, Ben squinted against the bright afternoon sun as he finally escaped the crowded airport. Stepping out into the fresh Boston spring air, he wearily headed for a water taxi to take him to his hotel, a shower and exhausted oblivion.

Six hours later, he surfaced to consciousness just as the last light of sunset faded to dark. He knew that at his age it was going to take at least a week to re-set his body clock and groaned at the thought. But, right now what he needed was food and then hope for more sleep. Time for room service.

After ordering up his first USDA prime burger in almost four years he geared up his computer and turned on the TV. Free WiFi, a phone that worked and satellite television. It was worth it to be in a hotel, let alone one with hot water and regular electricity. Years of living in hotels that charged for things that didn't work made this feel like heaven. And, after spending more nights than he could remember in a freezing tent on a mountain somewhere or blistering under a relentless sun in the desert, anything with a roof had to be heaven.

A knock on the door had him almost running to get his food. He could already smell it. After signing for his meal he closed the door and opened a cold one he'd bought on his way in. The all-dressed burger went down well with the crisp hot fries and cold beer. He was feeling more and more human by the minute.

As the last fry disappeared and a second beer cap hit the waste bin, Ben went over to check his email. He could call Mark. But he wasn't quite ready to talk to him. He wanted their next conversation to happen in person.

Hi Mark. Got in at 1:30 on the flight from London. Been sleeping ever since. Just polished off a fine burger. How about we meet for lunch tomorrow? I'm at the Doubletree on Washington St. Be good to see you again! Dad

MARK SAW HIS DAD'S EMAIL POP UP, READ IT AND REPLIED: *Just landed a full-time job today and start tomorrow. My hours are 7-4. How about I give you a call when I'm leaving work and we'll figure out where to meet for dinner? Mark*

Walking into the small bathroom, he took out his medication and fingered the bottle. He'd have to talk to his psychiatrist about adjusting the dose if he was going to be doing a lot of physical activity. And he'd definitely have to wear a hat and sunscreen. On top of being a blonde with a fair complexion, his medication made him very sensitive to the sun. To care for the grounds at Brentwood he would slather sunscreen all over and wear a parka if he had to.

He was itching to get started.

BEN SAW MARK'S REPLY and sent him the hotel phone number and his room number. As he did, he saw the email folder marked 'Heather'. For some reason, he'd kept her emails all this time. There had been many times he wouldn't see them until they were a few weeks old. He felt completely powerless, plagued by delays in communication and sheer distance. He couldn't bring himself to delete them yet. They were all he had left of her.

Ben took another pull on his beer and closed down his email.

I really let her down, he thought. She had every right to ask for a divorce. I can't imagine what she thought of me for not being there when they needed me.

With fatigue and jet lag kicking back in, Ben shut down his computer and got ready for bed. In less than twenty-four hours he'd be seeing Mark again. Lying in the dark he could hear street noises far below. The noises were almost comforting. He was in Boston. No-one wanted to blow him up or kidnap him. And he was back in the same city as Mark at last. *I hope the boy can forgive me,* he thought and buried his head in the pillows.

MARK'S ALARM BUZZED HIM AWAKE AT 5:30 A.M. This *is going to take some getting used to,* he thought, as he stumbled to open the blinds and let the morning sun signal his brain to activate. One of his treasures was his mother's automatic coffee maker with timer. He could already smell the fresh brew and sent up a silent prayer of thanks to her.

By 6:30 he was on the bus that would take him to Brentwood. He'd checked on-line and discovered it shouldn't take more than twenty minutes or so to get to and from work. His backpack held a thermos of apple juice, his sunscreen, meds, an apple, a granola bar and his cell phone. Kathy had told him he could pick up anything he liked from the breakfast table in the staff kitchen but it didn't hurt to have spare supplies.

At the gates to Brentwood, Mark got off the bus along with more than a dozen staff. They walked up a lane that would soon be fully shaded by the maple trees on either side. Ahead was the main building with a long, wide veranda and a scattering of chairs and tables.

Following the other staff, Mark went around to one side of the residence. Benches were dotted along the path close to the flower beds. Already, there were a few residents out for a pre-breakfast stroll. Further back the telltale glass roof of a hot house glinted in the sun.

Going in the staff entrance, Mark made his way to a table with a basket of fruit, muffins and a coffee service. He got a coffee and muffin and found a table to sit down.

"You're new here aren't you?" Mark raised his head and saw a pretty nurse with her thick ebony hair in a ponytail. She was holding a tray with contents similar to his. "Mind if I sit down? My name is Lana, Lana Fitzpatrick."

"Nice to meet you Lana. I'm Mark Powell, the new groundskeeper." Mark stuck out his hand to shake hers. Others joined the table and soon Mark had been introduced to half a dozen people. Everyone told him about old Fred, the former groundskeeper and his love for the property, its plants, wildlife and people.

"We were all sad to see Fred retire but he deserves it. He designed most of what you see here and kept it all in top condition until the day he left. You have inherited Fred's pride and joy." Lana finished her cup of tea and picked up her tray. "See you around."

Mark finished his coffee, put his tray on the rack near the kitchen entrance and went off to the human resources office.

JENNIFER WALKED SLOWLY FROM THE PARKING LOT to the residence so she could soak in the sunshine, savor the smell of nearby roses and listen to the burble of hundreds of birds high in the trees around her. It was one of those early spring days that make you forget the short gray wet days of winter and hanker to be outdoors.

As she rounded a corner, she was surprised to see Mark Powell walking towards her.

"Mark," she called out. "Hold up a minute."

Mark turned at the sound of his name and broke into a broad smile. "Hey Jennifer. Thank you so much for helping me get an interview with Kathy Hunter. We got along really well. She likes some of the ideas I came up with to refresh the gardens."

"You didn't waste any time that's for sure. You're already dirty." Jennifer was pleased to see how relaxed and happy he looked.

Mark grinned. "I spent a couple of hours going around and looking at things. Just getting the lay of the land and figuring out what needs to be worked on first. Setting priorities." Already his new work gloves showed he'd been poking around in dirt, machine oil and sawdust. His boots wouldn't look new for much longer either.

"Oh yes. My dad emailed me last night that he's in town. We're going to try and get together for dinner tonight. He's staying at the Doubletree for now. I don't know what he plans to do next but I'll have a better idea by the time of our next appointment." Mark frowned. "I'm working full-time now. People will wonder when I have to disappear every week. What do I tell them?"

Jennifer raised her hand to stop him. "We'll schedule your group counseling after work.. Also, you can choose to tell Kathy that you're going for counseling without saying why. She would understand and support that I'm sure. Some employers want to know some of your medical history and there's no law says they can't ask. But I suspect Kathy won't do that." From what Jennifer knew of Kathy she was sure it wouldn't be an issue.

"When you feel comfortable, you may want to let a few people at work know that you're on special medication for a health condition. That way, if anything happens, you'll have a support network of people who will know what to do. I suspect that won't happen but it's always good to have a Plan B."

As Mark and Jennifer parted, he held out his hand to her. When she went to shake his hand he took it in both hands. "You've helped to change my life in the most amazing way in just the past twenty-four hours. I can't thank you enough. If you have a garden, I could help you with it on my time off."

Jennifer smiled and put a hand over his. "I just might take you up on that Mark. Mine is like a jungle these days. No self-respecting Bostonian would let their garden get out of control the way mine is. My father would be appalled if he saw it." With that, she went into the building to see what kind of day her father was having.

A few minutes later, Mark pulled off his gloves and stood in the doorway of a room that Fred had turned into a small office. The sun-filled glass-walled room in the greenhouse had been wired for lights, heat, phone and computer along with a desk, filing cabinet and a couple of chairs. Sunlight streamed through the glass ceiling and walls. Bamboo shades were rolled up at each range of glass panes. Mark unfurled some and soon the office was shaded.

Sitting at the old wooden desk, he pulled open the drawers on each side and located some basic office supplies. Fred had been a tidy and spare grounds keeper. There was nothing extra, only the essentials: some pens and pencils, a clipboard, paper, post-it notes, scissors. Then he saw them. Several diaries. They were in the bottom drawer all stacked up neatly.

He leafed through the pages and was taken back years and decades to freak snow storms, torrential rains, planting schedules, mite infestations, sunny days, rainy days, squirrel damage and anything that affected the gardens. Fred had meticulously documented the life cycle of the Brentwood gardens on virtually a daily basis for the better part of thirty years. In all, there were seven thick diaries.

"I like gardens and tending to plants but this must have been a passion for Fred. It must have almost broken his heart to retire." Mark spoke to the glass walls around him.

By four o'clock Mark had his list of things to do: job poster for the local high schools; call the fertilizer company to order fertilizer supplies for the coming months; contact the nurseries in Fred's list to see how to order new plants; have the tractor mower engine inspected and check the battery; check the tires on the tractor, trailer and wheelbarrows. He called the Doubletree as he gathered up his backpack.

"Dad. Mark here. Just getting off work now. I need to go home for a shower. Meet around six at your hotel and go from there?" Mark heard his dad's agreement and signed off.

"How was your first day on the job?" Lana pulled up beside Mark as he was walking down the drive. "Where are you headed? Can I offer you a lift somewhere?"

Mark thought, "What a pretty face".

"Why thank you!" Lana grinned as Mark blushed brightly. He'd said it out loud.

"I'm picking up my son at day care. We live in Southie. Whereabouts are you?"

"I'm on the East Side. I have a little apartment there."

"Hop in then. We make one stop to get Danny and then I'll give you a lift home." Mark climbed into the passenger seat. Lana eased the van out onto the street and picked up some speed.

"How did your first day go?"

"A bit overwhelming to be honest, but amazing. Did you know Fred kept a gardening diary with a notation every day for the weather, temperatures, precipitation, which gardens he'd worked on, which plants did well and which didn't, where to plant what and which plants didn't like to be planted together? It's almost an encyclopedia in seven volumes."

"I knew Fred was devoted to his gardens." Lana could hear the excitement in Mark's voice. "He always worked long hours. I think his wife died fairly young and they had no children. The gardens were his life. He knew every plant and when it had gone in."

Mark and Lana chatted as she worked her way through the heavy afternoon traffic. When they pulled up at the day care centre, a number of small children were in the yard. Danny caught sight of his mother's van and dashed for the gate. "Mom, over here!"

Lana stepped out and waved to a worker to let Danny through. He ran full out for the van, his backpack and art of the day waving around him.

He stopped short abruptly when he saw Mark.

"Who's that?" he demanded.

"This is Mark Powell. He's the new groundskeeper for the residence. He just started today. He lives pretty close to us so we're giving him a ride home."

"Mark, this is my son Danny."

"What's a grundkeeper?" Danny struggled with the unfamiliar word.

"I'm a gardener. I'm going to take care of the trees, shrubs and flowers at Brentwood."

"Does that mean you dig in the dirt and stuff?" Danny looked at Mark closely.

"Yep it does. Every day. And they pay me for it. How's that for a great job?" Mark smiled as Danny expertly did up his seatbelt and leaned forward to shoot out another question.

"Can I come and help you when I'm there?"

Lana smiled at Danny through the rear view mirror. "How about we let Mark settle in for a few days and then see?'

Mark smiled his thanks to her. His 'to do' list didn't include shepherding a small boy around machinery, equipment and tools just yet. "Tell you what Danny boy. Let's make a date for you to shadow me for a day. Do you know what that is?"

Danny shook his head, eyes wide.

"It means you would stay with me for a whole day as my assistant and see all the things I do for my work. Sometimes I would ask you to help me with things. That okay with you?

"For sure! My mom has a garden. I know what weeds look like. I pulled out the raditches by mistake last year."

"That would be radishes Danny." Lana corrected gently. "Okay Mark, where do we turn? I'm not really familiar with the streets here." Lana was soon pulling up in front of an old four-storey brownstone. Stepping out of the van, Mark stuck his head back through the window.

"You pick a date in a couple of weeks with your mom Danny boy and you can be my assistant for a day. If it works out, maybe you can come and help me other days too over the summer. Sound good?"

"Cool!" Danny enthusiastically waved goodbye to Mark and then tapped on the back of his mother's seat.

"Why did he call me Danny boy?"

Lana smiled warmly. "Danny Boy is a very, very old and popular Irish song. And you are a Fitzpatrick so that makes you very Irish indeed."

Chapter 4

It had been almost twenty-fours since his return. Ben felt out of sorts from the jet lag. Coffee didn't help. He'd just have to weather it through. Knowing he was seeing Mark in a couple of hours helped send some adrenalin into his system. How much it helped he wasn't sure but at least he was awake, dressed and moving.

The thought of seeing Mark rattled him. It was the first time he'd seen Mark since the days after Heather's memorial. Then, they were both immersed in a grief they'd been unable to share. Ben knew and adored Heather as a lover, friend and wife he'd lost through his own neglect. Mark knew her as his mother and the only parent he'd had for at least the last ten years. While both were in deep pain at the rapid progress of her disease and the inability of the medical community to cure her, neither had been able to connect emotionally. Ben had quickly retreated to his work and reporting on conflicts far removed from his family and former home.

He checked the mirror one last time. It was force of habit. Years of being in front of the camera had made him conscious of the need to look his best. Age was being kind. Despite his fifty-nine years he appeared youthful, toned and had a full head of hair. Not every man his age could make even one of those claims, let alone all three.

He slipped on a soft wool blazer over a golf shirt, patted his pants to confirm his wallet was in its pocket and headed out the door to meet Mark in the lobby.

Coming off the elevator he immediately spotted a younger version of himself coming through the doors. Whether it was fatigue or the lengthy separation or just his aging self, he suddenly choked up at the sight of his son – his own flesh and blood – walking towards him looking happy yet apprehensive. He hadn't known what to expect after all this time and was gratified by what he saw.

"Dad." Mark recognized him immediately.

"Mark, you look great." Ben stepped forward. Both men locked in an awkward embrace. "Sorry I didn't call last night but I was totally whacked. I don't travel so well anymore."

"No problem. I was out pretty late picking up some stuff for my new job and getting a haircut. Didn't want you to come back and think I'd gone hippy. And I wanted to make a good impression on the job my first day."

"So what's this new job? Wait – let's find a spot to eat and then we can talk." Ben was easy with small talk. It was the deeper conversations he knew would be a struggle. Sometimes life without a script sucked.

"What's your fancy? I'm into Thai, Japanese, Chinese, Italian. There are several good bistros around here." Mark led the way out of the building.

"Much as I love it, I've had enough Asian food to last me years. I'm starving for good old-fashioned American anything. Tonight I seriously need a very prime, very rare steak. I haven't had a good steak since I was in Gaza about three months ago. Impossibly expensive for the locals but not for the foreign journalists."

Mark and Ben headed off from the hotel and quickly found a restaurant that served the largest T-bones outside of Texas. A large frothy draft beer appeared in front of Ben while Mark opted for iced tea, remembering his alarm would be sounding reveille in a few short hours.

The men made small talk for awhile as they scanned the menu, made their choices and placed their orders. After Ben had taken a few good pulls on his beer he set it aside and looked at Mark.

"Mark, I have to be honest. I didn't know what I would find when I came back. Last time, at your mom's memorial, we were both in pain and you were so depressed. You were trying so hard to hold yourself together and I didn't help by not staying." Ben took another swig. "I didn't know you. You didn't know me. Your mom was really the only thing we had in common and it wasn't enough."

"Since then, I've avoided facing you, facing me and facing the relationship we don't have. But, I'm changing, hopefully for the better. I'm sorry for not being there for most of your life. I can't fix that part but maybe we can start from here?" Ben wasn't used to making speeches but realized he'd just made what might be the most important one of his life.

"Dad, four years ago I figured I'd be lucky to see you again. I figured between Mom dying and you barely knowing me it was a done deal. It would be over and I'd hear from you at Christmas, if that." Mark took a long drink of his ice tea before continuing.

"I've had a ton of counseling in the past four years. Your absence and its effects on me were a big part of my issues, apart from the divorce and my depression. We couldn't be having this conversation without all that counseling under my belt. The fact is, I had a very devoted mother who gave me all the care and nurturing I needed. It wasn't a substitute for a father but it was enough to know I was well loved and cared about." Mark's look was serious but not sad.

"During Mom's cancer we had a lot of conversations about life, love and living. I learned a great deal from her in those last months. She helped me understand there is no point in going through life thinking bitter thoughts about someone because they didn't live up to your standards, even if those standards weren't all that high to begin with."

Ben squirmed uncomfortably but waited for Mark to continue.

"The fact that you and I are having this conversation tells me there's some hope for us. It took a lot of courage for you to come back. I'm sure it would have been easier for you to just stay away. Less complicated for sure. You wrote you might get a job stateside. If you do, it will be the first one since I was about six years old." Mark saw his dad purse his lips.

"I was angry at you for not being there when I needed a father. What kid wouldn't be? But when Mom got sick, there was no room for that anger. We were in survival mode just trying to go from one day to the next. Now that I've come out the other side of that crisis, I've had counseling to acknowledge and deal with my anger. I know it was okay to be angry at you. I've let my anger go. It'll be up to you when you're ready to let the guilt go."

"Man. I deserved that," Ben felt gut-punched and hoped the steaks arrived soon so they could both retreat to more neutral ground. "I know we have to build a relationship and it will take time. But, I'm game if you are."

"I'm here, aren't I?"

Mark looked across the table at his father and met him eye to eye. Ben could see the challenge in his look.

"I'm here, too. And I plan to stay in your life for the rest of it in a more meaningful way." As he said it, Ben realized he meant it.

They were interrupted by the arrival of hot plates of steak with baked potatoes and the offer of sour cream, chives and butter. They took it all and dove into their food silently. As the restaurant filled with dinner hour patrons, the two men turned their talk to the safer ground of baseball and whether the networks were sacrificing journalistic accuracy to feed the 24/7 news machine and boost ratings.

Chapter 5

Jennifer slipped quietly into her father's room. It wasn't much after noon but she didn't want to disturb him if he was resting. Lana had told her he was sleeping more and more – another symptom of the progression of the Alzheimer's. But, as she entered the room she heard his familiar snort.

"Young lady, I am quite capable of getting into this wheelchair myself. There is nothing wrong with my arms you know." Jennifer smiled at a tone that instantly threw her back to her childhood. Art Severn had never been one to take orders or be pandered to. Whenever her mother had tried he was quick to cut her off.

"Your wrist is all better then? Maybe you could just use your walker."

The nurse looked up at Jennifer and shook her head.

"Jennifer. Tell this nurse that I do not need her help and resent it." Her father was not listening. "I do not know why she is being so insistent."

As surprised as she was, Jennifer didn't miss a beat. "Dad, I think she has to help you because of the residence policy. If you fall and get hurt, she could lose her job."

"Well, in that case, carry on young lady. I would not want you to lose your job but do step back a bit and give me some room to maneuver. I am not helpless."

Jennifer breathed out slowly. Her father was having a really good day. First time in months. Time for a celebration.

"Dad. I'm taking you to meet the new groundskeeper. Bet you can give him some pointers on how to maintain a proper Boston garden. What do you think?"

"I think you had better take me to meet this fellow." He started to grumble but fell silent as Jennifer went behind his chair to bring him outside.

Jennifer happily pushed her father's wheelchair towards the glass greenhouse off in the back corner, hoping she'd find Mark hiding behind his desk at high noon. As they approached, she saw a garden tractor parked at the door.

"Mark. Hello?" Jennifer called out as she wheeled her father into the building.

"Stop there Jennifer," her father commanded. He was peering at a range of young plants that had yet to be transplanted into one of the many flower beds. "Why are these coreopsis in here? They need to be in the ground now."

Jennifer was hoping to make this a pleasant outing for her father and grimaced as she heard the critical tone in his voice.

Just then, Mark stepped out from his office. "Mr. Severn, so nice to meet you. Jennifer told me you're an expert in all things about Boston gardens. Glad you dropped by. Can I show you around?"

Jennifer's father snapped back, "You need to get these coreopsis in the ground soon son. They need time to establish before the hot days hit. Need to keep the ground nice and moist under the roots to encourage growth and flowers."

"I know Mr. Severn. I'm trying to hire some high school students to come and help me but they're still in classes for a few more weeks. I'm on my own unless I can find someone to come on weekends."

"I could help some. Not much use from my wheelchair but I still remember what needs to be done and there are others here at the residence who have more years in their gardens than you have on this planet. You could take advantage of that you know."

Mark looked at Jennifer's father. "You're absolutely right. Bostonians pride themselves on their gardens. Getting older doesn't mean your gardening stops. Mr. Severn, you're brilliant! We'll still need the students to help with the heavy stuff like driving the tractor mowers and doing the tree pruning but you're absolutely right. We need a gardening club for the residents to give all our retired gardeners a chance to get back out and dig in the dirt. Maybe a vegetable garden. We'd have fresh vegetables every day. "

Jennifer hugged her father. He took her hand as she stepped back. "You're a good daughter you know. I knew you would find me".

Jennifer choked back hot tears as she moved behind her father's wheelchair. She hadn't connected with her father like this in over a year. She gazed over at Mark and signaled a teary thank you. He nodded in understanding. He'd been lost to his family too. Depression had become a mental prison he thought he'd never escape. This man would never escape his prison.

Mark had been on the job a few weeks when Kathy paged him to meet her in the Manor's sun-filled solarium. She didn't say what the meeting was about so he was curious as he dusted off his boots and cleaned himself up to go in the main building. He still had some overgrown hydrangeas to cull and hoped whatever it was wouldn't take too long.

Kathy was already there when he arrived. He gratefully took note of the fresh pot of coffee and plate of cookies on a small table by the window where she was seated. It had been a long and physical day and the coffee smelled excellent. She motioned him over to sit down. She began pouring when he agreed to a mug of the fresh-brewed Columbian.

Still mystified, he tried to get comfortable on the dainty antique chair. *Clearly not designed by anyone near six feet tall,* he thought, as he waited for her to lead the conversation.

"I hear you're a very talented piano player and singer."

"I play a bit, yes." Mark was actually itching to touch the gleaming black baby grand that held court in a bright corner of the room.

"We have a resident who will be turning one hundred in late June. Jennifer Barrett mentioned you're quite a Sinatra fan. Vera was a chorus singer back in the days when Sinatra sang at the Latin Quarter. Her family's hoping we can do a little concert to celebrate her day. When Jennifer mentioned your special talent, I knew my prayers were answered."

Mark stared as Kathy pushed ahead. "I know you're busy with the gardens and I'm guessing you don't have access to a piano. Not for what we pay you. Here's what I propose. You work one hour less per day in the gardens and come up here to the solarium to practice on this piano and put together a little show for Vera. We have three weeks to be ready and it has to be a surprise. Are you willing Mark?"

"Sure thing." Mark said it without even having to think about it. Play the piano and sing again? It would be like breathing again. Access to the piano every day while he was being paid? No question. Bring it on.

"When?"

"Well, it's three o'clock now. Do you need music?"

Mark looked lovingly at the baby grand. It was almost identical to the one that had graced the living room of his home while he was growing up. He and his mother had spent many happy hours tickling the keys together or separately. He went over and opened the glossy lid. He nodded at the crisp tone that came off each key as he played random chords. This baby was ready to play. He sat down. The hydrangeas could wait.

"Ladies and gentlemen. Welcome to the Brentwood Lounge. Time for a little smooth music and some easy sounds. Let's take it away." Mark had done this many times with his mum. He played a few intro bars and some trills as his fingers remembered the keys and then relaxed into one of his favorite Sinatra lyrics – the *Days of Wine and Roses*.

Next, he transitioned seamlessly and crooned *"Moon River wider than a mile..."*.

Mark kept on playing excerpts of Sinatra favorites, stumbling only slightly from lack of practice. An audience was collecting both inside and outside of the solarium. They came gradually. A resident in her wheelchair with her attendant. Another resident self-powered with a walker. A staff member walking by and just stopping to listen. Mark played on for a good fifteen minutes before stopping. Everyone around burst into applause.

Mark cleared his throat and smiled.

"Mark, we need to get some helpers hired so you can be involved in our summer entertainment calendar."

"Summer entertainment calendar?"

"Maybe you could do a couple of concerts?" Kathy smiled.

Mark couldn't resist. He smiled brightly and nodded.

"BEN, WHEN ARE YOU COMING BACK TO PAKISTAN? Things are heating up over here." The satellite phone crackled as a senior field producer shouted into the line.

"I won't be coming back." Ben let the sentence slink out over the connection and sink in.

"What? What're you talking about? You're our voice here. You can talk to the insurgents. I can't believe you could say this."

"Believe it. I'm done. It's been over thirty years. I have important family issues happening. I won't be back. Take that as a given."

"But you have a new contract."

"Which I haven't signed. My son needs me. I'm staying stateside. No negotiation. End of discussion." Mark thanked the producer for their work together and then quietly but firmly cut the connection and turned the phone off. He seriously doubted it would ever get turned on again if he could help it.

As he put the phone down, he realized he was drenched in cold sweat. His hands were shaking uncontrollably. Despite the warmth of the room he was shivering. *Take slow, deep breaths* he commanded himself. *Slow, deep breaths. Focus on where you are right now. You are in a safe place now.* He looked around the room in somewhat of a daze.

He could feel his heart pounding in his chest and took in deep calming breaths through his nose. *Whoah. Hyperventilating or what. Haven't had an anxiety attack like that in over a month,* he realized. He shook his head. *Guess my war isn't over yet.*

As his heartbeat and breathing gradually returned to normal, he turned back to his computer and opened an old email from Mark.

Hi Dad – Mom passed away this morning. I was with her. She was not in any pain. She'd been in a drug-induced coma the past week. All life support was removed three days ago. She had such a strong heart though. The doctors were surprised at how long she survived given that she was riddled with cancer.

I brought in my iPOD filled with the classical music she loved. The staff told me her blood pressure and respiration was calm compared to some of the other patients. They believe the music had to be part of it.

Mom planned her memorial. She told me what music she wants played, what singers to have perform, where to hold the service, who to invite, what caterer to use and what food to order. It will be amazing. The mayor of Boston will be there and many arts and culture luminaries. She would want you to be there. Let me know how soon you can get back so I can set the date. Mark

Ben closed the email. The attack had passed. He was back to himself. *Heather stayed in control one way or another right until the end,* he thought. *She was such an amazing woman.* He looked out the window at the bustling waterfront far below. He was pensive as he stared out the window. *I really should have tried harder as a husband and father. But I was damaged goods. I couldn't bring that into her life and Mark's. Not then. They had enough things to deal with without having to deal with my demons.*

For long minutes, Ben stared at the sunlight glistening off the water. Lost in his thoughts, he reached back to massage his tight shoulder muscles.

Chapter 6

Lana checked herself in the bathroom mirror and sighed. She hadn't quite figured out how to ask Mark Powell if he was dating anyone. *I've been so busy raising Danny and holding down a full-time job I haven't had any time for dating*, she rationalized. *Oh be honest*, she told herself. *There hasn't been anyone like Mark since Tim died.*

She took stock in the mirror. *I'm still under thirty, no grey hairs yet, my body's in good shape.* She smiled at her reflection. *I'm still an Irish rose.* She walked into her bedroom. Tim's face smiled up at her from the photo on the dresser. *I miss you big guy. But Mark and I get along so well. I really want to get to know him better. He's a baseball nut just like you.* She smiled back at the photo.

Lana kept in touch with friends from nursing school but everyone was busy with careers and young families. She'd met lots of great people at work but everyone tended to go their separate ways at the end of the day.

I definitely want to get Mark out on a date. Driving him to and from work is fun, she thought. *Danny likes all his dirt stories. We've become friends first. That's a good thing.*

She took a last glance in her dresser mirror to check her hair and make-up. She kept both simple and basic. Getting a four-year-old up and out the door shortly after six in the morning left her precious little time for herself. Even getting up an hour before him was usually spent dealing with laundry, making his lunch and straightening up.

Satisfied she was ready to meet the day, she went into Danny's bedroom. It was covered with Spider-Man posters, action figures and comic books. She smiled at him sleeping with one foot stuck out the side of the bed and an arm flung over his head. She watched him for a minute, treasuring this moment of complete peace.

"Danny, time to rise and shine kiddo," Lana tousled his hair and waited for his eyes to open. He wakened slowly, stretched and let out a huge yawn.

"Is it sunny today, Mom?" Danny was already asking questions and not even out of bed. "When can I come with you to work and hang out with Mark?"

"I guess we'd better get a date organized. He has helpers now. I'll ask him today I promise." Lana added it to her mental to do list along with a dozen other things.

IN HIS HOTEL ROOM, BEN GLANCED AT THE BEDSIDE CLOCK. *I need to get my act in gear.* He threw back the covers. *Finally, I can check out.* He grinned when he realized how his thinking had changed. *Just weeks ago I was beyond grateful to be in a hotel. I must be ready to settle down if I'm thinking a hotel is boring. I can't believe I actually want to move into Gord's condo,* he shook his head, scratched his head and grinned at himself in the bathroom mirror. The furnished condo overlooking the harbor belonged to a journalist buddy out on assignment. He'd offered to pay rent but Gord said it was just going to sit empty. Might as well keep it occupied. *Works for me,* Ben thought and set himself up for a steaming shower.

He was soon hailing a cab over to the studio to pick up the keys. He was still getting used to the pulse of Boston and being in a city where suicide bombers were unknown.

"Wait here, I'll be back in a minute."

"Meter's running. It's your dime." the cabbie kept the car running and the air conditioning on high.

Ben stepped out onto the crowded sidewalk. The air was hot and dense after the coolness of the taxi. The keys were with the receptionist. He'd deal with the human resources people another day. He still had a few weeks before he was scheduled to start the new assignment in Pakistan. He wasn't going there again. The country was still reeling from historically heavy monsoons. There was little infrastructure left in over one quarter of the country. And he could no longer take the violence and the constant threat of snipers and roadside bombs.

The taxi pulled up in front of a tall building with floor to ceiling glass windows. After tipping the taxi driver generously, Ben gazed up at his latest home. *I really need to figure out what to do with myself next. I can't keep living out of my duffel.* He lugged the stuffed bag and his cases across a spacious bright lobby and made his way to the elevator.

He was pleasantly surprised to find a very well furnished airy apartment with windows facing the harbor. *Must cost a small fortune,* he figured. It would be quite a panorama at sunrise and sunset. *Great place to bring a date if I ever find one.*

With his body recovered from his travels, Ben considered his next moves. As he stowed his belongings, he let his mind wander. *I'm not ready to retire completely but I don't want to work a full-time grind. And I'm definitely tired of travelling.*

He gazed out the window and watched the harbor with interest. *I can live quite comfortably on my savings and investments,* he thought, as he followed the path of a sleek schooner easing out of its berth. *Financially, I've done well.* He did a mental tally of his portfolio and realized he'd actually done better than well. He had no debts, no car and no mortgage. He was well set for whatever he decided to do.

For today though, I'd better get some supplies in. He opened the cupboards one by one. *Definitely a bachelor pad,* he reflected, seeing few ingredients for actually making a meal. *No more hotel food for me,* he smiled as he patted his flat stomach. Well, almost flat. *Time to visit the workout room and check out the equipment. Maybe Mark and I could work out together a couple of times a week and grab a homemade bite of something.* Ben rummaged around until he found some paper and a pen. He realized with a start he was actually planning some meals to make for himself and his son. *Now this is a first in a very long time.* He smiled again as he started writing out his grocery list.

"Hɪ Jᴀɴᴇ, ɢᴏᴏᴅ ᴛᴏ sᴇᴇ ʏᴏᴜ ᴀɢᴀɪɴ," Mark had already met the activity coordinator about the upcoming one hundredth birthday party for Vera. Kathy breezed into the modest meeting room with a phone attached to her ear. She waved them both to sit down and held up a finger to let them know she was almost finished the call.

"Whew, glad that call is over," Kathy rolled her eyes and explained that it was a long-winded board member who was constantly trying to micro-manage his board portfolio. "He doesn't seem to get it that he's there to guide us, not to run the place. We have an executive and staff for that. Sorry guys, didn't mean to vent on you."

Kathy turned off her phone. "So, what's this about a vegetable garden run by the residents? Tell me more." Both women looked at Mark.

"I was talking to Jennifer Barrett's father, Art Severn. He's a long-time gardener. We have over one hundred able-bodied people in the independent living wing. If even a fraction of them were interested in helping out we could develop a really viable garden. I'd have to speak to Vito about the volumes being ordered now for various vegetables and then do some homework on how large a space would be needed, how many plants and a planting schedule but I think we could have something really productive even this year. At the very least we could have an excellent salad garden." Mark pushed ahead.

"I walked around some this morning and have a good spot in mind that should be large enough. It faces south, there are a couple of trees to shade the gardeners and I know the irrigation system is in place." He handed out the notes he'd printed off.

Kathy and Jane both scanned the sheets in front of them.

"This is an excellent proposition." Kathy looked up at Mark and then Jane. "You really have thought this through. I'm impressed."

Mark smiled and blushed at the compliment. "It wasn't a big shift to go from thinking about residents working with flowers to working with vegetables. They're all plants and all need about the same care and attention and fertilizer."

"You have my full support. Jane, I can see you agree as well.

How about you two put your heads together and get things rolling. I really need to go and make a few calls. I'm sure you two can handle it from here. I'll let Vito know to expect you to come by with your questions and let him know I'm supporting it. Thanks Mark. This is definitely a good project for the residents." Kathy had her phone back on and was already scanning her caller list as she sailed out the door.

"I bet Fred would love this idea," Jane turned to Mark. "He had to slow down a bit the past few years. He developed arthritis and then had two hip replacements. I think the surgery was hard on him, although he was up and about quickly after each operation."

"I was thinking about asking him if he'd like to become a volunteer. He might like to come back a few hours or days a week."

"He and I are still in close touch. He's an honorary grandpa to my children so we usually see him every week or so." Jane noted 'call Fred' in her tablet. "He has always said that being paid to work at what you love is better than winning a jackpot and having nothing to do but spend it. I'm sure he'll be back in a heartbeat as a volunteer."

"I hope so. Between the vegetable garden and the concert I have a lot on my hands these days. I'm not complaining though. I love it here."

"I do too. It's one of the best places I've ever worked."

The two continued talking and sorting through who would do what to help get the project going. The main beds would need to be prepared, tools brought in and a group of silver-haired volunteers assembled and assigned.

Upstairs in the non-ambulatory floor, Lana expertly shifted Vera Easton from her wheelchair onto her bed. The elderly woman was still gamely dressing and getting into her wheelchair every morning to go to breakfast. Now, with her one hundredth birthday just ten days away, she was visibly slowing down. A series of small strokes had left her with limited speech and her arms were no longer strong enough to transfer herself. Lana knew it frustrated her to need more and more help and wasn't surprised when a flash of anger surfaced once in awhile.

"There you go Vera. All set for some quiet time before dinner." Lana draped a handmade crocheted throw over Vera's tiny frame. "I'll come back and get you out for supper before I leave."

"Where Danny?"

"He's at day care today. But he's coming here to shadow the new groundskeeper and be his assistant for a day soon."

Vera beamed. "He good boy. I much like him."

"He likes you too. He's really looking forward to spending the day with Mark Powell the groundskeeper. Maybe we can get them to bring you a bunch of flowers." Vera smiled like a girl about to receive a gift from a suitor.

Lana left her elderly charge propped up in her bed high enough to be able to see all around her when she wanted to but then rest or nap in comfort as the mood struck. Her pager went off. She checked up and down the hall for the flashing light over someone's room.

Jennifer arrived home after another long day and laughed as Charlie almost bowled her over. She put down her purse and bag of groceries. Squatting down to pat the wriggling dog, she was rewarded with tail-twitching, tongue-lolling love. *I wonder how people without dogs find joy,* she thought, as she let him into the yard.

Gazing around her kitchen and out to the back garden Jennifer realized she was torn. She had this big home all to herself and loved the old place. Apart from the colorful gardens and rich green lawn, the house was bright and cheery and full of happy memories. Everything in it had been with her since childhood.

A year after Jason and Kaylee died, she sold the home they'd made together for almost two decades. While she'd needed its solace that first year, she found she had to make a break. After weeks of teary sorting and smiles over cherished memories, Jason and Kaylee were at rest. She had to move on. Her father's health was deteriorating and he needed someone with him as much as possible. Now, Jason and Kaylee were with her in the many photos she had spread around the house on tables, bookshelves and walls.

She stepped into her back yard with a glass of lemonade and looked around in dismay. *I've really let this go*, she thought as she walked along the stone path that led to the back gate. The hostas were spilling over their border. *How can I ever get it back under control? Maybe Mark Powell could give me some ideas or even help.* She ran a hand through her hair and wondered again whether she should just sell and get into a lower maintenance apartment or condo.

"Jennifer?" Her neighbor Gerry rapped on the gate just as Jennifer was about to turn and go back to her kitchen.

"Gerry. Don't look at the yard. It's a disaster." Jennifer held open the gate as her father's gardening buddy received an enthusiastic greeting from Charlie.

"Saw your dad on Sunday. He didn't know me by name but he asked if I had been to our favorite nursery yet." Gerry accepted Jennifer's offer of lemonade and the two sat down at her patio table.

"He was still complaining about things, so that's a good sign." The two laughed in agreement. "He's always been such a curmudgeon."

Gerry looked at his friend's garden. "I don't know how you manage with your work, visiting your father, caring for Charlie and taking care of this big old place."

"I've been thinking the same thing." Jennifer set her glass down. "To be honest Gerry, I don't feel I'm managing all that well, especially in the gardening department." Jennifer waved her arm at the yard. "You and I both know what it used to look like. It wasn't that long ago either."

Gerry watched Jennifer closely. "You thinking about selling?"

"The thought has crossed my mind more than once," Jennifer was relieved to have it out in the open. "It isn't about money. My father was very frugal."

"Be honest. Art's a cheapskate."

"He is, isn't he?" Jennifer laughed. "My mother put a roll of duct tape in his Christmas stocking every year. He was always taping something so he wouldn't have to replace it. But seriously, even with a private room at Brentwood, he will never go through it all even if he lives to be a hundred."

"What about you Jennifer? This place was always way too big for even the three of you."

"This house has been such a refuge for me since Jason and Kaylee died. Being able to help my father gave me a new purpose and it let him stay here a few more years."

"But…"

"I'm wondering if it's time to move on. Get a smaller place closer to work." Jennifer gazed around, taking in the tall trees shading one end of the yard. "This house and the gardens are a handful for one person. At least the lawn is being mowed. My father would have a conniption fit if he saw what has happened to his precious perennials and shrubs. He'd lecture me for a week."

"As part of that lengthy lecture he might tell you to consider whether you're up to living in this house alone." Gerry finished his lemonade and stood up. "Ellen and I are here if you need to talk some more."

"Thanks, Gerry." Jennifer walked him towards the gate. "I may take you up on it."

As she locked the gate behind him, she looked around. Carol says this is a great market for sellers. Says she can get me top dollar. It's tempting. No more lawn to mow. No more gardens to tend. No snow to shovel. Maybe a swimming pool or an exercise room in the building. I have to think about this. I can't go on pretending I need a house and property like this, she mused.

JENNIFER AND CAROL WERE WORKING UP A SWEAT in their Latin dancercise group. As usual, Carol had on the latest workout gear, with her hair pinned back and diamond studs at her ears.

"I'm so glad we found this group Jen," They both watched carefully as the instructor showed them a new move. "This kind of exercise is so much fun and I love the music. I was thinking we could go to the farmers' market and get some fruit and a bagel. Maybe just hang out and watch the sailboats as the sun sets."

The two friends swung by Jennifer's to pick up Charlie for the outing. After scouting out some food, they were soon opening up their bags on a park bench and taking in the scenery while Charlie had a long wriggling roll in the grass.

"I've decided to kick Lance out," Carol picked up some grapes and popped one in her mouth. "It irks me to see him sitting around doing next to nothing while I'm busting my butt. He tells me he's going into consulting but all he's doing is calling around to buddies, going out for lunch and coming back with nothing but the bill. I shouldn't be surprised he never married or had a family. He's so totally self-absorbed. I have no idea what I saw in him other than good looks and smooth talk."

Jennifer let her gaze scan over the harbor as her friend continued to vent. "He keeps saying we should take a trip together somewhere. With whose money? I'd love to go on vacation but not with him. No sir. He's out. I really have to do this once and for all. It's driving me nutty."

"Do you want me to be with you while he clears out his stuff?" With her years of counseling experience, Jennifer had visions of a nasty confrontation. She'd met Lance enough times to know he expected everything and everyone to revolve around him. She suspected he could have a mean streak when thwarted. He had clearly decided that living with Carol and her paying the bills was his preferred lifestyle. Jennifer had never met a man who could look so good, sound so charming and be so completely shallow. She was surprised when Carol had let him move in with her. Her friend usually had stronger radar.

"No, he knows it's coming but is just too lazy to move out until he absolutely has to. He'll go bunk in with one of his brothers until they kick him out."

The two friends took Charlie for a walk along the sunny path.

As the shadows lengthened and the temperature gradually cooled, they drove back to Jennifer's.

They made a date for dinner and promised to keep in close touch. Until Lance was out and the locks changed, they both knew Carol needed her friend more than ever.

Chapter 7

"I'll check with my father's lawyer but let's do it." Jennifer checked the treadmill speed and adjusted it up slightly to match the cadence of Carrie Underwood smashing the headlights of her boyfriend's sporty little SUV. She loved that song of the cheatin' man. Especially the part about the Louisville Slugger. Really ramped up the treadmill experience.

She was ambivalent about selling her paternal home and her only piece of permanency. But, she had to set aside her worries about the changes ahead to think about finding a new normal and new stability. More change. The more she thought about it the less sure she was. *What am I getting into?*

"There's a lovely condo on the inner harbor I want you to see. When you see what the building has to offer you won't have any qualms about selling, trust me. It would be the perfect size for you, you could bring Charlie and you can most certainly afford it. The asking price is below what your house will bring. And I'm sure you haven't touched Tim's insurance money right?"

"I make enough from my work. I've invested it." Jennifer knew almost to the penny what her investments were worth. She could afford to retire but didn't want to. She liked having a purpose to each day and enjoyed meeting and helping her clients.

"You'll be amazed at the view. When would you like to see it? It won't stay on the market more than a week."

"How about after lunch? A friend and her son are picking up Charlie later this morning so I'm free for the afternoon if you like."

"Let me call the client and see when we could drop by."

BEN CHECKED OUT THE CONDO and noted with satisfaction that it was neat and clean. A little sterile even.

Not enough photos and what Heather called brick-a-brac. *She always liked to have little collectibles on the windowsills and corner shelves.* He always thought of them as dust collectors but now realized they gave a room character.

This place's only character was that it was a well-paid journalist's bachelor pad with a giant plasma screen television dominating the living room. *Heather would never have had a television that size,* he thought with a smile. *And certainly never in the same room as her beloved piano.*

Mark was on his way over. When the buzzer sounded, Ben keyed him in and waited with his door open. A minute later, he heard the quiet swoosh as the elevator doors opened and watched his tall lanky son step out and head towards him.

"Hey Mark! How's it going?" Ben stood back to let him through the door.

"It's going amazingly well all things considered." Mark moved past his father, let his bag drop and walked over to the windows to look out at the inner harbor. Even on a weekday, it was dotted with dozens of sailboats of all sizes. But on this warm breezy Saturday morning it seemed everyone in Boston had become a sailor. "This view is so incredible." Mark accepted a bottle of water. The two men stood side by side scanning the watery panorama in front of them a dozen stories below. "You ever sail?"

"I used to when I was much younger. Your mother and I took you sailing when you were a baby. You started to help steer when you were about five or six."

"I remember that! I had completely forgotten. I sat on your lap." Mark grinned as the memory came back. "I thought Mom wasn't much for it. She was usually pretty busy with weekend concert dates here and in New York. But when you were here, we did a lot of sailing. I'd like to give it a try again."

"I have a very dusty sailing certification. I'll get in touch with one of the sailing schools and see what would be involved in bringing me up to date. I'd need to know the latest sailing regs and how to read the current navigation displays. Like I said, it's been a few years. At least I'm handy with a GPS."

"We could always go on one of the harbor tours in the meantime."

"No thanks. They talk at you through loudspeakers.

I remember hearing them out on the water and vowing I'd never go on one. I prefer the peace of being out on a boat with people I know and like." Ben thought about the many weekends he'd spent in his youth helping friends to crew their parent's boats. He'd crewed some pretty large watercraft. "I'll check into getting recertified so we can rent a boat and go out on our own. Sound good?"

"Sounds great. I can't afford it but I'll be happy to let you pay and tag along any time." Son and father grinned their identical grins at each other.

"Speaking of water, how about we go for a swim and then head out for food?" Domesticity was not returning easily after years of living out of hotels, tents, trains and planes. Ben really didn't know how to run a kitchen and plan and shop for food.

"What's happening with the vegetable garden project at Brentwood?" Ben held the elevator door as Mark stepped in.

"It's taking shape faster than I could have imagined. We've been given a small grant to start it up as a community garden project. It'll pay for almost everything we need for this year. Over the winter I'll do up a full plan so we can apply for a larger grant. I found out today the former head groundskeeper is willing to come out of retirement and help coordinate. He just can't stay away, which is lucky for me." In the locker room, Mark slipped off his pants and put them in the locker with his bag and other clothes. He already had his trunks on.

"The summer students have done all the heavy work with supervision from two of the residents. Over two dozen people turned up for the first meeting." He pulled out his goggles. "I couldn't believe how quickly they organized a couple of committees to deal with buying and organizing supplies, tools and schedules.

They walked out to the pool deck with their towels and found they were alone. "Give these folks a piece of ground to work with and they're out at seven in the morning waiting for me to open the doors to the tool sheds."

They did some stretches before sliding into the crystal clear water.

LANA GAVE A LAST CRITICAL EYE TO HER NOW TIDY LIVING ROOM. She'd gotten up early to get some housework out of the way so she and Danny could have the rest of the day to themselves. With them outdoors, this room would stay tidy until Danny reassembled it.

With a load of laundry in the dryer, she opened the fridge door and started packing up a colorful cooler bag with a couple of water bottles and their sandwiches. They were going for a picnic in the park with Charlie.

"Mom?"

"I'm in the kitchen." Lana was trying to get Danny to move in closer instead of yelling from anywhere in the house. With all the windows open these days, half the neighborhood must hear his constant string of questions. She popped a tube of sunscreen into her bag.

"Can we fly a kite today? Do you know where it is?" Danny's voice moved a bit closer without any reduction in decibel level. "This looks like a perfect day to fly my kite. Don't you think so? Mom?"

Better get this child outside soon, let him run off some steam, Lana thought as she closed the cooler and tried to remember where she'd stored the kite over the winter.

"Check the basement closet where we keep the winter boots and coats. I think it's up against the back wall behind the coats." A moment later Danny emerged triumphantly, holding a kite almost as tall as him.

"Found it. And the string is attached. Are we ready to go now?

"Got your ball cap? Let's go get Charlie and get that kite in the air."

AFTER A SWIM AND SHOWER, Mark and Ben emerged from the

condo building into another glorious spring day. The trees, shrubs and spring flowers had exploded with growth in recent weeks. The long, hot days of summer were now only weeks away.

As the two men walked towards a stall to buy their lunches, they chatted amiably about the weather and the new baseball season.

"Too bad you weren't around for the home opener," Mark perused the offerings in front of him and chose a thick sandwich made with olive and rosemary bread filled with a mixture of sliced meats and havarti cheese.

"Yeah, well at least we scored those tickets to the Oakland game. That should be good." Ben eyed Mark's sandwich in some surprise and picked up something with sun-dried tomato and basil bread, smoked turkey and emmental. "Sandwiches have come a long way since the nineties. What happened to plain old ham and cheese?"

Ben plucked a bill from his wallet to pay for them both as Mark picked up sodas.

"Let's grab a bus and head over to Deer Island. I haven't been there for years. This is a great day to be by the water."

"Sounds good." Ben scanned the street for a bus stop. "Beats the heck out of the condo."

"LANA. DANNY. COME IN." Jennifer opened the door wide as Charlie launched himself at his young friend. The pup ran in doggie circles of delight as Danny ran into Jennifer's spacious living room and collapsed on the floor. Charlie climbed all over him, licking his face, arms and hands.

"Charlie!" Danny tried to restrain the only living thing in the Boston area that had more energy than him. "Sit. Charlie. Sit."

The two women smiled and chatted as they waited for the dog to settle enough to go out for his time in the park. Jennifer gave Lana a small bag of dog treats and enough scoop bags to ensure Charlie left no gifts behind.

"Someday we'll have to pack us all up and take Charlie to one of the off-leash parks." Jennifer watched Charlie obediently sit while Danny put on his leash. "We're going to Deer Island today. He'll still be on leash but we'll all have an afternoon of fresh air and exercise."

"He gets lots of exercise running around the house and back yard but it'd be good to get him out for a real run." Jennifer hesitated and then plunged ahead. "I'm thinking about putting the house on the market and buying a condo. If I do, I'll really have to organize to get him out for regular walks."

Lana was the first person besides Carol to hear about the house sale plans. "You're selling? But you were raised in this house weren't you?"

"I love it here. But my father can't come back and it's too big. Also, a condo would mean a lot less maintenance. I think it best I sell now while the market is good. Who knows when that might change." Jennifer knew she didn't sound convincing.

"Oh Jennifer. Promise me you won't rush into anything. Why don't you come with us and we could talk about it some more?"

"I'll take a rain check. I won't rush, I promise. I'm going to see a condo this afternoon with my friend Carol. She's a real estate agent. She says once I see this condo it will convince me. We'll see. I've never lived in anything but a house so it would take some getting used to for sure."

Jennifer watched as Lana bundled boy and dog into her van. "Have fun you two."

As Lana put it in gear, she leaned out the open window with one last piece of advice. "You and I both know what it's like to lose a husband years too early. This house has a special feel to it. Maybe because the people in it loved and cared for it and each other. I can't imagine a condo ever being that special."

Jennifer looked back at the house and knew Lana was right. She had some serious decisions to make. But first, she had to meet up with Carol and visit this condo her friend was so excited about.

A SHORT DRIVE LATER, Lana found a visitor parking spot. Leaving the food and kite in the van, she, Danny and Charlie set off for a walk to build their appetites.

"Danny, it's way too windy here for the kite. We can go over to the Common after lunch and fly it there." The offshore breezes were fine for the sailboats but would likely carry off the kite and its pint-sized owner.

Even as Lana and Danny were strolling the Island's paths, Mark and Ben were enjoying the bus ride over to the island.

"Did you bring sunscreen son?" Mark dug a tube out of his knapsack. "Good. I'll need to borrow some. Forgot mine."

"I have to be really careful. The anti-depressant I'm taking makes me sensitive to the sun." Mark handed the tube over to his father.

Mark looked out the window as they approached the causeway. "It's been a long haul but my doctor thinks I can gradually wean off them in the next few months. Now that I'm working outdoors a lot and playing the piano again I feel great. Mom really pushed me to get help. She could see I was having real emotional problems."

"It must have been so hard on you watching her lose her battle. You must have been scared too, knowing you'd be alone."

"Mom was my beacon of light. She was the only person who could get through the blackness. The only person I would listen to." Mark shoved a hand through his hair. "She arranged with Dr. Emery to get an emergency consult with his psychiatrist golf buddy.

I went to see him three times a week at first. He helped me get through when Mom went into full-time palliative care."

The bus reached the end of the line. The two men took a moment to decide which way to go. They decided to walk into the stiff breeze to find a good spot to eat and watch boats.

"Were you in the hospital?"

"No. Dr. Emery is a strong believer in talk therapy and staying connected to your real life. It took about three months for the medication to really kick in. I started to feel better mentally and emotionally just around the time Mom died. She got me to find treatment just in time.

"Were you ever suicidal?"

"Yeah. You?"

"A few times." Ben looked out over the water at the dozens of sailboats bobbing on the sparkling water. "How are you these days?"

"I haven't felt this good in years. Working outside is the best therapy there is. That and my music." Mark smiled. "Dr. Everest told me as long as I take my medication, continue with therapy, get proper rest and exercise, eat a balanced diet and avoid too much stress I should be just fine. He told me I need to get on with my life and plan for my future."

"That's a prescription most of us need to follow, myself included." Ben gazed out over the shimmering waves nearby. "I'd like to meet this Dr. Everest some day."

"Better take up golf. When he's not at the hospital, he lives on the golf course."

They were walking along, chatting about sailing and baseball, when Mark saw a woman, boy and dog ahead of them. As they drew a bit closer he could see the cocker spaniel's nose was in highest gear, snuffling from right to left and then suddenly stopping and practically yanking his young owner's arm off.

"Lana. Danny. Wait up."

Lana turned around to look at the two men now almost abreast of them and broke into a warm smile of recognition when she saw Mark.

"Well hi there. Fancy meeting you here." It was evident Mark was related to the older man standing next to him. "Is this your dad then?" There was a tiny remnant of Irish left over from hearing her grandparents lilting talk as a child.

Introductions were made all around, with Danny and Charlie quickly becoming the center of much adult attention as the two raced back and forth along the path. By mutual agreement they all went back to the van to pick up Lana's picnic supplies.

After finding a shaded spot where they could spread out, Danny collapsed beside his mother. Charlie crept under a bench to cool down in the shade. "Why is this called Deer Island? I haven't seen any deer. Lotsa dogs but no deer."

"Hundreds of years ago the deer used to swim over here to get away from the wolves," Mark saw Lana searching for an answer. "Wolves do swim but not unless they're really hungry. A few wolves probably swam after the deer but most would have given up and gone looking for easier prey."

Lana smiled her thanks at Mark over Danny's head. "Guess we'd better hope all the wolves got back to the mainland. Wouldn't want some big old bad wolf sneaking up to steal our lunch, right Danny?"

"Mom. There are no wolves here. Charlie would have smelled one by now." Danny dug into the bag of carrots and celery and came up with a handful. Charlie poked his head up when a carrot stick waved in front of his nose. He ate it like it was the finest of dog biscuits and then stood to beg for more.

"So, Mr. Powell, will we be seeing you back on the news again?"

"Call me Ben please, and no, I'm hanging up my news hat to develop a couple of documentary projects and maybe a memoir. Never had the time and wasn't in the right places the past few years." Ben gazed out over the harbor and watched a sailboat skittering along in the brisk breeze near the harbor entrance. "This sandwich is really good." He opened it up a bit to check what was in it and then took another man-sized bite.

"I never asked you Mark but is your mom here in Boston?" Lana had noticed that Ben didn't have a wedding ring on.

"My mother passed away four years ago. You may have heard of her. Heather Arlington." Mark put his sandwich down for a moment as Lana spoke. "She and my dad had been divorced for awhile."

"Heather Arlington. I went to some Philharmonic concerts where she was the guest pianist. She played beautifully. I remember hearing she died."

Ben glanced over at Danny who was feeding Charlie more carrot sticks. He didn't seem to notice the conversation between his mother and Mark.

"I'm so sorry Mark. She must have been quite young. An accident?"

"Breast cancer. I miss her, but it was for the best. She was suffering."

"It's so hard to lose a parent. Mine both died in a car accident." Lana shifted the conversation from its serious heading. "How did you folks get here? I know you don't have a car Mark."

"Took the bus over."

"I can give you a lift back then."

"That would be great Lana. Thanks for the offer." Mark smiled again. Lana thought his eyes perfectly reflected the brilliant blue water in front of them. She smiled back, wondering again how to go about getting a date with him.

"Say Mark, do you and your dad have any plans for dinner? I have a barbeque in my backyard that we don't use nearly often enough. We could pick up some steaks and beer. I have all the fixings for a salad. What do you say? Shame to waste any of this gorgeous day."

Mark and Ben stared at each other. Steaks and beer. This was no ordinary woman. This was a food angel sent from heaven. Both men nodded in unison, the awkward conversation all but forgotten.

"Sure. Sounds great! I'll buy the steaks now that I have some money in the bank. Can't think of a better thing to spend it on. Hope you have some onions and mushrooms. If not, I'll get those too." Lana smiled at the enthusiasm in Mark's voice.

"Put me down for the beer. And I'll throw in some chips and salsa to snack on." Ben patted the pocket with his wallet in it.

"What kind of chips Ben? I only like barbeque and jalapeno. I won't eat the ketchup ones. Yech." Danny screwed up his face.

"You can choose the chips then. Do you like salsa?"

"I think so. Do I like salsa, Mom?"

"Yes. It's that tomato sauce stuff you dip the tortilla chips in."

"I 'member that. Yep. I like it. Can we go now?"

"We just ate lunch. How about we all go to Boston Common for an hour and fly that kite of yours?" Danny was going to be one very tired little boy by the end of this day.

"Let's go!" Danny jumped up. Charlie wiggled and danced around the excited child, happy to be part of whatever adventure was about to come. As the adults packed up from the lunch, boy and dog prepared to lead the way back to the van.

CAROL GAVE JENNIFER'S HOUSE A CRITICAL ONCEOVER as she waited for her friend to come out. She quickly appraised its curb appeal. It would need a few touch-ups before the listing went live. The house was in almost but not quite perfect condition outside. Roof looked to be in good shape. New windows would be nice but not necessary. The front yard could definitely use some touching up to put it in top condition for showing. She could get top dollar for the property and already thought of two couples who would be very interested.

"Sorry to keep you waiting." Jennifer eased into the BMW. "I lost track of time this morning for some reason and ran late."

"No worries, Jen. We have lots of time. The owners will be out all afternoon. We'll grab a late lunch after." Carol shifted into first and briskly pulled away from the curb. Moments later they were crossing the Charles River and headed for the North End.

"This property just came on the market. The paperwork's barely done so it's not up on the Internet until tomorrow. You're getting first dibs on seeing it." Carol liked to be first off the mark with a new client. Showing it in under twenty-four hours of listing proved she had a network of buyers.

"It's right on the waterfront. Just over thirteen hundred square feet. Beautifully maintained." Carol was ready with some key highlights.

"What floor is it on? I've never lived in anything taller than two stories." Jennifer stiffened slightly as Carol sped around a slower driver. "I've been to your place and visited other friends in high rises but I'm not convinced I want to live in one myself.

"It's only the tenth floor. There's a spectacular view of the harbor from the living room, dining area and bedroom. The balcony overlooks the harbor. You can watch the sailboats come and go with your morning tea." Carol zoomed up the ramp to the visitor parking and swung into the only space left. "There's a pool, Jacuzzi and exercise room on the lower level. The kitchen is a galley type. Very compact and well designed so you get maximum space in the living areas."

"Let's have a look-see." Carol put her GPS in the glove compartment, picked up her smart phone from the console and shoved it in her over-sized bag.

Jennifer got out of the car slowly and gazed around. She knew the neighborhood. It was very tony and expensive. But, so was much of Boston these days. The two women strolled to the front of the condo building as Carol retrieved the pass card for the entrance. Soon she was opening the door to lead Jennifer into the unit's entry hall. She showed her the kitchen, bath and bedroom to save the living and dining areas last.

"And here is the million dollar view for a lot less than a million." Carol swept her arm across the view from the floor to ceiling windows. In front of them was the harbor with Logan airport off in the distance. Dozens of sailboats dotted the water at their moorings. Looking towards the southeast they could see the wharves and make out vehicles moving about.

"It would be gorgeous at night with all the lights." Carol waited for some reaction from her friend. "Isn't this breathtaking? Let's see the balcony." She slid open the door. "Here's a perfect spot to sip your tea and read the morning paper." They both stepped out onto the little balcony with its café table, two chairs and a pot of geraniums.

"What do you think? I can see your furniture fitting in here. Well, some of it."

"Do you realize there isn't one picture or photo anywhere in this condo? What kind of people don't have anything at all on the walls?" Jennifer found the place cold and devoid of any warmth.

"The unit was staged. They took their art down to make it more neutral for showing. It was a little off the wall, if you'll pardon the pun."

"Well I've been in this unit for about ten minutes and I'm ready to leave. View or not." Jennifer wanted out. "I'd like to think about this some more before listing the house. I didn't realize until now what's involved, including how I feel. I'm not ready for this Carol."

"Okay, Jen. You let me know when you're ready and I'll be there. Time for some lunch?"

Jennifer shook her head. "I'd like to go home and spend the afternoon doing some gardening. I've had enough for today thanks." She wondered how Carol could have ever thought she could move into this fish bowl. And the kitchen! It would have been crowded with one person in it. She wouldn't have been able to open the fridge and oven doors at the same time. Who designed these things?

THE TWO TALL MEN WALKED MEEKLY BEHIND LANA AND DANNY as she guided them from aisle to aisle in the unfamiliar country of her neighborhood grocery store. They exchanged bemused looks and shrugged their shoulders as if to say any sacrifice was worth the meal to come.

"Mom, can I get a soda?"

"Yes, as long as it doesn't have a lot of sugar." The last thing she needed was Danny to go all hyper before bedtime, even on a Saturday night. She pointed to a few choices and let Danny select from them. It worked. He was on his best behavior with Mark and Ben.

"Okay, let's see. We have three T-bones – Danny and I will share – mushrooms, a couple of Vidalia onions, chips, beer, soda. I have everything for the salad already, potatoes and a dessert we can thaw for later. That's it then. Gentlemen, open your wallets please."

As they reached the cash, the cashier finished making change for a customer and then looked up with a smile to greet the next customer. Her eyes widened when she saw Ben.

"Do you know who that is behind you?" Lana and the cashier chatted regularly.

Lana grinned. "Actually, I do. He's with me."

"Oh my. Ben Powell. Sir. Welcome to our store." The middle-aged cashier kept staring at Ben as she fumbled the groceries over the scanner. Two other cashiers looked over as did other customers. There was a small island of silence in the busy store, quickly broken when all the folks at the cash realized who was there.

Mark rolled his eyes and grinned. "Is it always going to be like this dad? Guess I'd better get myself a big pair of dark shades when I'm around you."

Ben hung his head. "I didn't encounter this when I was in the field. Not even in the London area really. This is news to me."

After signing some hastily-produced pieces of paper and calmly asking who to write the autograph to, Ben was finally left to pick up a grocery bag and flee to Lana's van.

"They'll forget you in a few months. Someone else will come along to take over the spotlight." Lana smiled over at Ben.

"Just what my ego needs. Thanks Lana." Ben's tone was lightly teasing. "I hope they forget me soon but not before they buy the book I'm going to write."

"People will start looking at you and know they've seen you somewhere. But they won't remember where. Be patient."

"You speak from personal experience?"

"Must be from a previous life. Or the Irish second sight." Lana chortled.

"Mom. Can Charlie stay with us for dinner? We don't have to take him home yet do we? I'm sure Aunt Jennifer would let him stay. Please?"

"Sure he can stay. We'll call her when we get back and see if he can stay overnight." Having the dog would keep Danny occupied until dinner was ready. She figured he would be conked in a couple of hours. Lucky to make it through dinner probably.

While the men brought in the groceries, Lana called Jennifer.

"Sure Lana. I'm just having a quiet evening here. Been doing a little gardening out back this afternoon and feel a bit stiff. I'm going to feel it tomorrow for sure. But, Charlie will have fun re-marking all his bushes and shrubs now that I've cut them back. Might as well give him a rest for tonight. How about I pop by after breakfast tomorrow to pick him up? Maybe have a cup of tea?" Jennifer had needed to physically reconnect with her home and garden after the condo experience. What was she thinking?

And what was Carol thinking? Did they not know each other's tastes well enough to have at least some idea of what would work for Jennifer if she decided to sell and move? The tenth floor. *No way,* Jennifer thought, *I need to have my feet on real ground. I need to hear and see the birds, see the trees, smell the flowers and feel the breezes. I need a Plan B,* she mused.

Chapter 8

"Salad's ready. Time to man the barbeque gentlemen." Lana noted that both Mark and Ben had their beers in hand and had been standing by the barbeque looking very manly while they waited for the go-ahead to put on the steaks. The foil-wrapped potatoes were almost ready. They could smell the warm butter.

She did a last check. The patio table was set with her favorite Mediterranean-style tablecloth and bamboo placemats. She'd brought out paper napkins, cutlery and a generous glass of Shiraz to go with her steak. The men declined the wine and were staying with beer.

Ben and Mark exchanged a look, suddenly realizing neither of them knew how to barbeque the steaks to the right doneness. They turned towards Lana.

"How do you like your steak Lana?"

"I like mine medium-rare." Lana was pretty sure she'd detected some hesitation over the steak cooking business. "Say about four minutes per side for steaks this thick I think. What would you say?"

"Sounds about right to me." Mark eyed his father, who smirked. "Perfect. We all like them the same way."

"Who's going to time these?" Lana pulled out a digital timer.

Mark seared each steak around the edges and set it on the grill, turned down the heat slightly and closed the lid. "All right. Steaks are on. Four minutes please."

Some time later Ben pushed back from the table with a satisfied last lick of his fingers and swallowed the last of his beer.

"I have to say that is the best meal I've had since I got back stateside. Can't chew at the bone in any decent restaurant. The steak's not finished until you do. By the way, will you marry me Lana?"

Lana laughed out loud. "Can't marry you Ben. I'm already in love with another man."

Mark almost choked on a mouthful of mushrooms and onions. "I didn't know you had a boyfriend."

"Not a boyfriend silly. Danny here." Lana grinned and shifted her gaze to where Danny had dozed off on a lounge chair. Charlie was curled up behind the boy's knees and already sound asleep. "No dessert for this boy tonight."

"Is there a Mr. Fitzpatrick?" The meal had been so casual and friendly that Mark felt comfortable posing a question that had run through his mind several times in the past few weeks. He wanted to know more about this lovely Irish beauty and her spunky little boy. And a big question was where was his father. He couldn't imagine anyone ever leaving her.

"His name was Tim," Lana said quietly. "He died in a military training accident when Danny was eighteen months old." Lana started collecting dishes to bring back to the kitchen. "Danny can't remember him but I tell him stories to help keep his memory alive. I keep a picture of him in Danny's room."

"My turn to say I'm sorry for your loss Lana." Mark stood to help. "It's a lot of work raising a child alone, especially a curious and energetic kid like Danny."

Ben cleared his throat and stood up.

"Mark. Another beer?"

"No thanks. I'm good."

"I'll just grab another beer for myself then. I'm not driving." Ben got no reply as he sauntered away towards the door off the patio.

"I didn't realize you'd been widowed. I assumed you were divorced or never married. Not sure why. You're so young." Mark picked up the salad bowl. "You must have family to support you though right?"

Lana started for the door with Mark beside her. "I lost my mother and father years back when I was in nursing school. They were hit by a drunk teenager with no driver's license. They both died at the scene.

I'm an only child. My mother was an only child too. Tim's parents and my only uncle and his wife all live out west so I'm alone here with Danny. Jennifer Barrett is the closest person to family for me."

"I know Jennifer. She told me about the job at the Manor." Mark opened the door as he digested this new information. He didn't know what he was feeling at this moment but he knew he yearned to put his arms around Lana and hold her close. As he opened the door for her, he glanced back at Danny. He realized he wanted these two people in his life. In the second before he stepped into the kitchen himself a wave of emotion washed over him so powerful he thought he might crush the salad bowl. He couldn't say where the feeling came from but he felt a sea change in his feelings about Lana and Danny.

Lana lit candles as dusk descended. Danny hadn't even blinked when Mark picked him up to carry him to his bedroom. The boy would be sleeping in his clothes tonight. When Mark glanced at the photo of Tim on Danny's dresser, Lana picked it up and brought it into the hall.

"He was handsome. Danny has his eyes for sure." The smiling man in the photo gazed back at Mark. He looked like he'd spent a lot of time outdoors. "It must have been such a terrible shock when you got the news."

"I was doing my clinical placement at the VA Medical Center. Someone from UMass tracked me down. I got called to the nursing director's office. Everyone was so good to me. Someone drove me to the day care to pick up Danny and then drove me home. There was always someone with me until Tim's parents arrived the next day. Everything was a complete blur for weeks afterwards. I don't know how I made it through. But, I had to. For Danny." Lana stroked her fingers over the photo. "He was so proud to be a father and was just waiting for the day Danny would be old enough to play ball."

Lana gazed up at Mark, her eyes glistening. "He would have been so proud of our little boy."

Mark put a hand on Lana's shoulder. "He sure would."

Lana nodded tearily and put the photo back on the dresser. Together, they went down to the kitchen and found Ben eyeing a blueberry pie Lana had warmed. The aroma of fresh-brewed coffee mixed with the smell of warm blueberries. Following Lana with the pie, both men took their coffee out to the backyard patio. Stars were just beginning to twinkle in the darkening sky as they had their next taste of heaven on earth.

"That was excellent Lana. But, it's time to get going Dad. It's been a long day. I'm about ready to crash." Mark stood up and carried his mug and plate into the kitchen.

"Thanks for such a great day and excellent dinner Lana. You sure you don't want to marry me?" Ben stood at the door to watch for their taxi. "It was great to meet you and Danny. Maybe we could take you two out sailing with us some time. Or come over for a swim at my building."

"You would be Danny's best friend for life if you took him sailing or swimming. He loves both, although he's never actually been sailing. He sure loves to watch the boats though." Lana and Mark stood next to each other in the small entrance. The two tall men made the space seem tight and cramped.

"How about I pick you up for work on Monday morning?" Lana looked up into Mark's eyes and felt the warmth of his gaze. She realized with a little lurch, that it was the look of a man who wanted to kiss her. She hadn't seen that look since Tim. She realized with another little lurch that she wanted to kiss him too. Here. Now.

When the taxi pulled up, Ben stepped out the door with a wave and a last goodnight. Lana reached up to plant a light kiss on Mark's cheek. Mark reached down to cup her face in both his hands and gave her a warm kiss on the mouth. Eyes wide, they stared at each other, both acutely aware that the earth had just shifted orbit. Ben walked towards the cab oblivious.

"Monday morning it is." Lana spoke softly. "I'll call you as we're leaving."

"Why don't you bring Danny with you to work on Monday? He

can spend the day with me. I promised him." Mark stepped out the door. They were both reluctant to let this moment pass.

"If you're ready for it." Lana stood in the doorway wishing they could be alone to savor what was passing between them.

"I'm ready for anything." Mark looked back once before getting into the taxi. Lana waved. He waved back with a wide grin on his face.

"I think you two need to have a real date without a chaperone around," Ben teased. "And you look adorable when you blush."

"Was I that obvious?" Mark felt a bit giddy and it wasn't from drinking one beer.

"Son, you would have to be crazy not to fall for a woman like Lana. If I were twenty or thirty years younger I'd do the same and give you a real run for your money." Ben gave the cabbie his address.

"I don't think I've ever felt such a strong attraction. She's so feminine and pretty. She's a lot of fun as you know. And she's so good with Danny. He's a great kid. She's a real take charge type. I like that. And did I say she's pretty? Man she's pretty."

"Wonder where I stored my tuxedo."

"What?"

"Sounds like you want to marry her."

The taxi pulled up in front of his apartment.

"Dad. She doesn't know enough about me. When I tell her, she may run for the hills."

"If Lana is the kind of woman I think she is, she won't run. You know that."

"Yeah. I think I do. Thanks Dad."

Lana thought back on the day with pleasure and a sense of wonderment. She mentally hugged the warm feeling surrounding her heart. As she got things out for breakfast and set the table, she thought of Mark in this room and the warmth of his kiss at the door. She put her hands up to her face where he had touched it and smiled dreamily as she drifted up to her bedroom.

"I think Mark's going to be a special person in my life and Danny's." Lana picked up the photo of Tim from her dresser. "He's really great with Danny and Danny adores him. I like that he works with his hands. He's musical too and a good kisser. Correction. He's a very fine kisser. At least as good as you were." She smiled brightly at the memory of that kiss at the door.

As Lana turned off her light and cuddled down into her bed, she fell asleep thinking of Mark. It was the first time she had thought of another man since Tim.

Chapter 9

"Danny, you ready?" Lana hadn't had any peace since telling him he would be shadowing Mark. Her Sunday had been spent being grilled about what he would do, what if he needed to pee and they were far from the buildings, where would he eat lunch, did they have any work gloves like Mark's, was it okay to get dirty. On that last question, Lana made Danny sit down.

"Part of the fun of gardening is getting dirty Danny. I thought you already knew that." Lana put her hands on both his shoulders as he squirmed. "You're going to have fun tomorrow. It's supposed to be nice and sunny. We're starting a vegetable garden for the residence. You already know a lot about vegetable gardens so you can be a real help."

"I like Mark. He's really cool. If I could pick a new dad I would pick Mark. And then Ben could be my grandfather. I'd like to have another grandfather. 'Specially one I could see more often." Danny peered into his knapsack to inventory its contents for about the fourth time in the past hour.

"How about we put that idea away for the time being? We don't really know Mark that well yet." Lana was astounded and impressed with the direction of Danny's thinking. He was a whole step ahead of her. She was still working on the idea of Mark. She hadn't even considered the Ben part of the equation.

"Mark." Lana called him and warmed to the sound of his voice so early in the day. "We're on our way. Be prepared for a gazillion questions. Danny's been at me since yesterday breakfast. You have no idea what you're in for. I hope you know all the places a boy can pee outdoors."

"I'll be outside waiting for you. Danny will be a busy boy today. I had all day yesterday to plan." Mark smiled and put down the phone.

"Hi Mark! What are we going to do today? I've never been a gardener for a whole day. Do I get to drive the tractor?" Mark was barely in the van when the questions started.

"We'll see." Mark turned to look back at Danny, who was strapped in behind his mother's seat. "Gimme five big guy."

They slapped palms together as Lana pulled into traffic.

By the time Lana swung into her parking space, Danny and Mark were in a deep discussion about how to make the best soil combination for a new vegetable garden. For some reason that escaped her, they both liked the part about mixing in rotted vegetable compost. Seems the rotting part held a special allure for them.

Lana gave Danny a light kiss on the head and walked away briskly to start her shift. Danny and Mark aimed for the garden sheds where half a dozen residents were already waiting with hats and gloves at the ready.

"Well, who is this?" Art Severn had been brought over by one of the other residents who knew he wanted to join the club.

"This is Danny Fitzpatrick, Mr. Severn." Mark figured they had met before but he knew Jennifer's father wouldn't remember.

"You ever worked in a garden young man?" In his wheelchair, Art was almost eye level with Danny.

"Yes. I helped my mother with our vegetable garden last year. I wasn't even four years old then. I'm almost five now."

Mark smiled. He was opening the door to the main garden shed and could see Danny was itching to see inside.

"Well then maybe we could work together. I've planted a few gardens myself. We could swap some stories." Art was in his element when it came to anything about gardening, even with this young boy.

Within minutes, the gardeners were fanning out in various directions, some to help with weeding in the flower beds and others to continue the main project of producing fresh vegetables that would soon grace the tables at Brentwood. Mark watched as his two student helpers rolled out boxes of bedding plants he'd bought at a discount from an area nursery. The owner had enthusiastically supported the idea, knowing it would boost his business to be known as a supporter of this special community garden. He even offered to donate a bench with a small plaque naming his business, which Mark gladly accepted.

He watched Danny struggle a bit to angle Mr. Severn's wheelchair next to a mock orange that needed some trimming. The plant had almost finished flowering and was looking leggy. Mr. Severn instructed as Danny held a pair of small clippers in both hands and chose his cuts. Mark marveled yet again as he watched Danny with the elderly man. Even though he couldn't hear the conversation, he could see Danny was peppering Mr. Severn with questions. The boy was a sponge for new knowledge and old Art was getting a level of mental stimulation that was probably rare for him now.

As the students began transferring the boxes of tomatoes, various kinds of lettuce, green and red peppers, eggplant, zucchini and a wide range of herbs, Mark went into the shed and brought out a bag with the seeds he'd bought to grow snow peas, carrots, radishes and more lettuce along with a bag of seed potatoes. Chef Vito had given him a detailed list of what could be used in the kitchens and was especially looking forward to having eggplants and zucchini to make into Italian delicacies he was sure the residents would enjoy. Mark had offered to start a composting area near the kitchen with a wooden frame and mesh cover to keep rodents away. Vito had quickly agreed.

Mark had been helping organize a few things for about half an hour when Danny appeared at his side. "I trimmed back the mock orange bush just the way Mr. Severn told me to. He said I did a real good job. He told me to come see you to find out what we do next. He couldn't remember your name so he described your hat."

Danny looked up at Mark's old-fashioned farmer's straw hat with its wide brim.

"What kind of hat is that anyway? I've never seen one before. Do you have another one?"

"I don't have another one but I know where we can get you one." Mark reached down and pushed Danny's ball cap down to his nose. "I think there may be a couple of rows ready to plant now. Why don't you and I push Mr. Severn over to where that guy is hoeing a row? I think we're ready to put in the tomato plants." Danny straightened his cap, grabbed Mark's hand and pulled him towards Mr. Severn.

The new garden construction brought out residents and staff alike to watch the progress, offer encouragement and make observations. Everyone was enjoying the spring weather and this project touched many who had tended their own gardens in younger days.

It was mid-morning when Jane arrived with Fred, the former groundskeeper. As they walked over, Mark was on his knees planting green peppers with Danny while Mr. Severn looked on and provided instructions. There was a general buzz as the residents and staff recognized Fred and started calling out hellos to him. Mark stood and stretched and watched Fred visibly straighten up at the friendly calls and greetings.

Mark reached out to shake his hand as Jane introduced them. "I've heard so much about you sir. Your diaries have been a major help while I was figuring things out. I'm really glad you could come and help."

"Call me Fred. If you call me sir I'll be peering over my shoulder for my old army sergeant. And he was a mean one. Nope. Fred'll be just fine."

The two men discussed the plans for the vegetable garden while Danny was set to work planting snow peas. The rows would be carefully marked so that trellises could be added to make the plants climb and leave their neighbors alone.

"Looks like you've had a busy morning." Jennifer arrived to have lunch with her father and found him resting in the shade. "This is going to be a major garden. I had no idea it would be so big."

Art peered up at her. "I'm hungry. Will you be taking me to the dining room soon? I hope they have something I like today." He was clearly tired and hungry.

Jennifer commented on the progress in getting the plants in and called out a hello to Danny and Mark as she pushed her father's wheelchair in the direction of the aromatic smells coming from the main building. Whatever is on the menu it sure smells good from here, she thought, thinking of the tossed salad and sandwich she had packed for herself.

Jennifer had just about reached the entrance with her father when she heard it. It was a cross between a scream and a howl. The howling got louder. Then it stopped. Everywhere, people were looking for the source of the strangled sounds. Mark was among the first to realize that Danny had been stung. Bee probably. They were all over the place when the mock oranges were in bloom. He ran in the direction of the sound and, as his eyes found Danny, he could see something was very wrong. The boy was clearly having problems breathing. Mark ran, scooped him up and kept running towards the infirmary.

He spotted a nurse. "Kerry help! Danny's allergic to the bee sting. He's going into shock." Mark sprinted through the entrance and headed to where he knew the infirmary was. Kerry ran behind him. Both reached it at almost the same time. She quickly located the epinephrine.

"Know how much he weighs? I've never used an adult EpiPen on a young child. We don't stock pens for children. We're going to have to take a chance with the adult one."

Mark figured max forty pounds as Kerry instructed him to pull down Danny's jeans. Kerry agreed and quickly injected Danny in the thigh, pulling it out when she hoped enough adrenaline had gone into his system for a child his weight.

The effect was almost immediate. Danny started to take in longer and deeper breaths. His head began to straighten and then his eyes fluttered open.

"What happened?"

Mark laughed with relief as Danny's first words were a question. "You and bees don't get along Danny. You ever been stung before? "Nope. The bite's on my neck. It hurts!" Danny's eyes filled with tears as he gingerly felt behind his head. Mark eased Danny forward and found the red and swollen area. The stinger was still there. Kerry pressed around the area until it moved up and she could tweeze it out. Danny sobbed in pain. She swabbed the site to ease the inflammation and prevent more venom from going into his system. By this time, Danny was crying and snuffling and clinging to Mark, who enfolded him in his arms.

Lana ran into the infirmary just as Danny pulled up his pants. She crouched in front of him with her hands on both his shoulders and then took her unhappy little boy in her arms. She kissed the side of his head and rubbed his small back.

"You okay big guy? Heard you had a nasty run-in with a bee." Lana drew on all her training and experience not to become a panicked mother as she realized how close Danny had come to dying.

"It hurts." Danny cuddled into his mother's embrace and sobbed. He took the ice pack the nurse brought him and sniffled as he put it against the throbbing spot where the stinger had been.

"That's it for you in the garden today. We have to keep a close eye on you to make sure you won't need another injection. Doc Anderson is on site today too so we'll ask him to check you over just to be sure."

The three of them huddled together until Danny felt ready to face the world again. Danny and Mark went hand in hand to the men's room to wash up before lunch. When they came out, Lana smiled at her men.

"Hey you two. I can't stay and eat with you but I didn't want to leave until I give you another hug." Lana hugged Danny even as she visually examined him to make sure he was all right. "My lunch break isn't for another half hour. What's with the hat at the table?" Lana flipped Danny's ball cap onto the table and tousled his hair.

"Mom. Puhleeeeeze!" Danny ducked away from his mother's public display. He was recovering quickly.

Lana sighed. He'd only recently started to become self-conscious if she tried to hug him in public. Despite his tears earlier, her little boy wasn't so little any more. She smiled over Danny's head to where Mark was grinning at her.

"We had a busy morning between the gardening and the bee sting. Vito will be thrilled when he sees everything we've planted already. Danny's becoming quite an expert on planting seeds just the right distance and depth."

Danny preened visibly at the praise.

"That's my guy. He's getting some pretty expert instruction from what I can see. The Brentwood Garden Club members have a few hundred years of experience between them. So, are you having fun then Danny?"

Danny's head bobbed a vigorous yes. Despite his close brush, he had recovered completely. He'd be fine to go back to the garden.

IT WAS SHORTLY AFTER FOUR WHEN MARK AND DANNY WENT INTO THE SOLARIUM.

"I guess you're old enough to keep a secret right?"

"Of course." Danny's eyes were wide as he looked up at Mark. "I know lots of secrets. I could tell you some but then they wouldn't be secrets any more right?"

Mark chuckled. "Yep. I'm sure you can keep this secret." Mark explained to Danny that he was practicing to do a little surprise concert for Mrs. Easton's one hundredth birthday. "So don't say anything right Danny boy?"

Danny sat quietly beside Mark and watched him play and sing Mack the Knife. Between the work and the bee sting, he had finally run out of energy. He sat without twitching or squirming as Mark sang the lyrics to the song made famous by so many, including his idol Frank Sinatra. As he played and sang, Mark felt the boy's small frame relaxing beside him.

The minute Lana came off shift she aimed for the sunroom to find Danny and Mark. They'd agreed to fast food take-out for supper so Danny could eat before fading from fatigue. Lana had made the offer with another, more ulterior motive. She wanted to get Mark alone and see what would happen next. Once Danny was asleep, a freight train whistle wouldn't wake him. Mark wouldn't stand a chance once she lit some candles and put on some mood music. She wasn't just thankful to him for saving Danny's life. She had already crossed the line. She was falling in love with the blue-eyed crooning gardener.

"OH MAN THAT WAS GOOD PIZZA. I think everything tastes better now that I'm working outside all the time in the fresh air." Mark had eaten half the pizza single-handedly. Lana had hinted at a special dessert too. Danny only made it through one piece on the half that had no mushrooms, onions or green pepper. Lana made do with the rest of Danny's selected toppings while stealing pieces of mushrooms and green pepper from Mark's side.

It was nearing seven o'clock as the pizza made its final disappearing act. Danny had been yawning for the best part of an hour already. Lana knew he'd be asleep sooner rather than later and smiled at the thought of stage two for this evening. She gathered up dishes and tidied the kitchen.

"Danny. Time for bed. What say we get you into the bath and soak off some of today's gardening efforts before you get under the clean sheets?" Lana knew there would be no argument. Danny was totally exhausted and happy. "Would you like Mark to help you out while I clean up and get our lunches ready for tomorrow?"

Mark smiled at Danny. "Guess if I helped you get all that dirt on you, I should help you get it off right?"

"Mmm… yes. That would be great." Danny wasn't going to be awake very long.

"I'll be up to tuck you in and say goodnight whenever you're ready." Lana turned her back and left Mark to organize her boy for his bath and bed. *This feels so right,* she thought. *Now, Mark needs to know just how right it is for him and me and Danny.*

As Mark and Lana came down the stairs after tucking Danny in and saying goodnight, their arms brushed against each other. Mark coughed and sputtered. Lana smiled and floated down the stairs into her cozy living room.

It wasn't large. There was an entire corner devoted to Danny's toys and games. The television was bracketed by two bookcases holding a variety of books, DVDs, pictures and figurines. With a large leather chair and roomy sofa, the overall effect was casual and comfortable. She lit half a dozen candles on the coffee table and a couple of side tables. And then sat on the couch and patted the spot beside her when Mark came down.

"So, what's for dessert?" Mark sat down.

"I thought maybe we could start with me." Lana snuggled up against him, her petite frame small against his long lanky one. She wrapped an arm across his chest and hugged him. The physical labor of the past few weeks had hardened his muscles and broadened his chest. Lana was tingling with desire to explore him without benefit of clothes.

Mark stared down as Lana lifted her face up to gaze up at him. He stared into the liquid pools of her blue-green eyes. He gathered her gently into his arms, bending his head down to kiss her forehead and then her eyelids. His tongue found a sensitive spot under her right ear as Lana moaned softly against him and arched into him for a long, deep kiss that spoke of things to come.

She led him back up the stairs but this time they turned into her bedroom. Lana cupped her hands around Mark's face to draw him down for a kiss. Then it was Mark's turn to cup her face in his hands and deepen the kiss. Without a word, they moved in unison to the bed to explore, to touch, to murmur and explore further.

As they lay together bathed in moonlight, Mark slowly undid the buttons on her shirt and gently pushed the fabric away to stroke her bare skin. He looked at her trim figure and small but generous breasts.

She was wearing what could only be described as a naughty confection that hid little and promoted much.

Lana looked into Mark's eyes and grinned with delight at the reaction she saw. She loved her lingerie collection and was thrilled to see that Mark did too. "I may be a conservative nurse by day but under that uniform lies a wanton woman."

Mark groaned, "I'll never be able to be around you again without wondering what's underneath. I'm doomed." He stroked the lacey edges of the bra and let his fingers brush across the top of her satiny breasts.

"Right now, what you are is hot." Lana pushed him up and helped him take off his shirt. Before it slid to the floor she was rubbing her hands up and down his chest and leaning in to take in his scent. She loved the smell of him. He smelled like the gardens at the residence but in a subtle and very manly way. "Do you mind if we just go straight to animal lust? It's been so long and you smell so wonderful. I can't help myself." Lana was surprised at the strength and even determination of her desire.

In answer, Mark got her shirt off, took one good look at the bra that almost wasn't, unclipped it from the front and took each breast into his work worn hands. For Lana, the raspy touch of his hands only fuelled her desire. She pressed towards him.

Kneading her small breasts in his hands, Mark pushed her back onto the bed and bent in to kiss each tight nipple. His tongue moved slowly over and around each one and then traveled downwards. Lana arched as his gentle but demanding ministrations sent jolts of desire through her. She was feeling decidedly wanton and pushed him over to explore with her tongue and hands and lips.

Together they playfully wrestled the remaining clothes off each other as the heat rose between them. Lips found lips, hands found places to touch and rub. Mark moved over Lana as she melded her body to his. As he entered her warmth, Mark thrilled to the way she kneaded his shoulders and then slipped her hands down to cup his buttocks. They moved together in a dance as ancient as humanity.

Lana curled her legs around him and urged him deeper. Her eyes were half-closed as she let herself be swept in the tide of their love making. She rode on and on as the waves of pleasure and desire swept her towards her climax. And then her body crested. Mark felt her release and rode with her until they both felt the last ebb of his release and lay wrapped together as the moon looked on.

Lana caressed Mark's chest, smiling dreamily as the moonlight bathed them both in its soft light. Mark stroked her thick waves of hair, looking at her smooth skin glistening in the pale light. She trailed a finger lightly back and forth across his chest and then up to an ear lobe, which she rubbed.

"That was a great dessert but I'm still hungry."

"For more of me or actual food?" Lana reached up to run her fingers through his hair.

"The night is young and so are we. What say we have a bit of both?" Mark rolled over on his side and made to pull up the covers but instead flung them back. "I need food, woman. Take me to your fridge!"

They crept down the stairs giggling and shushing each other like little kids early on Christmas morning. Mark strode to the fridge wearing only his jeans and opened the door wide to survey the contents. Suddenly, he reached in and emerged triumphant with a strawberry and apple cobbler.

"Is this what I think it is? Have any ice cream?" Mark set down the dish almost reverently and opened the freezer door. Success again. He pulled out a tub of Ben and Jerry's cheesecake brownie. "Oh rich. So rich. Now I know who's in heaven. You, me, Ben and Jerry for sure."

Lana watched his foray into her fridge with amusement. *Almost like a kid*, she thought. And then thought, *that was no kid in my bed a few minutes ago.* She'd have to stay away from the ice cream or she'd melt it as she remembered their almost feverish lovemaking. She'd been sex deprived for way too long.

Lana handed Mark a couple of bowls and spoons and began to busy herself with making a pot of tea. Minutes later the two of them were sitting at her kitchen table, eating dessert and thinking about getting back to bed.

Mark watched Lana and listened to her lilting voice telling him about Danny playing with Charlie. "I'm just going to get a glass of water. It's time for me to take some medication." He went to the front hallway for his backpack and brought it back to the kitchen.

Lana was curious but said nothing. She knew he was about to tell her something about himself that was important. Lots of people took medication for any number of conditions. Maybe he had epilepsy. She could deal with that. Maybe he was bipolar. She didn't think so though. He seemed too balanced.

She waited for him to tell her but instead he just handed her a bottle of pills. Lana looked at the drug name and recognized it immediately. "How long have you been battling depression?"

She looked straight into Mark's eyes as he pulled out a bottle of anti-anxiety medication.

She pushed away what was left of her dessert. The ice cream had melted and was puddled around the plate.

"Since I was about twenty. When I learned my mother was dying.

"I wanted to tell you before this but I didn't know how. I wasn't sure where we were heading and I didn't want to scare you off before you had a chance to get to know me better. You're the first woman I've become romantically involved with in all these years. I don't have an instruction book on how to deal with this."

Lana smiled at Mark and put her hand out to him. "Getting to know you these past weeks has been wonderful. It's been life-changing for me. I feel wanted and cared about the way I did with Tim. I didn't know when or if that would happen for me again. You are such a kind and caring person and Danny adores you. You don't seem at all depressed. Are you?"

"I can honestly say I have never felt better in my life. Working outdoors is perfect for me. Being able to play and sing again has given me my life back. My doctor figures I'll be off both meds within a few months." Mark shifted in the chair to face her directly. "When my mother's cancer advanced we both got so focused on her health that I didn't realize what was happening to me. She was the one who realized I had lost my *joie de vivre* as she called it."

Lana glanced up at the clock and realized they wouldn't be getting much sleep before the alarm went off. But, she wanted to find the common ground that would let them both look to the future and worry less about the past.

"How are you doing these days? I know some days you seem tired as if you haven't had enough sleep."

"I have a few side effects like fatigue. Mostly I can handle them without it interfering too much with my life. I'm going to ask the doctor if we can start weaning me off the anti-anxiety drug. Working outdoors has been really therapeutic. I was really lucky when Jennifer Barrett suggested I apply at Brentwood."

Lana perked up when she heard Jennifer's name. "Jennifer is your social worker then? I know you said she told you about the job opening. I just didn't connect it to her work."

"Yes. She's found me group counseling after work and steered me to Brentwood. She's been great." Mark looked down at their clasped hands. "You and Danny have become very important to me. So important that I would sign a contract to keep stress under control and not take on more than I could handle. I make that promise to you." Mark covered her hand with his other one. "I'm making a new life for myself. I want you and Danny in it."

Lana took her hand away from his and reached up to gently caress his cheek. She made a decision. "Take your medication and let's get to bed. We have a lot more to talk about but now we need to sleep if you're going to keep that promise."

They stood up and hugged in silence for a long moment.

THE NEXT MORNING BROUGHT A CHANGE IN PLANS. As Mark was showering, Lana woke Danny up and explained they'd be taking Mark to get a change of clothes. She had long since given everything of Tim's to the good will.

"Mark slept over? Where'd he sleep, Mom?"

"He fell asleep on the couch so I put a blanket on him and let him stay over. He felt a bit silly when he woke up here this morning." She mentally crossed her fingers over the little white lie.

"Can he stay over again soon?"

"I hope so. You'd like that then?" Lana smiled dreamily, remembering how they had quietly cuddled before falling asleep wrapped in each other's arms. The man she was coming to love was coping pretty well with the hand life had dealt him.

"Do you think he could teach me baseball?"

"He's from Boston. Of course he can teach you baseball." Lana handed Danny clean socks and scooped away the dusty ones he'd been about to put on.

Lana and Danny dropped Mark off at this apartment. Moments later he emerged with fresh clothes. To her trained eye, Danny seemed to be right back to normal when she dropped him off at day care. She made a mental note to call the pediatrician as soon as his office was open and get a prescription for a junior EpiPen today. She was beyond grateful that Danny had been so close to medical help with his first sting. She knew from what Mark had told her that her son had a severe allergy. Nothing to play around with. He would need to learn how to inject himself as soon as possible. In the meantime, all his caregivers would need to know about the allergy and have a couple of EpiPens available at all times during bee season. She'd lost her husband to a stray bullet. She wasn't going to lose her son to a tiny insect.

Chapter 10

Ben didn't know exactly where he was going when he stepped outside that morning. He just knew he had to get his new life organized, whatever it might be. Years of tracking down hot stories and putting them through production had provided a routine he could depend on in a quirky kind of way. The routine was that there wasn't one until he was on the story and moving towards deadline. The deadline provided the sharp focus he needed to get the job done.

Now, deadlines were in his past. He felt at sea for the first time in decades, he realized. He'd given himself a few weeks to think about what he wanted to do next. Now those weeks were adding up and he still didn't have a plan.

I need to see Mark, he thought. *Just bounce some ideas around with him. Time to see where the boy works.* He changed direction to catch the bus that would take him to Brentwood. *Fine day to see how the old folks live.*

Getting off the bus at the entrance half an hour later, Ben was immediately struck by the beauty of the property. The long driveway lined with mature Norway maples and flower boxes offered a cheery welcome that was not lost on him.

Looks like a great place to live or work, he thought as he strolled towards the large front verandah. His cameraman's eyes appreciated the casual array of garden chairs and tables bracketed by boxes overflowing with colorful mixtures of flowers, ivy and spikes. He decided to stay outside and walk around the building, figuring he would find Mark at the greenhouse office he was always talking about. He saw the building over on the south side and was only half-way there when he heard someone calling out "Dad".

"Took you long enough to come out here for a visit." Mark couldn't hide the beginnings of his trademark grin.

"I was just waiting for the gardens to be in full bloom before hiking out here." Ben saw the grin and knew Mark was teasing.

"Actually, you're right. I'm just noticing this week how everything is really starting to fill out with both the late spring and early summer blooms. This is probably one of the best times of the year for a garden. Not too hot yet and enough rain to keep all the plants happy."

"So, other than seeing some of the prettiest gardens in Boston, what brings you here today?" Mark steered his father towards the bench donated by the garden supply store. Both men sat down, shaded by a large chestnut tree.

"I'm feeling at loose ends. I have no job. I have no place to live I can call my own. I'm still relatively young and healthy but I have no desire to go back to doing what I was doing before. I'm open to new ideas." Ben shoved his hand through his hair. It was an unconscious habit when he was trying to focus his thinking.

"Well, you've come to the right person. I know what it's like not to have a job, no place to call home and not want to go back to what life was like before. I know all about that."

Ben glanced sideways at Mark. "You're so right. You have been there already. I really did come to the right person didn't I?"

"How about we talk over lunch? I'll double check but I don't think there would be any problem in you having lunch here. I know friends and relatives of the residents can call ahead and join them for a meal from time to time." Without waiting for an answer, Mark pulled out his cell phone and dialed Reception. He spoke for a moment and hung up.

"No problem. All taken care of. Let's go before it gets crowded." He motioned his father towards the back entrance off the garden.

"Mr. Severn. Jennifer. Hi!" Mark smiled as the two men easily overtook Jennifer wheeling her father towards the dining room. "Jennifer, meet my father, Ben Powell."

Jennifer glanced up into the face she had seen on her television news over the years and hoped she wasn't blushing. She'd had a schoolgirl crush on Ben Powell for years. She loved the deep gravelly voice that carried such authority you just knew he was telling you the truth. And, in person, he exuded a presence or power she couldn't quite identify. She tried to give a word to how she felt to be near him. The only word that came to mind was protected. It wasn't a word she had ever thought she would need or want. She was quite capable of taking care of herself.

She reached out to shake the large hand in front of her. "Mr. Powell. Ben. Good to meet you. I've been hearing about your long overdue reunion with Mark. I must say you two sure look alike. Clearly father and son. I'd like you to meet my father, Art Severn."

"Miss. Can you please take me into the dining room? I like to eat my lunch promptly at noon." Art ignored the familial reference. He was hungry.

"Good to meet you Mr. Severn. How about I get you into the dining room? I'm hungry too. Much as I love talking to a beautiful woman out here in the sunshine, food comes first." Jennifer stepped back as Ben moved to take the wheelchair. She quickly found herself trailing behind three men bent on finding food.

Despite the schoolgirl crush, she was prepared not to like Ben. He had abandoned his son for most of his childhood and neglected his wife to the point she divorced him. Then, when his son was battling his way back through depression, he'd hightailed it off to the mountains of Afghanistan to report on another man's war. What kind of man could be so shallow?

Yet, here he was, an older and equally charming version of his son. There were no celebrity airs about him at all. He spoke to her father with respect and wheeled him off to the dining room as if it was the most natural thing to do.

JENNIFER, MARK AND BEN CHATTED QUIETLY OVER THEIR LUNCHES. As Mark and Art started an animated discussion about the gardening projects and the best location for some new flowering bushes, Ben and Jennifer found themselves sliding into an earnest conversation.

"What are you doing now Ben without a camera and microphone in front of you every day?" Jennifer tucked into a crunchy garden salad.

"That's what I came out here to talk to Mark about. I refuse to go overseas again and chase the headlines. I'm ready to leave that to the younger folks. And, I don't want to anchor. It's not my style. I need to do something completely different. Not full time. Just to keep my brain engaged."

"I know what you mean. I'm doing the same thing. I work enough to pay my bills, stay connected to my networks but still have time to do the things I want to do. The trick is to find a balance."

"Funny you should say that. I think that's what's been missing most of my working life. There was no balance. I was too busy chasing stories. Never had enough time for myself. Certainly didn't make enough time for my family."

"I'm glad to hear you say that. When Mark told me how absent you've been from his life I couldn't imagine you as anything but hard-hearted."

Ben blinked at her candor and put down his fork. "I had to be pretty hard-hearted when it came to what I was seeing. That's for sure. But my network pushed all of us to give two hundred percent. It was costing them a pile of money to have us over there. We weren't given a lot of choice about how often we could fly home."

"But Mark says he hasn't seen you since his mother's memorial service. I'm sure you've had a few weeks of vacation in all that time."

Ben looked directly into her eyes. "I didn't know it at the time, but I was suffering from post-traumatic stress disorder. The thought of coming back here to Mark's depression was too painful. I couldn't bring myself to book a flight home. I know it was cowardly but I just couldn't handle any more."

Jennifer could see Mark was listening closely.

"Dad. You never said anything about PTSD. I met a few people being treated for it. It's serious."

"Tell me about it. You and I should compare meds sometime. "

Ben grimaced. "I had to keep working. It's not like I could go to my boss and say I was afraid to get out of bed in the morning. I doubt there's any career more macho than television journalism. I kept my head down and got away to civilization whenever I could. I spent a lot of time in England off in the countryside, away from cities and noise. I couldn't even watch old war movies or westerns. The gunfire set me off."

"How are you now?" Jennifer realized she couldn't begin to imagine what Ben must have seen and heard.

"A lot better than I was even a month ago. I realize now I was completely burned out. At least now I don't walk around looking up for snipers but I still feel more comfortable with my back to the wall in restaurants. Just coming back, resting, exercising and eating properly has made a huge difference. I feel like I'm standing on firm ground that isn't going to blow up when I least expect it."

Jennifer noticed her father had dozed off in his wheelchair. She tried not to look at her watch. Ben's revelations were more than she ever expected to hear on their first meeting.

"There are some places that are just too dangerous to send in a journalist." Ben spoke to both of them. "Journalists aren't safe any more. I know some who've been attacked and beaten up by mobs. There was a case of a print reporter who had his hands hacked at with a knife. They were trying to prevent him from sending in his stories. Female journalists have been raped."

Jennifer smiled warmly and reached out to touch Ben's hand. "Thank goodness you came back before anything else happened to you. You found Mark. And he's found you. It sounds like you both have a lot of catching up to do and some new memories to start making together."

"Are you free for dinner tonight?"

Mark grinned at the wide-eyed look on his father's face.

Jennifer smothered a laugh. It was clear Ben had just blurted out the invitation. "Actually, not tonight. I have a Yoga class and then dinner with a friend. How about tomorrow night?" It was so easy, Jennifer thought.

They had both just nimbly cleared the hurdle of whether either or both of them were single and available.

"Tomorrow it is. Is there any food you really don't like?"

"I eat everything."

"My kind of girl." Ben slid the piece of lemon meringue pie in front of him and attacked the yellow and white confection.

Jennifer gave him her business card and signaled an orderly that she needed help with her father. He woke up groggily, thanked her for visiting and said he hoped she would come again. He thanked Mark for visiting too.

As the orderly wheeled her father away, Jennifer smiled at the two handsome Powell men. "See you soon Mark. Ben, look forward to dinner tomorrow."

He seems to be handling the PTSD as well as could be expected, she mused. *Wonder if he's getting any counseling.* Walking towards her car, she felt a lightness in her heart she hadn't felt in five years. Ben was real and warm and completely human. It felt like the door to a special room in her heart that had abruptly slammed shut when Jason and Kaylee died just might be ready to open again.

"I'VE GOT A DINNER DATE TOMORROW." Jennifer opened her eyes slowly and rose from her final moment of Yoga meditation. The words were out. She hadn't meant to say anything but she was too relaxed to stop the flow.

"Say that again? I'm not sure I heard what you said. Who is he? Do I know him?" Carol was slowly rotating her neck. "This is headline news."

Jennifer smiled at Carol's comment. "You will know who he is but I don't think you know him. And I'm not ready to say just yet. It's a first date." Jennifer rolled up her mat and strolled dreamily towards the change room.

Carol caught up quickly. "What do you mean I will know who he is but not know him? That's not fair. That's being a tease to your best friend. C'mon, dish. Who is it?"

"I'm not going to say just yet. I want to get to know him better before I decide if I want to let him into my inner circle."

"Just tell me he's not a gangster or something. I would worry about you going out with some shady character."

"He's not shady and I don't think he's a gangster." Jennifer teased and watched Carol furiously trying to figure out her puzzle. "Let it be, Carol. For me. When I'm ready you'll be the first to know."

"Promise?"

"Promise."

BEN SURVEYED HIS BORROWED PAD. He'd had a good workout in the building's gym followed by a hot shower. Now he needed some good old fashioned protein to feed his muscles.

Good lord, he thought, *if I'm old enough to call it a pad, I must be old.* He thought of meeting Jennifer and brightened. *I may be getting older but I still have a way with the ladies.* Opening the fridge, he peered at its meager contents. Two apples, half a jug of orange juice, cream cheese, two stale bagels and a container of yogurt. He raised the lid and quickly snapped it back. It was definitely a different color from when he'd bought it. *I need to get some real food in here,* he thought, closing the door and chucking the yogurt into the waste bin. He grabbed an apple and padded across the carpet to his laptop. *Must be someplace close by I can get decent takeout.* He Googled "restaurants", "takeout", his address and hit enter.

A half hour later he was back with an assortment of boxes that would tide him over for a couple of meals, including breakfast if he was inclined to eat reheated Pad Thai in the morning. *Why not,* he capitulated. *It used to be leftover pizza back in the day. Just got more interesting,* he thought, as he forked out veggies and chicken cubes redolent with eastern spices and curries. *Can't eat steak for every meal,* he reasoned. *And Asian is really pretty damn good.*

Finding a ball game on one of the cable sports channels, he tucked into his dinner and thought about Jennifer. As the innings progressed, he finally realized he was paying less attention to the game and more to the story unfolding in his head. *You're slipping buddy*, he thought. *Must be sex deprivation. Since when did a date trump a ball game?* He fingered the business card he'd pulled out of his jacket pocket. Too bad she hadn't given him her home phone number.

Back at the laptop he Googled her on 411. Nothing came up. He tried variations. Still nothing. Stumped, he went back to the ball game only to see it had ended and he didn't know who'd won.

I'm going out on an official dinner date. Jennifer rolled that thought around in her head as she closed up for the night and got the kettle ready for her morning tea. *A real date with a good-looking man who looks to have some fire left in him.*

Getting ready for bed, she wandered over to her closet and turned on the light inside. *What to wear tomorrow night?* She dug into the back of the closet and drew out her favorite little black dress. It was a classic. She checked the size tag and realized with some surprise it might actually be loose on her. Between yoga, spinning and all her other activities she had come down at least one size and maybe two.

Oh happy day, she thought. *At last, a dress that didn't shrink in the closet when I wasn't looking.* She decided to try it on just to be sure. A moment later she looked at herself in the mirror. Even without makeup she had to agree she still looked pretty good. No high heels any more but the copper-toned patent pumps looked pretty. Add a bit of jewelry, a wide belt to show off her trimming waistline and she might turn a head or two. *Just one certain head would be fine.*

I have a date! Better get my beauty sleep, she thought, and ambled off towards the large roomy bed that might have a visitor soon. She mentally wiped out that thought, ordering herself to get her mind back into safer territory. But, the idea snuck right back in. The handsome man she'd secretly lusted after for years was now flesh and blood. And, he was a completely down to earth human being who was fascinating to talk to and very easy to look at.

Who knew a man could be eye candy at his age?

Jennifer mentally chided herself for letting her imagination run wild. But, it wasn't her imagination. Ben was very real, very male and very, very tempting. *Who could resist?* She smiled dreamily and snuggled into her pillow.

"Hop up on the table Danny. Let's have a listen to your heart and lungs." Danny's pediatrician moved the stethoscope around to listen to Danny's breathing and heart rate.

"As you suspected Lana, Danny is just fine. None the worse for wear after the bee encounter." Dr. Morley checked the bite site and noted the swelling was almost gone. "I'll give you an open-ended prescription for the EpiPen Jr. You'll need to keep two on hand at all times but I would recommend four. Two at home and two wherever Danny is at all times. He's on the borderline for moving up to the adult one within a year at most."

Dr. Morley was writing the prescription as he spoke. Danny was already off the table and exploring.

"Am I gonna die Dr. Morley? My father died when I was a baby and left us alone. I don't want to die and leave my mom alone."

Dr. Morely smiled at his young patient. "Danny. You carry those pens with you everywhere you go whenever the bees are out. You do that and you'll be just fine. Lots of people are allergic to bee stings and most of them don't die. You got that?"

Danny nodded but went over to his mother and hugged her anyway.

Lana was more than a little surprised Danny had made the connection between losing his father and his mother possibly losing him. She returned the hug and tried to remember if she was wearing waterproof mascara. She grabbed a tissue from the box on the doctor's desk and dabbed her eyes carefully.

"We'll get six of those pens just to be sure we have all we could ever need."

After dropping by a pharmacy to get the prescription filled, Lana took Danny to his day care and explained the new situation. She felt confident when she left that the director would make sure all the staff knew about Danny's allergic reaction and what would need to be done if he was stung.

Later, after parking at Brentwood, Lana went to find Mark. She wasn't going to use her mobile to ask him out for a date when he was so close by.

"Danny's doctor said he should be fine and gave me a prescription for junior EpiPens. By the way, you're officially invited by Danny and I for a sleepover on Saturday night after spending the day with us doing something fun. How about you plan the day and I plan the food and everything else?"

"Danny invited me too?" Mark felt a special warmth near his heart at the thought of the little guy inviting him for a sleepover. As a child, he'd had several friends but the parents didn't seem to think about sleepovers. And definitely not one that included a pert nurse with sexy lingerie.

Mark shifted his thoughts and grinned like a little kid at the thought of spending a day and night with Lana and Danny. He glanced around to see if anyone could see them and saw the coast was clear. Bending his sandy-haired head over Lana's, he planted a resounding kiss on top of her ebony waves.

"Do you think Danny would like to go to a ball game Saturday afternoon?"

"You know he would." Lana tossed back her head to smile up at him. "We could snack at the game and then have a light supper after. We'll have to decide on a dessert though."

"Same one as last time works for me. You got any more of that cobbler?" Mark winked and got a lilting laugh in return.

JENNIFER STARED AGAIN AT HER COMPUTER SCREEN, willing herself to concentrate. Stop thinking about tonight, she commanded herself. All morning she had struggled between the thoughts racing through her head and the work that needed to be done. She was going on her first date since Jason and Kaylee died. And, she told herself, they would not only approve but cheer her on. She remembered a conversation she'd had with Jason. They were walking along the waterfront in early fall. They both agreed that if anything happened to one of them, the other should find happiness in a new relationship.

Jason said the wife usually outlived the husband and she should go out and find a new love to spend the rest of her life with. Neither of them realized his throw away comment would become her reality. But now, for the first time, she understood what he meant. She didn't want to be alone for the rest of her life. She was ready to share her future with a new love.

Chapter 11

"Jennifer. How about I swing by your place and we head over to Boylston Street? Shouldn't be too busy on a Thursday. We can stroll around and drop in to whatever place takes our fancy."

"That would be great Ben. I'll wait outside so we don't give the cab driver a wait fee." Jennifer was nothing if not frugal and didn't waste time or money. In this, she was definitely her father's daughter.

"Sounds great. I'm really looking forward to seeing you Jennifer."

"See you at six. And Ben? You're paying right?" Jennifer smiled as she teased. "I'll have you know this is my first date in many years and I plan to make the most of it. Make sure your wallet is well-stocked with cards or money."

Ben laughed out loud.

"Hi Mark, are you ready for Mrs. Easton's birthday concert next week?" Kathy had stepped out for some fresh air before her next meeting. "Everyone is talking about your singing and playing. I'm starting to wonder if we can keep the party secret for even a few more days."

Mark smiled as he stood up to talk with her. "I've planned about a twenty minute set. I'll play in the background after I have a bite of lunch and until it's time to sing happy birthday. Then I'll sing one last song to Vera to end the party. But you already knew that. Jane has everything and everyone organized. This will be such a treat for Vera. Does she have family coming?"

"Two of her great-great grandchildren are flying in with their parents from Arizona. She's never met the children. Most of her family will be arriving a couple of days before the party and staying for a week.

She won't see them until the party to keep it a surprise. Apparently Vera's birthday has sparked a family reunion. We're expecting about thirty relatives spanning five generations. It's pretty amazing."

Mark thought about his family as he and Kathy parted ways. Strolling back towards the greenhouses and his office, he realized that even if he lived to be a hundred, it was unlikely he would ever have a family big enough to produce that many relatives at a reunion. He wondered how many children Vera had raised those many decades ago and what life must have been like in the early years of the twentieth century.

He came up short in his imaginings as he realized that Art Severn was waving him over to where he was weeding along the edge of a bed full of fledgling tomato plants.

"Young man. Come here, please. There's something I want to show you."

Mark smiled and changed direction slightly. "What's up Mr. Severn?"

"Look here." The elderly man bent over stiffly in his wheelchair and poked his trowel into the rich soil near a plant that had been almost ready to be staked and was now almost cut in half. "We have cutworms." As he turned over the soil, an ugly beige slug could be seen trying to nose itself back down in the soil.

"I don't have much experience with vegetable gardens but I don't like the sound of the name." Mark lifted his hat, shoved his hand through his thick blonde hair and set the hat back on his head. "What can we do about it Mr. Severn?"

"We will need to put a collar or barrier around each of the plant stems. We can use nails, popsicle sticks, anything that sticks into the soil and out of the ground a few inches. When the worms encounter the barrier they can't wrap themselves around the stems. They feed at night so we need to get as many plants protected as we can before dark." There was no hesitation or fumbling for words as Art instructed his pupil. "We also need to check other plants, especially the eggplants and sweet peppers. They really go after them."

Mark glanced around for one of the summer students and called him over. "Dan, if you go in the shed where we keep the tractor mower, at the back you'll find a pail full of old nails. They're six-inchers. Bring that pail and find a couple of small buckets to divvy them up. And ask the other guys to come over. We have a job that needs doing pronto or we could lose a bunch of plants."

Within minutes, a new team had sprung up to do battle with the slugs. Mark strode back to his office and Googled cut worm on the Internet, quickly learning that Mr. Severn's techniques were not only the most humane but perfectly safe for the environment. Sometimes the old ways were still the best ways.

JENNIFER GLANCED AT HER WATCH FOR THE UMPTEENTH TIME and told herself to stop acting like a breathless teenager. Time to take a break, eat her lunch and plan how to best spend her time until the end of her work day, she told herself sternly. She decided to eat lunch at her desk and then go for a brisk walk in the warm June air to recharge herself for the afternoon.

She was just finishing a large salad with fresh strawberries and roasted pecans when the phone rang. Looking at the call display she immediately recognized the Brentwood number and grabbed for the phone.

"Yes. This is Jennifer Barrett." She anxiously waited to hear the next words.

"Mrs. Barrett? This is Kerry at the Brentwood infirmary. Your father was brought in with what we think is a bit of heat exhaustion. We wanted to let you know he'll be fine. Dr. Anderson has already been by to see him. We've taken him back to his room."

Jennifer took a deep breath and sighed with relief. She knew it was only a matter of time before she would lose her father. But, she just wasn't ready to let him go.

They spoke for a couple more minutes. Jennifer gratefully hung up the phone. She decided she now needed that walk more than anything. The call had started her adrenaline flowing.

SHE HAD JUST ENOUGH TIME TO GET HOME, take Charlie for a quick walk and change for her big night out. She was ready and waiting outside when Ben arrived. The warm evening air carried the smells and sounds of her neighbor's gardens, of cars being washed, a basketball hitting a hoop somewhere and dogs barking. Jennifer inhaled the sweet scents and smiled when Ben got out of the taxi to hold the door for her.

"Well hello gorgeous." Ben gave a low whistle of appreciation. Jennifer blushed and lightly slapped the back of his hand.

"I'm not sure Boylston Street is good enough for that dress."

"I warned you to bring your cards and money. There's a few pricey places on Boylston. I'm sure I can find one." Jennifer relaxed into the seat and smiled over at him. "Not often I get chauffeured around Boston. I could get used to it very quickly."

"Hmm. Pricey restaurants. Chauffeurs. Should I be worried about whether you're after my money?"

"Maybe just a little." She winked and smiled coquettishly.

They were soon walking past restaurant after restaurant gradually filling with people out to enjoy the warm evening. As they walked, they discussed various cuisines. Jennifer quickly realized Ben had personally tasted most of them in their native countries. She saw more than one person do a double take when they realized who they had just seen. But they were left alone to agree on a seafood restaurant with outdoor seating.

After a bit of a wait they found themselves seated at a table near the sidewalk, with menus in front of them. Their pert young waitress wasted no time and soon they were each sipping, a beer for Ben and a glass of Chardonnay for Jennifer.

"I don't think the waitress recognized you," Jennifer teased. "But then she probably isn't old enough to stay up that late on weeknights."

Ben smiled broadly, "She's certainly not the demographic the program is after."

After choosing an appetizer to share and cedar-planked salmon for the main course, they settled in to people watch and chat.

"Your father must have been quite the gardener back in his day. I heard him talking to Mark yesterday and it's clear he knows his stuff. He certainly knows more than I've forgotten. I haven't been around a garden in decades." Ben looked into Jennifer's eyes as he talked about her father. Her eyes suddenly teared up and she looked away.

"You miss him don't you?" Ben instinctively covered her hand with his across the table.

"We see each other often and have wonderful conversations at times but he rarely recognizes me. I've come to terms with it most days. Others not so well, like now." Jennifer carefully dabbed at the corner of her eyes and deliberately watched a couple of kids trying to skateboard among the pedestrians. She liked the feel of Ben's hand over hers but couldn't bring herself to look into his eyes again just yet.

"He's happy at Brentwood even though he complains. The staff is friendly and caring. And I know the food is good, which is very important to him. But, he's always liked to have something to complain about. My mother really pampered him. He was completely spoiled for over fifty years."

"Your mother is dead then. How did your father cope?" Ben left his hand over hers.

"I moved in for a couple of years when his dementia was still quite mild. At first, he never wandered off the way some people with Alzheimer's do. But when he finally did, it was serious." Jennifer well remembered the episode that showed much more than mild memory problems. "At one point he was stopped by the police because he was driving too slowly on the interstate. He couldn't tell them his home address or where he was going. He sounded so confused they wouldn't let him drive. Fortunately, he had my business card in his wallet and I was at my desk when they called. Ten minutes later and I would have been in a meeting."

She took a sip of wine and then looked at Ben directly. "He lost his license that day and never drove again. Less than a year later I had to get him into residential care. He'd forget to eat. One time he doubled his dose of blood pressure medication and almost passed out on me. That really scared me."

Ben sat back as the waitress put a generous bowl of fragrant mussels in the middle of their table.

Jennifer spooned up some broth and savored the light taste of the shallots in white wine and a blend of herbs. "This broth is divine. What do you like to do when you aren't working?" She didn't want to turn her first date into a counseling session.

"To tell you the truth, I don't have any hobbies. Never played golf. Where I was reporting from was far away from the country club life. Tennis was never much of an option either, for the same reason." Ben plucked a mussel from the bowl. "Other than jogging when it was safe to do it, my favorite has always been swimming. When I was out on assignment I would track down the nearest hotel with a pool. Even if I couldn't get there more than once a month, it was something to look forward to."

The evening light was gradually waning but the warmth of the day remained. It seemed half of Boston was strolling on Boylston Street as Ben and Jennifer's entrées arrived.

"I haven't had a serious date for several years." Ben smiled across the small table. "How am I doing so far?"

"I'm not the best judge. I haven't had a date for awhile myself." Jennifer leaned forward, looked at Ben and pursed her lips. She nodded slowly. "Overall, I'd say you're doing fine. Great restaurant. Great food. Stellar conversation. And the evening is still young."

"I wouldn't say my conversation is stellar. But thanks for the compliment." Ben grinned and cocked one eyebrow. "And the evening is still young. What does that mean?"

Jennifer tilted her head and smiled brightly. "Well, after dinner we could go for a nice long stroll, then you take me home, give me a very chaste kiss and we set up another date."

"Now that sounds like a fine plan. Gets my vote. Except the chaste part. I don't do chaste."

"We could skip chaste and go for steamy if you like." Jennifer threw back her head and laughed. Ben grinned.

After lingering over coffee, he generously tipped the waitress, waved to someone who had recognized him and took Jennifer's hand in his. He led her out to join the colorful human stream for a leisurely after-dinner stroll.

"Tell me something," Jennifer wasn't sure about asking this question so soon but she plunged ahead. "Why did you come back now? I don't mean to pry. Don't get me wrong, please. It's just that your return seems to have come at just the right point in Mark's recovery. Even six months ago, I don't think he would have been quite ready." Jennifer was very careful not to say anything that would breach client confidentiality. She figured her observations were neutral enough.

She glanced at Ben sideways as he pondered her question.

"Good question," he said. "It was a combination of things I guess. I realized I had seen too much violence and death. I was becoming very depressed. Everything was a major effort. I had sleep problems, insomnia mostly. My PTSD was nowhere near as bad as some others I knew. Some committed suicide rather than face their nightmares. I was starting to get some myself from the sheer brutality of what I was seeing."

Ben thought further, "I think it was also that Mark's emails led me to believe that he really had his depression under control and was ready to give me more space in his life. Even though I had promised his mother not to let him out of my life, I think it was really more the fact he was reaching out for more contact at a time when we were both ready.

"I had faced the fact that I couldn't really relate to him when he was a child. I could never leave my work behind and focus on the interests of a young child, let alone a teenager. It seemed to me that the problems in the world took precedence. I know now that I needed an attitude adjustment. But, at the time, it seemed more important to get my big stories out to the world."

Ben dragged his free hand through his hair. "By the time Mark hit his teens, I was basically out of his life. I set myself up just outside London, as close to Heathrow as I could get but as far from noise and violence as possible." Ben shook his head, "I came back because I finally realized it was more important to help my only child make his way in this world than to try and change the rest of the world.

"I figured the best way to make a real difference was to become the father that Mark still needs and be there to support him whenever he wants it. You should have been a journalist Jennifer. Talk about asking the one knock-out question." Ben looked down at Jennifer's upturned face.

Jennifer recognized a look that she could only describe as tender. She liked that look in his eyes. She wasn't sure exactly what had just shifted in their short relationship, but it suddenly felt warmer. *Not bad for a first date*, she reflected, as they walked toward the Common.

"You haven't mentioned anything about family. I'm sure someone like you must have one tucked away somewhere."

"I did have a family." Jennifer spoke quietly, almost reverently. "My husband and daughter were killed in a small plane crash." Jennifer hadn't wanted to speak of it during dinner at a busy restaurant. Here on the Common, among the trees and lawns and fresh spring smells, she felt more comfortable.

"Oh Jennifer." Ben was shocked. "When'd it happen?"

"A bit over five years ago."

"What happened?" They stopped and sat on a bench.

"Our daughter Kaylee was being wooed by a couple of universities. She was very bright and was hoping to go into medicine." She hadn't told her story to anyone in a long time. It felt right to be telling it to Ben, even on their first date. "They could have driven to Syracuse easily but Jason loved to fly. He rented a plane. They ran into engine trouble and crashed. I was told they would have died instantly."

"I can't even imagine how devastated you must have been. How did you find out?" Even after thousands of interviews, Ben found it hard to ask these simple questions of her.

"I was at work. It was a Friday. They were going to make it a father-daughter weekend." Jennifer looked up into the trees to where dozens of birds were warbling among the branches. Ben had taken her hand in his. She felt its warmth. "My director came to the door with a police officer. These two large men crowded into my office. I knew without either of them saying anything that something was terribly wrong. I think I started crying even before the officer told me."

Ben gently put his arm around her.

"They were so full of life. For weeks and months I couldn't believe they were gone forever. I would wake up in the night, feel the empty side of the bed and cry myself back to sleep. It was a nightmare for a long time." Jennifer looked at people walking by and realized she felt sad but completely at ease with Ben.

"This is my first date since they died. Sorry to take the sizzle out of the evening."

"Don't be sorry Jennifer. We both had a life before we met. There are many warm and wonderful stories we can tell each other, but this is the most important one of your life. It had to come out before we could really be friends." Ben patted her shoulder gently and was rewarded as Jennifer sighed in to him.

"Thank you for that Ben. It really is the worst story of my life. All the rest are better."

Ben stood up and held out a hand to her. "Let's keep walking. I'd like to know more about Jason and Kaylee. What were they like?"

"They were my geeks." Jennifer smiled and chuckled. "Jason was a chemical engineer at MIT. Kaylee liked nothing better than to go with him to his lab on Saturdays and holidays. Sometimes, they'd hole up there so long I'd have to call them to come home for dinner.

"Kaylee had top marks all the way through school. Picked up every science prize along the way. And she loved music. She loved the mathematical order of a composition. I couldn't really figure out what she meant by it. She didn't get her musical side from me I can tell you."

They were walking along the waterfront in the dimming evening light. Lamps cast soft pools of light along the path as they talked.

"How did you and Jason meet?" They stopped by a pond to watch the ducks gathering together to settle in for the night. The birds tucked themselves down on the ground in close proximity. Some had already settled their heads down and didn't move as runners and walkers passed by.

"We met on the Boston University Bridge. We were both out jogging and stopped for a stretch break. We started talking and the next thing I know, we're jogging over to MIT to see his lab." Jennifer smiled. "Had to be the oldest pick-up line in the book, but Jason was perfectly serious. He had just gotten his own lab area for his doctoral work and wanted to show it off.

"We kept on meeting and talking. I was at Boston University doing my master in social work. We compared our teaching and class schedules and set up a jogging schedule together. We just hit it off really well." Jennifer smiled as she remembered. "At one point, I went away somewhere for a week, a conference probably. When I got back, Jason had really missed me. He proposed to me in my parent's back yard."

The sky was darkening as they reached the edge of the Common. Lights were twinkling on in the buildings around them as they looked for a taxi to take Jennifer home. Ben was only a few blocks from his building.

"I really enjoyed this evening Jennifer."

"I did too."

"Are you going to give me your home number or do I have to get in line and call you at work?" There wasn't enough light for Jennifer to see the teasing sparkle in Ben's eyes.

"Well, you behaved yourself admirably. I've completed the criminal records check on you so I think it's safe to give you my number." Jennifer was smiling as she found paper and pen to note down her number.

"By the way, I tried to find your phone number on 411 and no J. Barrett came up."

"The phone is listed under my father's name." Jennifer smiled smugly. He'd tried to look her up right after they met.

"Severn. Of course, I didn't know then about you living in your parent's home." Ben flagged down a taxi. As he opened the door for her, he reminded, "You said something about a chaste kiss and setting up another date."

Jennifer laughed and put her arms around his tall shoulders and surrendered her face. Ben leaned down and kissed both her cheeks lightly. Before she could even register her surprise, however, he turned in and gave her a full-fledged Powell kiss that left her dizzy.

"Mmm. What was that?" Jennifer looked up into his face, hazy in the muted light.

"That madam, you will learn on our next date, which would be…"

"I'm free all weekend."

"It's a date. I'll call you. Think of what you'd like to do."

Jennifer sat back in the taxi and reflected on the evening. She felt a warmth in her heart and body that she hadn't felt in many years. Their first date. She could hardly wait for the second.

LANA WAS DOING SOME LAST MINUTE THINGS IN THE KITCHEN when the phone rang. Who would call at this hour? she thought and thanked her lucky stars that the phone never seemed to wake Danny up. The call display wasn't displaying any number.

"Hi Lana. I knew you'd still be up."

"Is everything okay?" Lana couldn't think of the last time her phone had rung at ten o'clock at night. Everyone who knew her also knew that Danny was asleep and would never call this late. She decided to make an exception for Mark.

"It's fine. It's actually great really. I just wanted to hear your voice for a few minutes before I go to my lonely bed. And, I just wanted to warn you of something in case it becomes an issue."

"What's that?" Lana stopped what she was doing. "Is everything okay?"

"Just wanted to give you a heads up that I'm not sure how I will react to the noise level in the stadium and the crowds. I talked to my counselor about it. I've been doing fine on buses and at malls. But Fenway is major league for me in more ways than one." Mark combed his hand through his hair and looked at the three tickets on his dresser. "I'm sure I'll be fine but I wanted you to know. I did go through a period when I was super sensitive to noise levels. That seems to have settled."

"We'll deal with whatever comes along. If you're not comfortable you let me know. Don't be a hero. We'll work it out." Lana hoped she could count on Danny not to make a scene if they had to leave. He had never made a scene before. They'd be fine. All of them. She hoped.

"Only two more sleeps before you come here for another sleepover." Lana walked over to the couch and curled up with the portable. Next time you call this late we should set a time so I can have the phone right beside me or I could call you."

"Even better, just let me stay over and I won't have to call you." Mark grinned into the phone. "You rolling your eyes?"

"How did you know?" Lana clutched a pillow to her chest.

"You roll your eyes when I say something cheeky."

"Have you made all the plans for Saturday?"

Lana decided to deflect.

"Yes. And I know Danny will be one very happy camper."

"What'd you do?"

"It'll be a surprise. Wait and see."

"Give me a hint?"

"Okay, think Jumbotron and almost birthday boy."

"Oh my god. He will be absolutely blown away. Where'd you get that kind of money?"

"It's only a fifty dollar donation to the Red Sox Foundation. It goes to support programs for children. I'm all for that."

"I can't wait to see his face when his name comes up." Lana smiled at the thought. "He'll be doing a major dance for joy."

"By the way madam, money is no object. I'll have you know I'm a very eligible Boston bachelor. Much sought after by society matrons who have heard of my modest wealth and impeccable lineage."

"Why I had no idea sir, that you were such a catch. I'll just have to pull out my pearls and white gloves and get in line with all the young debutantes." Lana was batting her eyelashes at the phone when she looked up and saw the clock. "Okay Boston bachelor boy. Time to say goodnight and get some sleep. I need you to be in good shape for Saturday."

"Yes Lana. I will be a good boy and get to bed. But don't expect me to be sleeping at this hour on Saturday night."

"Saturday night you will be busy bachelor boy. Count on it."

Chapter 12

Jennifer had just opened the front door when her phone rang.

"Jennifer, is this a good time to call?"

"I just walked in. Hang on a second." Jennifer put down the phone to unlock the back door and let Charlie out.

"My dog needs to get out more." Jennifer laughed. "You should see him Ben. My neighbor's cat is already up the tree at the end of my yard with Charlie circling it at high speed."

"I need to meet this dog. I hear him barking. He sounds like a real character."

"Oh he is that. Have you decided what we're doing on Saturday?"

"I was wondering if you'd like to go sailing?"

"That would be wonderful. I haven't been sailing for years." Jennifer stopped herself from saying since Jason and Kaylee died. She didn't want anyone, especially Ben, to think that her life had somehow stopped when they died. It had just changed. A lot. "I didn't think you'd be finished your course so soon!"

"I have my days to myself now and not much to do other than keep the condo tidy, take care of myself and go for workouts. That doesn't take up much of my day. Besides, the course was only seventeen hours." Ben was now a certified sailor. "How about we go out somewhere for breakfast together first? I can't pick up the boat until nine. It'll still be a little cool in the early morning too, although it's been pretty warm this past week."

"I'll pack us something to nibble on and some sunscreen." Jennifer couldn't help thinking of the practical details. She hoped he didn't mind. It was just her way.

"Now we're really getting a plan together."

"Saturday's supposed to be lovely. Do you like Greek salad?" Jennifer was already thinking of what enticing food she could pack into her picnic basket and cooler bag.

"I love it. You make your own?"

"From scratch. Add a roll and it's a meal."

"You do the salad then and I'll pick you up around eight. I'm renting a car for the weekend."

"I'll be ready".

"HEY MARK. COME OVER HERE AND TRY THIS." Vito was using the break between breakfast and lunch to experiment with a new vinaigrette. The stocky chef looked more like a middleweight boxer than a European-trained chef.

Mark changed course for the kitchen's back door and followed Vito into the cool and brightly lit interior. "What are you trying to foist on the old folks this week?" Mark towered over Vito by a good six inches.

"Thanks to all the herbs and vegetables coming out of the gardens, I had to think of what to do with it all. Making my own dressings makes sense when there are such fresh ingredients right out the back door." Vito stirred the bowl in front of him, smelled it and added a grand splash of white wine vinegar to his latest concoction. He dipped a spoon in and tasted it. Nodding, he gave a spoon to Mark and motioned him to do the same.

Mark sipped a small amount of the vinaigrette and his eyes widened. "I'm no food expert but I know what I like. This tastes great. What's in it? I can pick out the vinegar and that must be extra virgin olive oil. Basil. But what else?"

"Ah. That I cannot tell you. This is a secret family recipe handed down from my great-grandmother in Italy. If I tell you then I would have to kill you. Since I like you, I won't tell."

"Seriously Vito, some of the recipes you've had me taste should be bottled and sold. You could make a mint with some of your recipes."

"I like what I do right here. I don't need or want to be a big successful chef or a millionaire businessman. I like to feed my family. The people at Brentwood are my family. I'm happy."

Mark nodded in agreement. "I get you. I feel the same way about Brentwood." As he stepped back into the sunshine, he added to no-one but himself, *especially one person in particular.*

"DANNY, COME WASH UP FOR SUPPER." It was Friday at last Lana thought. One more sleep before a day out with Mark and another sleepover. She had just changed the beds and launched a load of laundry. They were having a summer supper tonight to taste test a couple of salads she was making. Her new favorite, and Danny's, was a broccoli-cauliflower salad made with some cheese, fresh lemon juice and mayo. The crunchy salad would go perfectly with the rib steaks now marinating in the fridge.

"Mom? When are we picking up Mark?" Danny whirled into the kitchen, headed for the sink and wet his hands.

"Wash Danny. Use soap please. We're picking Mark up a bit after eleven o'clock. The game starts at one-thirty. We need time to find our seats and get some lunch." Lana smiled as she relayed the information for about the third or fourth time.

"Can I have two hot dogs?"

"Let's see how you do with one first."

JENNIFER WATCHED IN AMUSEMENT as Charlie treed her neighbor's long-suffering cat yet again. It almost seemed a game between them. The cat would sit nonchalantly on the low fence separating the two properties but always within easy reach of the nearby tree. As Jennifer opened her back door, Charlie always looked in that direction, never any other. He would literally skid in his hurry to get through the yard and jump up at the fence. Before his paws left the ground, the cat was out of reach.

Today was no different. As Jennifer brought out her gardening basket and gloves to tackle yet another overgrown flower bed, she looked up at the cat, who peered down at her with liquid golden green-flecked eyes. "Y'know Nemo, you and Charlie could be friends if you just gave it a chance." The cat blinked lazily, licked a paw and lay down on the branch to watch her.

Jennifer set to work. Since coming so close to putting the house on the market, she now saw it in a whole new light. Increasingly, she saw it as a haven and no longer a burden. This was where she had grown up. It was where she and Jason had stolen kisses on the bench in the back corner of the yard, with lightning bugs dancing away in the dark. It was where Jason had proposed to her, kneeling in front of her in the traditional pose. And, it was where they had filled the yard with family and friends for Kaylee's christening less than two years later.

This house and its gardens held so many warm memories. She could see Kaylee running between the flower beds along the flagstone paths her father had laid himself. She remembered Kaylee and her father huddled together over his grafting table as he explained what he was doing to the curious little scientist.

As she divided yet another of the many perennials to ease the crowding, she could hear her father's voice telling Jason how to prepare to transplant a young shrub. She could hear her mother calling out to them to have some fresh lemonade at the wrought iron table on the patio.

She stood up a bit stiffly and wiped her arm across her damp brow. The warm evening air was barely moving. She'd been working non-stop for almost two hours. She could taste her mother's lemonade but made do with a long drink from the thermos of cold water she'd brought out. *I must buy some lemons,* she thought.

She looked around and noted with some pride that the hours she'd put in were beginning to pay off. Easily half of the large yard was now looking more like it had when her father tended it. She had cut back overgrowth so that the edges of the beds were now visible. There was shape to the bushes that would encourage fuller growth. She'd divided out some of her father's beloved hostas and planted more along the side of the house facing the street. She'd always maintained the front yard out of respect for the neighbors. But, being on a corner meant extra work and the hostas would keep that side lower maintenance.

As she gathered her tools together and put them back in the old wooden apple basket, she thought about inviting Mark, Lana, Ben and Danny over for a Sunday dinner on the patio. She didn't have a barbeque but she could roast a chicken a day ahead so the house could cool down. Her parents had never thought of putting in air conditioning. There were usually good Boston offshore breezes to keep the air moving.

A couple more weeks and she'd have the entire yard in shape for company. It was a good goal to work towards, she thought, as the lightning bugs began to sparkle in the growing darkness.

Chapter 13

Jennifer looked at the clock and realized she had less than an hour before Ben arrived. They had agreed on a restaurant close to the wharf that was known for its breakfast crepes. Both had been delighted to learn they had yet another mutual food love.

After letting Charlie into the yard for a last run at Nemo, Jennifer locked up and surveyed her two bags. The cooler bag was packed with some cold drinks, water, Greek salad, cooked chicken and green grapes. She'd bought a new picnic knapsack that held utensils, plates, glasses and had space for her wallet, keys and sunscreen. She had a scarf and hat. She was ready for a day of adventure with her new beau. She felt energized, with a gaiety she hadn't felt in far too long.

"Madam." Ben arrived promptly at eight. He took her bags, escorted her to the rental and deposited them on the back seat. "Here, let me get the door for you."

Jennifer stepped into the gleaming car and watched him go to the driver's side. I like his old-fashioned manners, she thought, it feels wonderful to be treated like a lady.

Even though it was Saturday, the traffic was still quite heavy as they made their way closer to the harbor.

"Perfect day for the ball game. I gather Danny has never been to a game." Ben drove up to the restaurant he had in mind and miraculously found parking just a few car lengths away. "He'll love it."

"Mark's arranged for a happy birthday notice on the Jumbotron. I'd love to see Danny's face when that comes up."

"What a great idea. I wouldn't have thought of it."

"You have a very thoughtful son, Ben." They walked into the restaurant and found a table by the window.

"I didn't really have a lot to do with it though."

"I'm impressed with the way Mark has come to terms with your absences." They had discussed the reunion at some length. Mark had made it clear he wanted to move forward and not get mired in the past. "Learning about your PTSD helped I'm sure. It's clear you both need to look forward."

"Well I'm just looking forward to today and going sailing with my new best friend."

Jennifer smiled as a waiter came over to take their orders. "You are such a softie."

After their leisurely meal, Ben picked up the check for their breakfast and waved off Jennifer's offer to split the bill. "Just so you know, on official dates I pay. This is an official date. I'm very old-fashioned that way. Trust me, I need to find some ways to spend some money. The IRS already gets more than its fair share. I might as well have fun with what little they leave me." Ben grinned at Jen while writing in a generous tip to the friendly waiter.

"I can agree to that on one condition." Jen was used to being independent. She wanted to have some say in these dating decisions. "When you come to my place for a brunch or dinner you don't bring a thing. I take care of it all."

"Not even a good bottle of wine?"

"Only if it's a really good bottle of wine." Jennifer conceded.

"I'll make sure it has a cork. You do have a corkscrew."

"Even better. I have one of those new-fangled things you push in and pull out and the cork comes out by magic. Won it at an office party as a door prize. I don't think I've used it. I really prefer the basic kind. Guess I'm old fashioned."

"That makes two of us. Let's just say I'm not first in line for all the new gizmos and gadgets. I don't have any apps on my phone. I'm terrified at the thought of tweeting and you won't find me on Facebook."

"I actually don't know anyone who could be my friend on Facebook. Kinda sad when you think about it."

"Much better to talk face-to-face, especially when that face is so pretty. What do you say we mosey on over to the marina and pick up our boat for a little cruise in the harbor madam?" Ben stood up, pulled back Jennifer's chair and gallantly took her arm. "Follow the captain. Our ship awaits."

The marina was a hive of activity. It seemed everyone who could sail a boat wanted to be out in the harbor at the same time. They could already see dozens of craft out on the water in full sail. It was a perfect day. The brisk breeze would carry them along at a good clip.

Ben went into the club house while Jennifer waited with their bags and jackets. Within minutes he was back with the key to the engine and the slip number. They loaded their small amount of gear on board and Ben familiarized himself with the sturdy craft again. It was the same as the one he'd been training on the past couple of weeks. Once everything was stowed and the lines brought in, they motored out of the marina before Ben raised the mainsail. Soon they were skimming over the sparkling waters of the harbor to join the growing pod of water craft of all shapes and sizes.

GAME DAY PROMISED TO BE HOT AND SUNNY. Even though it was only the middle of June, temperatures were nudging into the high 70s during the day and staying in the mid-60s at night. While it was great for the lawns and gardens of Boston, it was a chore to keep the human population comfortable.

Lana had gotten up later than she would on a work day but still bright and early. She had collected everything they would need for spending a hot afternoon at the game. It was all in a gaily colored cloth tote that did double duty as a purse.

The minute Danny opened his eyes he jumped out of bed, ran to open the blind and looked outside. He grabbed his slippers and bounded down the stairs to the kitchen.

"We're picking Mark up at eleven o'clock right Mum?"

Lana smiled. Question one of a thousand. "Yes, so let's get some breakfast into you. We also have to tidy up a certain pile of toys in the living room before we leave. Don't want Mark to trip, crack his head open and bleed all over the place."

Danny laughed and climbed onto the tall stool in front of the small island in their kitchen. He grabbed a banana out of the fruit bowl and was reaching for a muffin when his mother tapped his hand.

"Have you washed your hands since you got up?"

"Aw Mom. I'm hungry." He slid off the stool and went to the sink.

Lana smiled. No arguments today.

After breakfast, Danny managed a messy pile of toys into their usual corner.

"Can Mark sit in the back seat with me today?"

"Sure. I'll just sit up front and be your chauffeur." Lana had a last look around. "You ready? Got your EpiPens?" With his allergy, every minute counted. She was glad he seemed to understand it. But she checked every day. Understanding and remembering were two entirely different things for a boy his age.

Danny stood between Mark and his mother holding their hands as they made their way through the crowds working their way into the stadium.

"Danny boy. Want to sit on my shoulders so you can see around?" Mark could feel how tightly the boy was hanging on to his hand. He found the noisy, excited crowd a bit much too. But, so far so good.

"C'mon up big guy. You have to see Wally the Green Monster." Mark squatted down so Danny could scramble up onto his broad shoulders. The bright green mascot was posing for photos with game-goers.

"He's huge! Why do they call him Wally?"

Mark looked at Lana. Lana looked back. "I guess that's the name his mother gave him." Lana figured simple was best.

"Wow. Is that ever a lot of people!" There were people everywhere as far as Danny could see from his tall perch. "Mark, how many people do you figure?"

"When I checked online this morning they were basically sold out, so almost forty thousand people with standing room only sections."

"You got us seats in the infield grandstand? I'm impressed." Lana was relieved to know they wouldn't be sitting in the blistering sun all afternoon. They located their seats and sat down to gaze around the sea of humanity in the now-crowded stadium.

"Actually, these are not expensive tickets. I bought binoculars to check things closer up." Mark dug them out of his knapsack and hung them around Danny's neck. The large glasses almost covered Danny's entire chest and stomach but he manfully heaved them up to spy around the field and grandstands. Although they were pretty far up and back from the playing field, the massive video screen would catch the main action and the announcer would fill in the rest.

"What time is it, Mom? When will the game start?" Danny had overcome his concern about the crowds and was looking around and taking everything in. The smell of hot dogs and popcorn wafted over them. Some people were eating nachos and some had bought chocolate chip cookies.

"Mom, can we get some of those chocolate chip cookies?"

"How about we all have a hot dog now and have a cookie later?"

"Hot dog. Yeah! Can we buy a Red Sox cap, Mom? I need a cap."

Lana laughed out loud. "Funny child." Mark looked over askance.

"I taught him the difference between needing something and wanting it. So now he *needs* a Red Sox cap."

"When's your birthday Danny?"

"It's June twenty-sixth. Not this Sunday but the one after." Danny had put a big circle on the date on the calendar in their kitchen. He was in the final countdown going into this weekend.

"Tell you what. How about I buy you a Red Sox ball cap for your birthday present? We'll call it an early present." Mark grinned down at him. "Birthdays should really last a whole week. Y'know why?"

Danny's eyes widened as he shook his head no.

"If you get your birthday to last a whole week, you get to eat more cake."

"Mom, will my birthday last a whole week?"

"Looks like it will now." Lana smiled across at Mark. She knew it was going to start any minute now. Mark already had the cap in his knapsack.

"You ready for the National Anthem? Game's about to start." As the entire stadium rose to its feet, Mark took off the cap Danny was wearing, pulled out the Red Sox cap and snugged it onto the boy's head. He pulled it off to look it over. Looking up at Mark, he grinned with delight and grabbed onto his arm. Lana smiled over at Mark and winked.

As the anthem ended, the crowd erupted into thunderous cheering and the game was on.

By the time the first inning was over, the Red Sox were down 1-2 against the Milwaukee Bears. Danny had peppered Mark with questions about the rules of the game, leaving Lana to watch the game and do some people-watching.

"So if the batter only gets to have three strikes how come that guy got to hit the ball about three times and it still wasn't a strike?" Danny was now sitting on Mark's lap and peering closely into his face.

"Those were foul balls. That means he hit the ball but it went outside the base lines. That isn't a strike. It's a foul. As long as no-one catches the ball in the air, which is an out, you can pretty well hit as many foul balls as you like."

As the teams exchanged places between the field and bench, the widescreen lit up with the first of the day's announcements. Mark pointed to the screen and told Danny to watch closely. Sure enough, within a minute or so, a new message came up: "Happy 5th Birthday Danny Fitzpatrick. You Rock!"

Danny peered at the screen for several seconds before he recognized his name being announced to the entire stadium. He leaped off his seat and started dancing in circles between his mother and Mark.

"That's me, that's me! Wow!" He kept jumping for joy. People around him laughed and chuckled and starting clapping.

"Oh wow. They said my name to everyone here. All forty thousand. Is that cool or what?" Danny waved at all the people around him.

"Mark did this for you Danny. What do you say?" Lana was grinning from ear to ear to see her little guy so incredibly happy.

"Thank you. Thank you. Wow. Now I really do have a whole week for my birthday. It just started today!" Danny climbed back onto Mark's lap and gave him a huge hug. Mark smiled at Lana who smiled right back and mouthed 'you're in trouble tonight'.

Mark grinned back and pulled Danny's new Red Sox cap down over his eyes.

Lana smiled at them. Mark was doing fine. There were no problems with the noise and the crowds.

"WHAT AN AMAZING DAY TO BE OUT SAILING. Thank you so much for inviting me Ben." Jennifer felt wonderfully happy and relaxed. "Jason and I never got much beyond doing a tour of the harbor. He wasn't all that comfortable on the water. Come to think of it, he wasn't that comfortable in the water either."

"I've always loved it. When I was a kid, my parents would rent a cottage for a few weeks on Nantucket Island. I'd play by the water and go swimming almost every day. I never got bored. There was always something to do."

Jennifer watched entranced as he lifted his face to the sun and the wind. They'd been out about an hour. He was clearly in his element.

"I know what you mean. When I was little we travelled to places up and down the coast. We always stayed somewhere near the shore. My parents kept a plastic pail and shovel in the car. They were almost the only toys I needed." Jennifer smoothed her white khaki pants and gazed around.

Ahead of them was the island that housed the Boston Lighthouse. Even heading straight into the wind they were fast approaching it. The boat hitting the milder waves of the inner harbor sprayed up sparkling diamonds of water. The two sat beside each other in companionable silence, watching the spraying foam, as seagulls glided and swooped above them.

"I'm so glad I got certified for sailing again." Ben steered them closer to the lighthouse. "It's just me and Mother Nature out here. And you, of course. My two favorite women."

"You're such a romantic. Let me know if you start to feel hungry and I'll pull out some goodies. Mind you, that was quite a breakfast you packed away." Jennifer didn't think she'd ever seen someone eat such a large breakfast. Unlike Ben, Jason had eaten sparingly. One egg. One piece of toast. Ben had wolfed down three crepes with ham and cheese, a side of Canadian bacon, a bowl of fruit salad and then polished off what she hadn't eaten from her plate. With him around, she'd have to adjust her food budget up at least three notches. The unbidden thought made her smile. I'd love to have him around for breakfast every day, she mused, and watched Ben as he confidently navigated them around the island. As they tacked towards a cluster of islands, they could clearly see the many skyscrapers towering over the Boston waterfront.

"Hard to believe how much the skyline has changed in the last twenty years or so. This city has really grown from when we were kids."

"It's so metropolitan now. It didn't look like that even when Mark was little. There weren't nearly as many skyscrapers then. I remember bringing him out here with Heather when he was a baby. We spent the day on the water. The fresh air and waves must have lulled him because he slept most of it." Ben grinned, "Hard to think of Mark as a small baby when you see how tall he is now."

"What was Heather like?" Jennifer looked up from studying his well worked hands to his face and saw a wistful look play over it.

"She was the one that got away I'm afraid. She was beyond beautiful, with a laugh that made you smile just to hear it. When she played the piano it was like watching a princess. She could be so regal. The reviewers always called her Miss Heather Arlington. And then, the next day she'd be in her jeans and one of my old shirts organizing her houseplants and patio pots. We had a rooftop garden that was her pride and joy." Ben angled the sloop towards one of the islands that had a park and boat slips.

"How long were you divorced before she died?" Jennifer had heard the love in Ben's voice and knew it wasn't his idea.

"Mark was going on twenty. It was a really rough period. His doctor was doing everything possible to help him deal with Heather's prognosis and his depression. Everyone wanted to help him find his feet." Ben shook his head ruefully. "I just wasn't there for either of them. My paycheck was deposited automatically by the network so money wasn't an issue. But my absence was. To answer your question though, Heather died about two years after we divorced. I hadn't seen her for the better part of a year before that."

"You never stopped loving her did you?"

"No I didn't. And I will always love the memories of her." Ben looked at Jennifer with sadness in his eyes. "I haven't told anyone this before. We never lost touch with each other until a couple of weeks before she died. She'd send me links to her latest review and tell me some of the back stage stories. Some were quite funny. She knew how raw it could get out in the field and made sure I had a dose of Boston reality every once in a while."

"She still kept in touch even after she stopped performing. Sent me updates about Mark's latest adventure." Ben tacked the boat to bring them closer to the island. "You really should have been a journalist Jennifer. I think you'd have given Barbara Walters a run for the money."

"How about we dock over at Spectacle Island and have our picnic there?" Ben aimed them towards an empty slip. "Thank you for asking about Heather. It's good to talk about her. I need to do that with Mark too."

"I think he needs to hear what you just told me. It would bring you both closer." Jennifer watched as the automatic winch lowered the mainsail.

"Did I tell you she thanked me for making the divorce easy as a P.S. in an email? I still have it. Kinda underlines what a shmuck I was, doesn't it?"

"I think I would have really liked Heather." Jennifer grinned at his obvious discomfort. "Sometimes where you put the words is just as important as the words themselves. Shmuck indeed. Sounds like Heather was one gutsy woman. And you, Ben Powell, were a definite cad."

"Oh thanks. You and Heather would definitely have got along just fine." Ben playfully poked her in the arm. She poked him back. A small speedboat zipped ahead of them into the last open slip. They made do with dropping anchor just off the island.

"It's so relaxing to get away from the crowds and noise." Jennifer set out their food and dishes as Ben stowed the sails for their break. "Hope you like the Greek salad. I made enough to feed a small army."

Ben peered at the brightly-colored salad. "If you're lucky, there's enough olives in there for both of us. I'm mad about olives."

"I'll fight you for them if I have to. They're one of my favorites too." Jennifer reached forward and popped one into her mouth and then popped one into his. "Next time, I'll put a whole jar of them in just to keep the peace."

Midway through their early afternoon lunch, a slip opened up at the island's marina. Ben motored them over for a leisurely walk. They chatted as they wound their way along the footpaths, watching butterflies flitting among the young plants even as large jets tracked in straight overhead towards Logan Airport.

"What attracted you to journalism?" Jennifer smiled as she watched a young family ahead of them. The father was skipping with two little girls. They were struggling a bit but dad was holding their hands. Mom was pushing a stroller loaded with supplies.

"I think it was in my blood. My mother wrote radio plays. She sold quite a few. She even wrote some television scripts that were picked up by the networks." Ben looked down at Jennifer. The sun was bringing out copper highlights in her hair and kissing her cheeks with a warm blush.

"Was she a strong woman? A woman writing commercially back in those days would have been a rarity." Jennifer pointed to a bench just ahead of them.

"Oh yes. In some ways she was much like Heather. She had a talent she put to work and it paid off in spades. Because of her writing, we had a lifestyle that many would envy even today."

"So where did you study journalism?" They sat on the bench and watched wispy clouds floating across the pale blue sky. Seagulls swooped back and forth in their constant search for food. Off in the distance they could see the Boston skyline in sharp relief.

"Syracuse. No scholarship, but between summer jobs and help from my parents, I was able to chase my dream."

"And what was that dream?" Jennifer listened to the sounds around her. No honking cars. No engines or buses. Just the wind in the trees, the cry of the gulls and laughter from children playing nearby.

"I wanted to see the world. I got a real travel bug after a few trips with my parents. I felt this need to get behind the tourist façade and meet the people and hear their stories. Between my wanderlust and my studies it was a natural step to go into reporting."

"Were you always in front of the camera?" Jennifer couldn't imagine him anywhere else.

"Actually no. I took several technical courses that taught me camera work, film and sound editing. I spent about ten years on the technical side, learning the latest techniques and advancements. I didn't get overseas and in front of the camera until Mark was about six years old. Up to that point, I was home much more than I was away. Those were the years when we had a real family life."

"How did you meet Heather?"

Ben smiled. "I was assigned as a cameraman for an hour-long special we were doing on Boston's arts and culture scene. I met her on the second or third day of shooting. It was all back stage at that point. When I first saw her she had no makeup and was wearing jeans and a sweater. I didn't know who she was." Ben grinned. "I asked her out. I thought she was one of the stage hands."

"What did she say?"

"She laughed and said how about we start with a cup of coffee. She had no airs at all."

"And then what happened?" They left the bench and started walking towards the boat.

"We had a great time chatting over a coffee. She still didn't tell me who she was. Just her name."

"When did you find out she was a concert pianist?" Jennifer tied her scarf around her head as they left the protection of the trees.

"We made a date to see a movie on a Thursday I think it was. We were standing in line for our tickets when these two women walked up to her and said they had really enjoyed her last concert."

"What did you say?" Jennifer could just imagine a cocky young Ben Powell being upstaged by his date.

"I can't remember now. Something like, what was that about."

"So what happened next?"

"We saw the movie."

"Oh c'mon Ben. Where was that journalistic curiosity you were just talking about?"

"Okay. I was embarrassed not to know who she was. My parents attended concerts all the time. But you have to remember I'd been away at Syracuse for four years. The same years Heather was making a name for herself as a rising star in the Boston music world. And, I was focused on building my career. I accepted every assignment day or night, weekends or holidays. I was busy getting work experience. I didn't have the time or money to go to concerts. And I wasn't interested in reading arts reviews in what little spare time I had."

They reached the boat and made ready to motor out into the harbor and set sail. For several minutes, their conversation focused on getting organized to depart. Once they were back out and the sails set, Jennifer continued her questioning.

"After the movie, what did you talk about?"

"The usual stuff I guess. I remember asking her if she was a member of the orchestra and she said yes. She kept it really low key.

I had to pry it out of her."

"What did you think when you found out who she was?"

"That she looked really good in tight jeans and a clingy sweater." Ben grinned. Jennifer burst out laughing.

"You're nothing if not honest Ben. No wonder Heather found you refreshing."

"She also found me intelligent, able to hold down a decent conversation and rather handsome." Ben was still grinning as he steered them towards Thompson Island to explore along its sandy coastline.

"And very modest. When did you see Heather the concert pianist?"

"The Saturday after I met her. We had come back to shoot portions of the concert to go with the back stage footage. When we arrived, I couldn't see her anywhere. I was busy and didn't really have much time to think about her. I was focused on getting my camera set up to film the orchestra from the wings. I had to get my shots and then go behind the orchestra to get some footage that would show the audience out front."

Jennifer scanned along the shoreline and followed a group of kayakers skimming the surface of the water. "What did you think when she appeared? It must have been quite a change from the jeans and sweater."

"I had taken my shots from the wing and was setting up for the rear orchestra shot. Heather didn't come out until the third piece on the program. By that time, I was shooting over the heads of the brass section. When she glided onto the stage I didn't recognize her." Ben chuckled as he checked the depth finder. "She floated onto the stage in a full length black evening gown. It must have had sequins because it shimmered under the lights. I remember she wore no jewelry other than earrings. When I realized it was her, I was awestruck and almost forgot about getting my shots. I had to yank myself back to the job at hand."

"Was it love at first and second sight?"

"Yep. You could say that for sure. If I had only seen and met her in her formal concert persona I don't think I would have had the nerve to ask her out. Getting to know her a bit before that concert made it easier to just accept she was my new friend who was all dressed up."

"I wish we could stay out here and watch the sun set over the harbor. I think we're going to have a spectacular one tonight. Either that or a spectacular thunderstorm."

"Wish we could too but the boat is due back by eight o'clock. I wouldn't be comfortable navigating at night just yet anyway. Later in the summer we'll be able to see the sunsets and still have the boat back in time." Ben made a quick decision. "Tell you what, as compensation for such a major disappointment on this our second official date, why don't I buy you dinner?"

Jennifer didn't hesitate, "As long as we go to my place first and let Charlie out. And, as long as it's obscenely expensive and involves vast amounts of wine, you're on."

Ben crooked an eyebrow. "Hmm. I thought so. You're going to be an expensive girlfriend. I can see it already."

"You said you needed to find ways to spend your money." Jennifer batted her eyelashes prettily and put on her most innocent smile. "I'm here to help is all. I hear Dom Perignon 1996 is a fine vintage."

Ben groaned dramatically and rubbed the back of his hand across his eyes. "It's entrapment I tell you. First you ply me with homemade Greek salad and divine roast chicken. Then you make me feel like an ogre for not giving you a sunset cruise. And then, when you have me neatly hog-tied into taking you out to dinner, you become a diva demanding only the best. What's a guy to do?"

"May I remind you that I am the hostage here?" Jennifer was enjoying every moment. "If you don't want to take me out for an expensive dinner, you can leave me on Spectacle Island to find my way home on the shuttle. Of course, I wouldn't go quietly. I'd make a major ruckus."

"And now you threaten me as well!" They could see the sturdy shuttle chugging its way towards the island. "You have won this round madam. You'd better enjoy it is all I can say."

"I'm sure I will. I'm sure we will." The two of them grinned at each other as Ben steered down the Inner Harbor towards the marina.

"This is my first major league baseball game since I was a kid. That's Adrian Gonzalez coming up to bat now."

"Who's that?" Danny was back on Mark's lap so he could see over the heads in front of him. The hot dogs had long since been eaten. They were happily munching on supremely gooey chocolate chip cookies and watching their team running away with the game.

"He's their top batter. If anyone can come up with a triple, it's him. Two down, bases loaded. Gonzalez needs to make it happen right about now." The words were barely out of Mark's mouth when a mighty cheer rumbled up from the front rows and grew to a roar as the big screen showed a solid hit over center field that sailed past second base and far beyond the nearest outfielder.

"It's a triple for Adrian Gonzalez," the speakers blared. "It's now 12-3 for the Red Sox in the bottom of the eighth," even as runners continued crossing the bases. Gonzie had hit an uncontested home run. He triumphantly danced over home plate as his delighted teammates crowded in to slap his back and feint punches at him.

"Y'know what? How about we make our way towards the exit?" Lana figured they could beat the rush. Others were doing the same. "I think we've seen the biggest highlight of this game."

"I'm with you Lana. We have seen baseball history right before our eyes. C'mon Danny boy. Let's help your mom find those steaks you told me about and celebrate." As they headed out of the stadium, Danny held hands only with Mark.

Charlie charged down to the end of the yard to harass Nemo as Ben looked on in amusement. "How old is he?"

"He's a bit over two now, so he's just coming out of listening when he feels like it and obeying commands without me saying them over and over. It seems dogs have their own version of the terrible twos." Jennifer handed Ben a tall glass of the fresh lemonade she had made and beckoned him to sit at her patio table.

"Your yard looks interesting. Half of it's almost picture perfect and half is looking pretty wild and woolly. What's with the Jekyll and Hyde look?"

Jennifer laughed. "I'm only part way through a major spring overhaul. I had neglected it for some time, partly because Charlie was young and a bit destructive. But also because I was mildly depressed and thinking about selling."

"And now?"

"I've changed my mind. I'm keeping it and I'm going to take much better care of it, including the flower beds. One of my goals is to bring my father here for a visit and have him like what he sees. Although that may be reaching since he's always liked to complain about something."

"Well, I like what I see. On the patio and in the garden." Ben put his glass down and went over to Jennifer and put hers down on the table beside his. "I'm going to take you out for dinner now as I promised. But before we go, I want you to know this has been a perfect day. And it's not over yet." And with that, he gently cupped her face with his hands, kissed her lightly on the forehead, called out to Charlie and led her back into the house.

Jennifer melted. The gesture was so gentle and sweet she could feel her heart expand. Charlie bounded through the open door oblivious to his mistress's swirling emotions.

"Let's go somewhere very quiet and romantic for dinner. No noise. No crowds."

"Sounds wonderful. Let me just lock up and turn on a couple of lights for later."

"I couldn't believe it when I heard my name at the stadium. That was so cool. Can I play that again?" Danny was holding Mark's digital camera, which he had used to videotape almost five minutes of the moments before, during and after the announcement of Danny's birthday on the big screen.

"Let's transfer it onto a DVD and run it through the television. And you can keep it forever." Lana shrugged her shoulders when Mark looked at her.

"Feel free to check our system. I'm pretty sure we can do it although I've never tried with my camera." Lana continued tossing ingredients into a large salad bowl. "Almost ready to put on the steaks. Let's get the barbeque going. Time to wash up men."

Mark and Danny obediently put down the camera and went over to the sink.

"We have to use soap." Danny told him solemnly.

Mark squirted some into both their hands. "Women are so picky about germs. Personally, I think germs are very manly. But then I work in gardens where there are lots of germs and dirt. Must be because she's a nurse."

Danny stared up at Mark. "You mean you don't always wash your hands with soap before you eat?"

"Nope. So I eat a lot of dirt, including worm poop."

Danny cringed and made exaggerated gagging sounds.

"Come to think of it, worm poop can't be good for us. Maybe we should just do what she says." Mark washed his hands vigorously.

Lana smirked as she transferred the salad from the mixing bowl to a pretty plastic serving bowl. *Worm poop. Who would have thought of it?* Danny had just learned a major life lesson he would likely never forget.

"Would you happen to have a bottle of Dom Perignon 1996?" Ben naively asked the waiter.

"Yes Sir. Of course sir." The waiter's eyes went wide.

In his innocence, Ben continued. "Please bring us a bottle while we look at the menu."

Jennifer didn't know what was happening. She could see the waiter was vibrating over the request.

"Can you please tell us what that bottle costs? This is only our second official date. I don't want my brand-new boyfriend to break the bank too soon."

The waiter began to wilt. "Why yes, madam. The Dom Perignon 1996 is four hundred and ninety-five dollars a bottle. It's one of the top vintages we have." Ben paled.

"If you don't mind then, I would rather have a nice Italian Pinot Grigio. I'm not in the mood for champagne. We've been out sailing all day. I don't think bubbly would sit well at this hour." Jennifer barely concealed her mirth as she watched both men squirm. "I'm not in the mood for champagne tonight. Next time perhaps."

Ben recovered visibly. The waiter saw a major tip fly out the window. Jennifer approved the suggested vintage and the world resumed normal orbit.

"You didn't tell me it was one of the most expensive wines they carry."

"I had no idea it was special. I just picked a good year by chance. I was joking. I don't even like champagne."

"Thanks for the great save. That would have been quite a shock to my credit card and my heart. I like good things but there is a limit and that would definitely be one. No wine or champagne is worth twenty bucks a sip."

"I'm with you. Twenty dollars a bottle on special occasions but not twenty a sip."

As their more modest wine was poured, they continued perusing the menu, laughing over how they had managed to avoid ordering the monstrously expensive wine while still maintaining some semblance of dignity.

Mark sat back from the table and rubbed his stomach. "I don't know about you Danny but that steak was excellent."

"For sure. Wish Charlie was here. He'd want my leftovers." Danny still had a good-sized chunk of the rib steak left on his plate.

"I'll take care it. Just don't tell Charlie." Mark speared the remaining steak onto his plate and tucked right in. "Oh. I hope you didn't have plans for leftovers." His mouth was full as he spoke.

"Go ahead and eat tomorrow's lunch. We'll survive on apples," Lana teased.

"Danny. When Mark is finished eating all our food, how about you bring the plates to the kitchen counter and bring out the dessert stuff?" Lana was giving Danny more things to do and he was happy to help her, especially in front of Mark.

"Do I bring out the cake too?"

"First, you take the dinner stuff away, then you can bring out the dessert. We don't want salt and pepper on the table with the cake right?"

"Okay. Got it." Danny made the first of several trips between the patio and the kitchen. Lana was counting on wearing him down. The giant chocolate chip cookie had given him a second wind. She hoped the banana cake wouldn't give him a third and mentally crossed her fingers.

"Lana, Danny is such a great kid. You are doing an amazing job." Mark reached across the small table to take her hands in his. "Today was phenomenal. I'm sure you know that."

"I do. And I hope what we're doing is going to turn into something very special for each of us." Lana smiled into his eyes.

Mark rubbed her hands thoughtfully with his work worn fingers. "You two are the best people to come into my life in a long, long time. Getting back together with my father is special but you and Danny are part of a future I really want. I'm ready to work very hard to have a life that includes both of you." Mark looked around Lana's yard strewn with toys and at the small basketball hoop nailed to her garden shed wall. "Today was incredibly special. I've wanted to be part of a family for years. And now that you and Danny have come into my life, I want it even more."

Mark pulled his hands back as Danny came out with the banana cake. "Dessert! Bring it on."

Mark took over serving as Lana watched Danny fade. It wouldn't be long before the night was theirs.

"He's out for the night now. I think that's one of the longest days he's ever had without any down time or a nap. My little boy is growing up all right." Lana and Mark finished tidying up the kitchen. They were close in the small sink area. Each time they brushed up against each other they could feel the heat building.

"The chocolate chip cookies helped no doubt." Mark put down the towel he was holding and put his arms around Lana. He bent over to smell the mild scent of her hair and plant a light kiss on the top of her head. Lana leaned back into his chest and figured the rest of the cleanup could wait until morning.

"I think it's time to get our sleepover started." Lana turned in Mark's arms and nuzzled in against him.

"Where do we start?" Mark tipped her face up and bent in to kiss her warm, inviting lips. He angled his face around to deepen the kiss and gently teased open her mouth and flicked his tongue over her teeth. Lana groaned and wrapped her arms around his neck and pulled him down to tighten the embrace.

When they finally broke free, Lana moved away reluctantly to lock the back door and turn down lights. Together, they went up the stairs to the bedroom and quietly shut the door behind them.

"You know what I'd like to do to cap off this amazing day?" Ben was utterly relaxed and mellow. The dinner had been excellent, the conversation never faltered and they were now sharing a sublime dessert that included more ice cream than fruit. "I'd like to take you home and go for a walk around your neighborhood with Charlie. Stretch my legs one more time before I call it a day."

"That sounds like a fine idea. Ready when you are." Jennifer felt the need to walk as well. She felt a bit guilty about how long Charlie had been cooped up alone. Ben paid the bill and led them back to the rental. Before long, Charlie had been released from his friendly jail.

"This is such a lovely evening. Everything smells fresh and fragrant." Jennifer and Ben walked hand in hand as Charlie strained forward to speed smell every tree trunk, bush and hydrant. "I've always loved the quiet of this neighborhood as it starts to get dark. It's like the whole energy level goes down with the sun."

"I guess I can't talk you into going to some hot night club to dance until dawn."

Jennifer laughed. "I wonder which one of us would end up on a stretcher first."

"I can't imagine pulling an all-nighter anymore. Don't know how I managed to do it so often for so long." Ben shook his head, "I remember many times I would fly in to some hot spot and not even unpack before heading out to find someone to interview."

"What was it like being in the thick of it?"

"Makes me tired just to think of it. It was just a job really. One that involved long hours and more than my share of sleepless nights." Ben pulled his hand through his hair. "At first it was exciting. I did network feeds. My stories were on the news several times a week. But after awhile it became tedious. Never boring. But tedious. I looked forward more and more to being away from it for a few weeks. But then, I'd get sucked right back in. It's like I couldn't stay away. The moth going for the light, getting burned and still going back."

"Why were you able to stop this time? What made it different?" Jennifer looked up into Ben's face as they walked under a street lamp. In its soft yellow glow, she saw the ruggedly handsome face that was beginning to slip into her dreams, both day and night.

"I won't say that it's because of Mark. Mark being ready to have me back in his life was part of it but it was also the timing. I'd known for some months that I couldn't take much more. When I first started out, the nature of conflict was somehow more civilized. Battles were fought, people were killed, yes. But there wasn't the level of senseless and brutal killing going on that we see today." Ben stopped to let Charlie sniff yet another fire hydrant. "And it's often child warriors now. Kids who get food and shelter in exchange for packing a machine gun and killing their cousins. When I started in journalism, I honestly thought I could make a difference. That I could tell stories that would make people want to change and make things better. I've reached the stage now where I need to pass that baton on and hope the next generation can do better than we did."

As they walked up to Jennifer's front steps, Ben handed her Charlie's leash. "This has been an amazing day Jennifer. I have the rental until tomorrow evening. Do you have plans?"

"I was going to work on the garden again. Maybe you'd like to help me for awhile and then we could take Charlie somewhere for a good long walk and grab a bite somewhere?"

"Sounds like a plan. I'll be here around eight before it gets too warm? Or should I come earlier?" Ben cupped her face in his big hands, then reached to run a hand through her hair. "I've been wanting to touch your hair since we met."

"You can touch my hair any time you like." Jennifer wrapped her arms around his sturdy back and lost herself in a deep kiss even as Charlie scampered around their feet.

"Mmm. You taste wonderful."

"Come by at seven. I'll make breakfast and coffee."

A couple walking along the street saw them kissing and reached out to take each other's hands in the waning twilight.

Chapter 14

"How do you like your eggs Mark?" Lana called out as she heard the bathroom door open.

"I'll take them any way you make them." Mark tousled Danny's hair as the boy bounced into the steamy room. "All yours big guy. See you downstairs. Remember the soap right?"

Mark pulled on a clean tee and followed his nose towards where he was sure there was coffee, bacon and something he couldn't quite identify.

"You made muffins? What kind?" Mark moved to give Lana a warm hug even as his eyes scanned the food on the table and stove. "What a Sunday breakfast!"

"Those are banana oatmeal muffins with dried cranberries. Made them a couple of days ago. Just warming them up." Lana brought out two coffee mugs and set them down as Mark picked up the carafe.

"Before Danny comes down. What's the plan for today?" Mark poured two steaming mugs and added milk to both. "Tell me you're not going to kick me out after breakfast and leave me to languish in my tiny apartment."

"I was thinking of calling Jennifer and seeing if we could borrow Charlie. Spend some time over at the Common."

"That sounds like fun. Is it too early to call now?"

Lana looked at the clock over the window. "She'll be up. She's a morning gardener plus Charlie makes sure she's up early. I'll give her a call." She put the drained bacon into the oven to stay warm with their plates and turned the heat down.

"Hi Jennifer. Did I get you in from the garden?" She looked over at Mark and nodded. "Great day coming up. We're wondering if we could borrow Charlie and take him over to the Common." Lana listened and mouthed to Mark "she's spending the day with your father. Shall we join them?"

"Jennifer Barrett and my father? No-one told me." Mark had been so busy with work, Lana and his counseling sessions, he hadn't talked all that often to his father in the past couple of weeks.

"I guess so. Sure." Mark put a bit more energy into his voice. "I never thought of double-dating with my dad. Kind of a weird concept but what the heck. It'll be fun with Danny and Charlie for sure."

As Lana and Jennifer agreed to meet up at Jennifer's later in the morning, they each offered up the fixings for a picnic lunch. Jennifer's new picnic kit was going to get another workout.

"Okay. Let's eat. Danny, you almost ready up there?" Lana was rewarded with the sound of something slamming open or shut and the thud of his feet as he barreled down the stairs.

"What's for breakfast?" Danny breezed into the kitchen and hopped on his chair. "What're we doing today, Mom?"

"First, we're having breakfast. Then we're going to pack up a picnic, go to Jennifer's and meet up with Mark's father and Charlie. And then, we're all going to the Common together. How does that sound?"

"Cool." Danny reached for a warm muffin as Lana served up their first meal of the day. She silently gave thanks that Danny had not even questioned where Mark had slept.

"Charlie. Hey Charlie." Danny jumped out of the van and ran around the side of the house to Jennifer's side gate. As he reached it, he could hear a scuffling sound and saw a wet nose pushing against it.

"Just a second Danny. Let me grab him before I open the gate." Jennifer caught the collar of the squirming dog with one hand and lifted the latch with the other. Soon boy and dog were reunited inside the backyard as Lana and Mark came in through the gate.

"Danny. Come here please?" Lana gathered Danny over to her. "You remember Mark's father Ben Powell. Remember we met him the day we flew your kite at the Common?"

"Hi Mr. Powell. I remember you. You coming with Charlie and me to the park?"

"Yes I am. I hear your mother and Jennifer have planned a picnic. I'm good at following food." Ben squatted down to look at Danny almost eye to eye as he patted Charlie. "How was the game yesterday?"

"It was awesome! I got my name announced to everyone that it's my birthday next Sunday. And Mark gave me my very own Red Sox cap. See?" Danny pulled the cap off and pointed to the logo.

"So who won?" Ben stood up.

"The Red Sox of course!" Danny said it with fervor, as if there simply wasn't any other possibility.

Lana accepted a cup of coffee and toured the garden with Jennifer. "You've put hours and hours into this. What a change!"

"I realized all over again how much I love this old place and all its memories. Once I got back into the garden I felt like I'd come home. I think I had a case of the winter blues."

"You're not selling then? Lana bent forward to smell a creamy white lily. "I'm glad to hear that. It really is a lovely home and property."

"I feel it's my home and garden now. A little bit more each day. It's almost like I'm taking over from my father and making it mine. It's what I needed to do but had put off. I think I was in some kind of denial that he would get better and come home to take care of it again himself." Jennifer was seeing the garden in a new way. "He taught me everything I know about gardens and gardening. I couldn't walk away from that kind of legacy."

Ben and Mark sipped at the fresh hot coffee and watched the two women chatting on the bench at the back of the yard.

"When were you going to tell me you're dating my social worker? Isn't there some kind of conflict of interest?"

"It happened so fast. I hope for both our sakes there's no conflict. Jennifer needs to check."

"It's that serious already?"

"We hit it off so well. It's like we've known each other for years." Ben took a cautious sip of the steaming liquid. "We didn't talk about you specifically but she did ask me why I had come back now. She really made me think all over again about what is important in life."

"It was the same for me the first time I met her. I actually told her less than ten minutes after meeting her about my dreams for a career in music. I've hardly ever told anyone."

"Then you know what I mean. She has a special quality that draws you in. You know you can talk about anything and she'll get it. I didn't realize you were hoping for a career in music."

"Told you I hardly told anyone." Mark finished off his coffee as the ladies came back up the path. "Listen Dad, I hope it works out for you and Jennifer. She's really special. Be good to her."

"She's special to me too. I know it's fast but there it is. I know I screwed up royally with your mom. I know better now. I know myself better now. It won't happen with Jennifer." Ben watched as she came up the path with Lana, her head angled to hear something she was saying, then breaking into a sparkling laugh as they shared some private revelation.

"Is now a good time to get going? Anyone need to go to the bathroom before we leave?" Lana suggested, looking pointedly at Danny.

"Okay, Mom. I'm going."

It was quickly determined that Ben would return the rental car and they would all pile into Lana's van for the rest of the day's travel. As Danny opened the sliding door, Charlie leaped in.

"Charlie. Come. Sit." Danny got into his usual seat behind his mother and buckled up. Lana had made it a rule not to turn on the van until his seatbelt was buckled. "How come dogs don't have to wear seatbelts?"

"Because they need to lie down and the belt won't stay on." Lana waved at Ben to pull out ahead of her as she followed him to the rental agency. She knew where it was and had the address. But, Mark had gone with his dad and she wasn't going to let him too far out of her sight.

As Jennifer and Ben strolled arm in arm on the Common, Jennifer wondered aloud, "What must have it been like when our ancestors first crossed the ocean? It was so treacherous. It took weeks and months to get here. And yet they came. They braved Atlantic storms in ships that were built for cargo, not people. They braved scurvy, starvation and sickness to start their lives all over."

"The human spirit is remarkable but it has its limits." Ben looked across the lush lawns to where a group of children were playing. "You have to wonder if they had any idea of the hardships they would face. On the ships and then after they landed."

"When you think about it, we must come from pretty sturdy stock to have survived and thrived all these centuries." Jennifer relished the feel of the fresh breeze on her skin.

"I've traced my family back and I'm damned lucky to be here for sure. My great-grandfather was the only son to live into adulthood. He had two sons who lived. One died in the first World War. My uncle died at Pearl, leaving only my father. I'm an only child and Mark is an only child. At the moment, Mark's the last Powell."

"So you and Mark have been quite alone in the world all these years."

"Yes. My parents are both dead. Heather's family is all over. Mostly distant cousins I never really had much contact with. I don't think Mark does either. I should ask. Her music was such a passion. I don't think Heather had time for more than Mark and her music. She tended to do a few things very well rather than many things not so well."

Ben had stopped to look out over a pond. "Mark said something this morning. When he learned that we're dating he asked if there's a conflict of interest since you're his social worker. Is there?"

"I'm glad you brought it up. I'm going to talk to my director about it when I go in on Tuesday."

Jennifer could see Charlie running with Danny and was pleased to see Lana and Mark walking hand in hand. "Looks like Lana and Mark have something going."

Ben looked at his tall son walking with Lana, who barely came up to his shoulders. "I've been so caught up in our relationship that I didn't see the signs of the besotted male known as my son. Actually, that's not true. The night we had dinner at Lana's, she and Mark were talking to each other like I wasn't there. I felt like a third wheel on a bicycle."

"So we have a relationship?" Jennifer smiled up at Ben and squeezed his hand.

"You okay with that? I don't want to rush anything." Ben stopped and turned to her. "I know it's early days yet but yes, we both know there is something good happening between us. No sex yet but we don't have to rush into anything. If you'd like to though, I'm game." He cocked his eyebrows suggestively.

Jennifer threw her head back and laughed. "I don't mind if you lust after me. But this is no twenty-year-old body under here y'know. Just a warning."

"And there is no forty-year-old body under here."

"How about endurance? I don't think I can manage an all-nighter any more." Jennifer stifled a pretend yawn.

"At my age I'm aiming for maintenance. Last I heard, there are no Olympic sports for people over the age of sixty. So no all night marathons for me either."

"We could always try for a half marathon." Jennifer winked at him and grabbed his hand to pull him towards where Mark, Lana and Danny were setting up for their picnic. "C'mon. I brought some of that roast chicken you like."

"Since I have done nothing but eat, sail, walk and eat some more all weekend why stop now? How about we all head back to my place and finish off with a light supper and watch my garden at sunset?" Jennifer no longer cared that her back yard wasn't in showcase condition. They had all enjoyed the day together and it seemed the right thing to do to stay together into this lovely early summer evening.

"Do you have any desserts?" Danny walked along beside her with

Charlie on his leash.

"Does sherbet count as a dessert?" Jennifer was pretty sure she had some in her freezer and maybe some fairly recent ice cream or was that from last summer. Must check, she thought.

"What kind of sherbet?"

"I think it's lime. Do you like lime sherbet?"

"Do I like lime, Mom?"

"Yes you do. It's a bit like green slime, remember?"

Danny jumped up and down. "Oh yeah, the green slime. I love it."

"Does that mean you'll come to my house for supper?"

"If you have slime sherbet, I'll be there." Danny looked around as everyone started chuckling. As if he had a choice.

"Let's bring everything back to the van and take one more tour along the paths before we head back." Jennifer was delighted with the way this day was turning out. She couldn't remember a more wonderful weekend in many years. It feels like family again, she thought and smiled as she watched Ben, Lana and Mark getting Danny and Charlie back to the van.

"Ben, would you like a lift home? I need to get going. Danny and I have to be up early." Lana could feel and see the warm vibes between Ben and Jennifer. They stayed close to each other. They touched often. Just a light touch. A shared laugh. A warm look.

Ben looked over at Jennifer, who almost imperceptibly shook her head no.

"I'll stay behind and help Jennifer clear up. I'll cab back no problem. You folks go on ahead. Thanks."

"All right then." Lana took some dishes to the sink. "Danny, grab your knapsack. We're on the road. Jennifer, thank you for a wonderful supper. We have to do this again real soon, right guys?" She was met with a chorus of yeses.

"Do you mind that I stayed behind?" Ben brought in the last of the dishes as Jennifer loaded her dishwasher. They went back to the patio and pulled their chairs close together.

"I would've been mad at you if you'd left. I told you to go ahead and lust after me and I meant it." Jennifer stroked his arm lightly. She felt warm and mellow after a couple of glasses of Chardonnay. "It smells so heavenly out here. I'm not sure which flowers give off their scent in the early evening but just around dusk the air smells amazing. Feels like rain soon. Did you see the buildup as we were coming back?"

"Hmm. Yes. Rain soon." Ben caressed her shoulder, then reached up to smooth back her hair. "Seeing you on the boat yesterday with the wind and sun was special. You looked cute with your little hat and scarf. How about we go and sit over on the bench and make out? It won't rain for awhile yet."

"Ben! You sound like a randy teenager!" Jen laughed as they strolled arm in arm toward the aging wooden bench her father had built.

"What'd you expect? I'm with a lovely lady who makes me laugh and helped me enjoy a great weekend. Now I'm going to kiss you thoroughly and see what comes next. So call me Randy." As they sat down, Ben put his arm around her shoulder and gave her a warm bearish hug. Then he reached up to run his fingers through her hair.

"Your hair is just as soft as it looks and so thick." Ben rubbed her earlobe softly. Before he could say anything, she reached a hand up to stroke his cheek.

"This is so new. And strong. Very strong." Jennifer tried to take a deep breath and found she couldn't. She was trembling but she couldn't resist the feelings that were awakening in her. She felt like a flower ready to burst into bloom.

She stroked Ben's face and threaded her fingers up into his hair.

It wasn't clear who initiated that first tremulous kiss but it quickly deepened. Jennifer felt a passion welling up in her that was frightening yet exciting. As Ben put his arms around her and rubbed her back with his large strong hands, she felt driven by a need she hadn't felt in so many years. She needed to be made love to. Physically, emotionally and even spiritually, she needed the act of making love.

Jennifer was only hazily aware of a bolt of lightning streaking across the sky. A loud crack of thunder followed almost simultaneously. Without a sound, Ben grabbed her and dove off the bench, dropping to the ground holding them both tightly. Caught completely by surprise, Jennifer wasn't sure which startled her more, the thunder or Ben's reaction to it. She stared at him. *Would it always be like this for him? How could a man of his strength and confidence be reduced to this?* She couldn't imagine what he had gone through. "Ben, are you all right?" She wriggled out of his grasp and sat up.

He looked at her. She could see a dazed look on his face. "Ben, it's Jennifer. We're in my back yard. That was thunder. It's all right." She reached out to touch his shoulder. He flinched but shook his head as if to clear it.

"It's an automatic reaction. I do it without even thinking. It's saved my life more than once." He stood up slowly, helped her up and looked around. "It doesn't happen very often. Usually I'm alert and on guard for it. My mind was on other things." He smiled thinly. "Sorry you had to see that."

Jennifer could feel his embarrassment. There were probably very few people who knew him as anything but the confident brave broadcaster they watched on TV. She sat back down on the bench and patted the spot beside her. "Let's see. Where were we? I believe you were very thoroughly kissing me. As I recall, you weren't finished yet."

"Thank you Jennifer." Ben sat down, put his arms around her and hugged her in close. "You are some piece of woman."

She could feel him trembling slightly and rubbed his arms. They were locked in a passionate embrace when lightening struck close by yet again. Even before the sound of the thunder rolled away, Ben was on his feet.

"That was close! Let's get into the house." He grabbed her hand and quickly pulled her to her feet. "I've heard there are kisses that set off fireworks but never lightning – until now."

"Charlie come." Jennifer laughed as they ran for the beckoning light beaming through her kitchen door. Before they could reach it, the sky opened with drenching rain and hail. As they spilled into the kitchen they burst out laughing. Both humans and animal were dripping wet. Charlie shook himself vigorously, spraying them with a thousand droplets of water, setting off more laughter.

"Still want to make out?" Jennifer was chuckling as she walked over to her powder room for a towel.

"Sure. Any excuse to get out of these wet clothes." Ben had already pulled off his shirt and was working on his slacks when Jennifer emerged with a towel around her head. For a long moment they just looked at each other. And then, like it was the most natural thing in the world, they started peeling off their dripping clothes.

Ben stared as Jennifer stood before him in a lacy turquoise bra and dainty panties. She pulled the towel off her hair and started to rub it briskly.

"Here. Let me do that." Ben felt his mouth going dry. *Damn if she isn't all woman.* He set his slacks over a chair and took the towel from her hands. As he rubbed and fluffed her hair, he could look her over up close. *Curves in all the right places and legs that never end. I have died and gone to heaven,* he thought gratefully.

Jennifer reached up and wordlessly ran her fingers over the wavy sea of grey hair on his chest and then wrapped her arms around his trim waist. Ben dropped the towel and firmly cupped his hand behind her damp head and pulled her close in a molten kiss. When they finally came up for air Jennifer hooked her finger in the waistband of his underwear.

"Follow me."

She had finally moved into the large front bedroom her parents had shared for some five decades. She had done little to the room other than give it a fresh coat of paint and updated curtains. The roomy four-poster bed was still covered by a large handmade Quaker quilt. A pair of colorful shams had been added, which she now set aside on a large armchair.

Ben didn't absorb much about the room other than it was large and comfortable. He noted with satisfaction that there was lots of wood and upholstery and no chrome. *A real bedroom*, he thought and then abruptly stopped thinking as Jennifer turned down the bed, got in and patted the spot beside her, still wearing her lacey under things.

"I hope you didn't make any other plans for this evening." Jennifer lay back on her pillow as Ben pulled the covers over them.

"I only have one plan for this evening and it requires your total attention." Ben traced a finger along the edge of the lace bra. As he pushed the slim straps off Jen's shoulders one by one he rubbed his hands lightly over her shoulders and lazily trailed his fingers down each arm. "So soft," he murmured, "Soft and lovely."

Jennifer closed her eyes and reveled in the touch of his cool hands. Her body had taken on a life of its own as she stretched and arched into his slow, almost methodical caresses. Her mind held only one thought. This handsome, sexy, warm, gentle man was making her body tingle with a heat that would scorch them both before it cooled. She wanted that heat. Now.

Outside, the rain that had been falling in torrents had settled into a steady and nourishing shower. Neither Ben nor Jennifer noticed. Charlie curled up quietly near the bedroom doorway.

Ben caressed and explored Jennifer until she thought she would explode with the heat of her need. He finally slipped off her bra and cupped her breasts in his hands before bending in to kiss each nipple. Jennifer felt his touch zing through her to ignite a new fire below. As Ben slowly laved one nipple and then the other, she groaned and kneaded his back with her hands even as she wrapped a toned leg over him.

Ben worked his way down to her abdomen, lightly kissing the length of her. He took his time and was rewarded with soft purring sounds and her exploring hands. When he was sure he had touched almost everything there was to touch, he looked to see her eyes clouded with desire.

Jennifer moaned as Ben entered her and felt her body pulsing with a need she thought she had left behind many years ago. As they moved together, Jennifer's whole body and soul was consumed by a rising tide of sexual energy and tension she couldn't control and didn't want to. As her body peaked under Ben she arched and shuddered as she felt wave after wave of pleasure.

Ben felt her peak and joined with her as she rode out the last waves of her climax.

It was still raining lightly as Jennifer stretched in Ben's arms and felt the steady murmur of his heart. She felt sated in a way she hadn't experienced in more years than she could remember. *There is something to be said about new lover sex,* she mused. But, she remembered there was also something to be said for long-time lover sex too.

She looked around and saw that her room was still the same as before. But she had changed. She was a well-loved woman again. She smiled, inhaled Ben's slightly salty scent, closed her eyes and drifted off to sleep wrapped in his arms.

When Charlie quietly jumped up on the bed and lay down beside Ben, he patted the dog and rubbed his ear. "Y'know what Charlie? You have a very special mistress. Glad you don't mind sharing her with me." Charlie licked his hand once and laid his head across Ben's hand. Soon all three were sound asleep as the rain gently fed the gardens of Boston.

Chapter 15

Sunlight bathed the bedroom in soft color as Jennifer pulled back the curtains. She peered at the clock and was surprised to find it was earlier than she thought. As she raised her arms over her head in a long stretch, she looked over at Ben, who still had Charlie sleeping beside him. The dog raised his head and looked at her.

"You like him too don't you?" Jennifer took her bathrobe off the back of the bathroom door and slipped it on. Sitting on the edge of the bed, she patted Charlie and then leaned over to plant a warm kiss on Ben's lips. His eyes opened sleepily as he reached out to caress the side of her face.

"Morning beautiful. What time is it?"

"Not quite six. I'm going to put Charlie out. Want coffee?"

"Yes, but first I want you. Meet you back here in five?" Charlie had already popped off the bed and was heading for the stairs as Ben turned back the covers, grabbed Jennifer in for a quick kiss, then stood up and padded off to the bathroom.

"I can be back in two." Jennifer called back, smiling as she went down the stairs.

THEY WERE SITTING ON HER PATIO enjoying their second cup of coffee as the sun reached the yard. It was past eight and they'd just finished breakfast. Ben had eaten enough for an entire army. He had downed the bowl of fruit salad she'd made. Wolfed down the two slices of toast and jam, then innocently inquired what she had in mind next. Since when had breakfast become a three-course event? She wondered how many more trips she'd need to the gym each week to survive his appetite.

Ben stretched his legs out and watched Charlie rolling in a patch of grass. "By the way, that was some breakfast you put on.

I like a big breakfast but I don't eat that much every day. Seems we worked up a good appetite between last night and this morning." He winked at her.

Jennifer shook her head. "You're incorrigible Ben Powell. What are your plans for today? I'm off today."

"What'd you have in mind?"

"I was thinking of putting you to work in the garden for one. Wear off some of that breakfast. After lunch, a very late lunch," she emphasized each word, "I was planning to visit my father. Maybe pick up some perennials to plant along the side of the house. I put in some hostas but something that flowers earlier would brighten it up."

Ben turned his face up to the sun. "I'm a big eater Jennifer. Always have been. It was actually an issue out in the field at times when we were short on provisions. I got to carrying around whatever local snack food I could find. I developed a real taste for figs."

"I'm just used to shopping for one. No-one I know can eat like you. It's amazing."

"With Mark and I around, you and Lana will need to adjust your recipes. A lot." Ben grinned. "You have Powell men in your life now. And Powell men love to eat. How about after we finish up in the garden we go over to my place for a swim and then see your father? I'll need to stop by for a change of clothes anyway. And work off some of your amazing breakfast."

"You mean Mark eats as much as you?"

"More."

"I need to warn Lana."

"Probably a good idea. I have investments to help pay for my food. She's still too young."

"I should have recognized the signs. They were all there. How could I have been so naïve? You and Mark targeted Lana and I. Easy foodie marks." Jennifer was laughing as she picked up their coffee mugs. "Actually, we should go swimming first. Your clothes are way too good for gardening and it's already getting too warm to work out here. I'm usually out before seven. Once the sun hits the yard it's hard on the plants to do much in the heat. Let me clean up here a bit, grab a few things and we can take off. As long as I'm back by mid-afternoon Charlie will be fine.

"WANT TO DRIVE?" Ben took the keys from Jennifer's outstretched hand.

"Prepare to be chauffeur-driven today madam. You relax and tell me where to go. I am at your command." Ben made a great show of opening the passenger door, handing Jennifer the seatbelt and closing the door before going around to get in the driver's side.

Jennifer chuckled. She hadn't been treated like this in years. Ben and Jason were completely different. Where Jason had been almost quiet and reserved, Ben had a definite dramatic flair she enjoyed. Where Jason was average height and started losing hair in his early forties, Ben had a thick mat of silver hair she loved to comb through her fingers. Where she and Jason had settled into a comfortable married sexual relationship, Ben was a new and exciting element in her life.

"You drive like you mean it." She sat back as Ben expertly backed the car into the street and set off for his building and pool.

"I drove jeeps a lot. Got pretty good at avoiding pot holes at high speed in some places. Maybe I just can't wait to see you in that bathing suit I saw you toss in your bag." Ben reached over to pat Jennifer's thigh, giving it a gentle squeeze. "I find women are more sexy when they have something on and leave something to the imagination."

Jennifer looked at Ben and raised her eyebrows. "Really. I thought most men just wanted their woman to get naked as soon as possible."

"Well yes. But, you have to be dressed first before you can get naked, right?"

"Beaten by male logic. I'm really out of practice." She chuckled and looked out the window. His hand was resting lightly on her thigh. She put her hand over his and felt the light hair and weathered skin of it.

Turning to look at him, she picked up his hand and rubbed it against her cheek. "Thank you for all this Ben. Thank you for you."

"I promised Mark I would be good to you. I like to keep my promises." Ben pulled into a visitor parking space. As they walked towards the high rise, he kept an arm around her shoulder. "As I told him, I know myself much better than I did when he was growing up. I think I have a much better idea of what my priorities should be. And one of my major priorities right now is spending time with you and getting to know more about you, including how well you can swim."

"I haven't been for a long time but I think I can remember how." Jennifer laughed. "I'm really good at the hot tub part. Is there a hot tub?"

"There is indeed. I'm also quite good at that part. I think we've found another common interest." With that, he grandly opened the front door, bowed and waved her to go through the doors.

"You look like the cat that got the cream." Carol and Jennifer were both relaxed after an hour of yoga. "Your dream man again?"

"No longer a dream. He's so real. We spent the entire weekend together. Went sailing. Toured Spectacle Island. I've lived in Boston all my life and have never gone to the islands." Jennifer briefly debated keeping Ben's identity secret and realized it was time to break cover with her friend.

"Remember I said you would know his name but not know him?" Jennifer laughed as she watched Carol perk up. "He's Ben Powell."

"The Ben Powell?" Carol had to admit she was impressed. "I haven't seen him on television recently. What'd you do, kidnap him?"

Jennifer chuckled. "No. He'd decided to retire from being a full-time correspondent just before we met. I met him through his son, who is one of my clients."

"So when do I get to meet him? Maybe we could double date."

"You mean you already have a new boyfriend?"

"At our age, we don't have time to waste. Yep. The new guy is wealthy in his own right. He's looking at harbor front condos in the high six figures, low sevens. He wants to shift his home base to Boston. He and his wife split. No kids. No support payments. It's been a few weeks. We're enjoying each other, if you know what I mean."

"Oh yes. I know what you mean." Jennifer didn't say anything more but couldn't help but notice her friend was almost floating on air. And it wasn't just because of yoga.

"When can we meet your beau?" Carol pushed again.

"How about I check with Ben? Maybe we could go out for dinner together. What's your friend's name?"

"Michel. He's French. From Canada. A corporate jet pilot. He's in town a few days a week and is tired of living in Montreal. I'm letting him bunk in with me when he's on layover until he finds the condo he wants."

"He's in town this weekend?"

"No. He's usually here in the middle of the week. And we haven't made any firm plans. Let's work on it."

Jennifer hoped Carol knew what she was doing. The other side of her bed had barely cooled from Lance the leech.

"When are we going to see Mark again, Mom?" Danny was zooming around the kitchen with one of his Spider-Man action figures. Lana had just put away a bag of groceries and was pulling out something for them to eat.

"He's coming to your party. Who would you like to invite?"

Danny slowed down and climbed on his chair. "How many can I invite?"

"I think we could fit in maybe five or six of your friends. How would that be?" Lana knew the boys Danny played with at day care. She wasn't sure she could handle that many alone but Jennifer had already asked if she could help. The child-adult ratio would be about two to one. They would survive. If Ben came too she was sure they'd make it through alive.

They started making their plans. They would have hot dogs, tortilla chips and salsa and lemonade. Danny wanted a Spider-Man cake. Lana had already ordered it as a surprise. And, she knew Mark was planning something special too but he wouldn't say what.

Jennifer had asked what her nephew would like as a gift and offered to get him the talking garbage truck from Barnes and Noble. Lana was considering buying him a bicycle. They lived on a quiet street and he'd started pestering her for one. She just wasn't sure she was ready to let him out on his own.

As Lana sipped lemonade and watched Danny play with his truck collection she made two decisions. The first was that she would ask Mark to come and live with them. *Danny deserves to have a father figure and Mark is the right person,* she reasoned. *I suspect he feels the same way.* The second decision: Danny would get his first bicycle.

"JOHN! CAN YOU HOLD UP FOR A MINUTE? There's something I need to ask you about." Jennifer caught up with her director, admiring the svelte suit he was wearing. "Got a big meeting today?"

"Yes, board meeting. We're having a presentation on launching a capital expansion campaign. We're running out of space. Next thing we'll be bunking people vertically. What's on your mind?"

"It's a bit delicate. Would you like to step into my office? We're almost there." Jennifer was humming with a newfound energy and vitality. Ben had stayed overnight again and she was thinking about asking him to make it permanent. The condo he was staying in was almost as bad as the one Carol had taken her to see. They had both agreed there was no view worth it if it meant living in a space devoid of warmth and character.

"The question is this." Jennifer felt mildly nervous. Any appearance of a conflict would mean changes would have to be made. "As you know, Mark Powell is one of my clients. His father is Ben Powell. Yes, the journalist. I've been dating Ben the past month or so and I want to be sure it doesn't present a conflict of interest."

"Have you spoken to Mark about this?"

"Not yet. But his father said that Mark supports our relationship."

"I'd suggest you talk to Mark. He may not need your services much longer if he's doing as well as you say. By the way, I did notice a change in you the past few weeks. Now I know why. Congratulations Jennifer. You deserve to be happy."

"Thanks John. Ben is a fine man. Perhaps I'll bring him around and introduce you."

"Are you asking for my blessing?"

"No, of course not." Jennifer smiled and shook her head. "But if you want to give it that's fine too. I consider you both a friend and a colleague."

BEN WAS GOING TO A BIRTHDAY PARTY. For a five-year-old. Why was he excited? It helped of course that Jennifer would be there, and Mark too. And Danny was a pretty cool kid. But when did a kid's birthday party suddenly become something he wanted to go to? Maybe because he had missed so many of Mark's? It helped that Mark's birthday was in mid-December and close enough to Christmas that he was home for some years. But, he had missed many for sure.

"Lana. I need your help. I have no clue what to get Danny for his birthday." Ben had gotten Lana's phone number from Jennifer. He could have asked Mark but it was a good excuse to call Jennifer and hear her voice.

"Oh Ben. There's no need to get him a gift. Go halvsies with Jennifer. She's getting him a talking garbage truck."

"A talking garbage truck? What does it talk about?"

"Garbage I imagine." Lana wasn't actually sure. "It's part of a series the boys all seem to want."

"Any other ideas?"

"He's really into anything to do with Spider-Man. He has a collection of games, toys, cards and, wait a minute! I know exactly what you could get him without breaking the bank." Lana almost pinched herself for forgetting. "There's a Spider-Man spelling game Danny's discovered. If you can track down a copy for the PlayStation 3 you would absolutely be his BFF."

"BFF? What's that?" Ben sounded baffled.

"Best Friend Forever." Lana laughed as she tried to imagine Ben leafing through the gossip rags. "Clearly we don't read the same magazines."

"Okay then. Put me down for the Spider-Man spelling game. See you Saturday at what time?"

"If you come by at about ten, you and Mark can put up the decorations and each have a fortifying glass of lemonade before the hoards arrive."

After they hung up, Ben opened his laptop and Googled the nearest Barnes and Noble. Time to go shopping.

"Mr. Severn. Good to see you sir." Mark straightened up from where he'd been pinching unwanted shoots off the tomato plants and wiped his brow. It wasn't even July yet and it was well up in the eighties. "Your solution for the cutworms has been working perfectly. We haven't lost any more plants."

Although he hadn't known him for long, Mark had seen a distinct decline in Art's health since his arrival. It was a bit like watching a failing plant wither. The elderly man's hands had lost much of their strength, he sometimes seemed to have trouble holding his head up and he didn't even attempt to walk any more. He knew from Jennifer there was a concern he would soon be completely bedridden. It was probably going to be his last summer of being able to be dressed and come outside.

Mark motioned to the attendant to follow him. "I'd like to show you something new in the greenhouse."

As they entered the relatively cooler building, Mark walked over to where he'd set up an area for doing flower arrangements. "I'm no expert on flower arrangements but some of the ladies are. It was Jane Gardner's idea. We often get flower arrangements from local funeral homes. The flowers are still fresh but you can tell where they came from." Mark could see Art was listening attentively. "Whenever we get a delivery, some of the ladies take them apart and rearrange them. I think last count we had about twenty flower arrangements in the main building."

"I have seen them in the dining room. They are beautiful and add some needed color." Mr. Severn's voice had lost much of its force. His words came out in more of a whisper. "My wife always had cut flowers on the tables around our house. She especially liked lilies. White lilies. They made our house smell so wonderful."

They chatted for a few more minutes but it was clear that even the short outing was almost more than old Art could manage. His head was drooping as the attendant wheeled him back into his building.

Jennifer watched the orderly pushing her father's wheelchair. She'd give them a few minutes to get him settled in bed before going up to his room. In the meantime, she had to talk to the residence physician.

"Hello Jennifer. Glad you could come by today."

"Hi Avery. I think I know what you're going to tell me. I've seen it coming the past couple of weeks." Jennifer was under no illusion about her father's health. It had slipped rapidly.

"I believe he's had a number of small strokes. He's lost just about all sense of balance. His legs are barely responding and he's having trouble feeding himself because his hands are so weak. We can try some physio but I think you have to be prepared to have him moved to the non-ambulatory wing."

With the rest of Jennifer's life taking such a positive turn, she knew she had avoided coming to terms with the deterioration in her father's physical health. It had been hard enough dealing with his mental decline but now his body was giving up too.

"Thanks for staying on top of this. I don't think you're ever ready to lose a parent no matter how poor their quality of life.

At least he can stay here and not be moved far." She didn't want to cry in front of this young man. She swallowed and stood up. "Please go ahead and move him. Will he still have a private room? The cost is not an issue."

"It will depend on what bed becomes available but probably yes. You've made the right decision. I can't say with any certainty how much longer he has but based on the past two weeks it may not be much longer." He opened the office door. "Someone will call you to let you know his room number in the medical wing."

When Jennifer walked into her father's room, he was asleep. There was little she could do but pat his hand and kiss his forehead. She watched him, noticing how drawn and pale he looked. Getting up, dressed and into the chair had worn him out completely. She walked out, realizing she probably wouldn't be visiting him in this cheery room for much longer. Stepping back into the sunshine, she looked over the grounds and the profusion of flowers and flowering bushes. She had found her father a wonderful place to spend his last years. She knew the staff would keep him as comfortable as possible in the coming days or weeks. Right now, she needed to go home, hug her dog and sit in her garden for awhile. It was her garden now. She would care for it with as much love and attention as her father had. Reaching into her purse for a tissue, she realized with sad resignation that her father would never see it again.

Chapter 16

Mark was up at his usual hour but today he dressed with a difference. No work clothes for him today. Today was Vera's birthday party. After showering thoroughly and scrubbing his nails, he clipped them carefully and filed them smooth. No-one was going to see the gardener today. Today it was Mark the piano man.

No need to pack any lunch or snacks. He'd seen the walk-in. Vito could feed half of Boston with what he had made up and stored in there.

He checked a last time in the mirror. He'd had his hair cut on the way home from work. He'd wanted to stay over with Lana but she'd made it clear she had a busy week with Danny's party coming up. He wasn't sure if she was avoiding him a bit. Maybe I need to back off and give her some room, he thought, as he checked his backpack to make sure he had his meds, water and the ever-ready apple.

He was standing outside when Lana and Danny pulled up. Danny was coming to Brentwood today to join the party and hear Mark play and sing.

"Hi Mark. This really is my birthday week just like you said. My mom says there's cake today and then I get more cake on Saturday. Today is not my party though but it still is one. How cool is that!" Danny was humming with the energy only an almost five-year-old could have just three more sleeps from his own birthday.

"Yep. Today is going to be really special for a lot of people Danny boy. Wait'll you see all the food Vito has ready for us. I hope you brought a major appetite big guy." Mark climbed in on the passenger side and gave Lana a quick kiss on the cheek.

"You kissed my mom. Why'd you kiss her Mark?" Danny was suddenly serious and quiet.

Mark looked at Lana. She winked at him and smiled broadly. Answer that one.

"I kissed your mom because she's pretty and she smells really good. But I've also been known to kiss ripe tomatoes and even cucumbers. Why do you think I kissed her?" Mark lobbed the question back to Danny who took it under careful consideration.

"Well. I think you kissed her because you like her a lot. Like I do. I kiss her because she's my mom. Sometimes I don't want to but I have to."

"See Danny, moms are more mushy and emotional than us men. You have to hug them and kiss them just because. Because they made you a good meal. Because they wash your dirty socks. Because they don't yell at you when you come in all dirty. A hug and a kiss is a whole lot cheaper than money."

"So if we keep kissing my mom she'll be happy and keep doing all the things I like, like making muffins and taking us on picnics?" Lana was almost at the staff parking area. She slowed as Danny processed this new information.

"You got it big guy. Women need to be hugged and kissed often to keep them happy. Remember that and you may have a good life."

"We're here! Let's go!" Danny jumped out of the van with his small backpack and his Red Sox cap firmly planted on his head.

"I brought someone who may be able to blow up some balloons." Mark had taken over Danny as Lana's shift started.

"Hey Danny. Glad you're here." Jane took them back to her office where two bags of balloons were stored. "If you guys don't mind, could you start blowing them up and storing them here where no-one will see them? We've arranged for Vera to be getting her hair done while we're doing the decorating."

"Leave us to it Jane. We'll do what we can but please send reinforcements as soon as possible. We can't do all these alone I don't think."

Danny had already opened a bag and was trying manfully to blow one up. Mark took a balloon out of the bag.

"Try stretching it a bit and then blowing just a little air in. No pressure. The heat of your breath will make it relax a bit and then you can blow it up more easily." Mark demonstrated his technique and soon the first balloon was flung into the air.

Danny tried to replicate what Mark had done. He managed to get it blown up about half way and looked to Mark for approval. Mark smiled. There would be a few small balloons today. He took the half balloon, tied it off and flung it in the air.

"What's next?" Mark and Danny left Jane's office and went into the sunroom. A couple of nurses were blowing up the rest of the balloons. Breakfast was finished and cleared. It was time to decorate in earnest. Fresh flowers adorned every table. Larger arrangements had been brought in as centerpieces for the two buffet tables. The flower ladies had been busy. One of Mark's helpers appeared with a stepladder. The three men stood in front of Jane and her tablet.

Behind her was a table with streamers, a 'Happy 100th Birthday Vera' banner and an assortment of party favors that needed to be put on every table. Danny was assigned to the party favors. Mark and his tall helper were assigned to the banner and streamers.

A couple of off-duty nurses offered to tie up bunches of balloons together to guide the way from the main entrance to the party room. Another off-duty nurse went back to the kitchen and offered to ferry food to the buffet tables. Other volunteers arrived and soon Jane and Vito had all the help they could possibly need. There was a definite party mood in the air.

Jane looked around. Everything had gone according to plan. Vera's family had all arrived and were clearly impressed with what they saw. Mark was playing background music as the guests and residents started to arrive. Vera was almost finished with the hairdresser and word had come out that she was having a very good day and was well aware it was her birthday.

"Ladies and gentlemen. If I could have your attention please." Jane tried to speak over the hum of conversation. Mark played a trill loudly enough to stop conversation. "Vera will be here in a couple of minutes. When she arrives, Mark will start playing Happy Birthday. Let's make sure Vera can hear every word."

Vera was slowly wheeled into the sunny room by Kathy Hunter. As the executive director smiled over the wheelchair, the room fell silent. Vera was clearly surprised. Then her eyes went wide with joy as she saw the large knot of her family who were smiling, cheering and clapping for her. It was several minutes before things calmed down enough for Mark to play the opening bars of happy birthday and give a middle C for everyone.

Older voices wavered some, younger voices did too. It all came out as a wonderful confusion of notes and words. Vera continued to beam, reaching up to pat her hair and touch her necklace like a young girl on a date.

Jane went over and put a sparkly tiara on Vera's snow white hair. Her youngest great-great granddaughter came forward shyly to give her a corsage. The child's mother helped pin it to Vera's best sweater. The whole room started clapping all over again. There were even a few whistles and cheers.

"Speech. Speech. Speech."

Vera smiled up from her wheelchair. Everyone went quiet.

"Thank you." She struggled but pushed it out. "Thank you very much. I ... very... happy... today."

Her oldest daughter, herself in her seventies, came forward. "My family and I cannot thank you enough for this wonderful party. My mother has loved living at Brentwood all these years. You've been her family and we know she is well loved and cared for. Thank you so much to you all."

Jane cued Mark that he was up. "Vera. Hi. I heard you used to be a chorus singer when Frank Sinatra sang in this area. I've put together a few songs I know you'll remember."

Vera cocked her head to one side and half-closed her eyes as Mark played the opening bars of a well-known favorite. As the room went quiet, Mark looked over to where his dad had just slipped into the room and was standing by the doorway with Lana and Danny. He realized he was playing as much for them as everyone else in the room. He also realized he wasn't the least bit nervous. This was part of who he was and the people he cared for the most were here to witness it.

"The days… the days of wine and roses…" Mark segued effortlessly through segments from a dozen of Sinatra's signature songs. Vera was given a tissue at one point. Her daughter and son also needed a tissue. Danny went over and climbed onto the piano bench with Mark.

Ben watched and listened as his son's singing held the room captive. "Did you know he could play and sing like that?"

"I've heard him practicing a few times. I'm no expert but I know what I like and I really like his voice." Lana relaxed against the door frame. "You've never heard him play or sing before?"

"The last time I heard him singing was before his voice changed. He was probably around twelve."

Mark played effortlessly, his hands gracefully floating over the keys. "I remember Heather and Mark sitting on the piano bench in our living room. He would have been about eight or nine. Heather was teaching him a Beatles piece. They were laughing because he kept hitting the wrong chords over and over. Heather said he'd have to start writing his own music if he couldn't learn somebody else's. I wonder if he's written some music of his own. There's so much I still don't know about him."

As Mark wound down the last words of "Did It My Way", Vera reached out her arms and motioned Mark to come to her. The whole room had exploded in vigorous applause as Mark made his way to the centenarian.

"Thank you. Thank you much. So happy. Thank you." Vera couldn't contain her joy as she hugged Mark. He bent way down to the tiny little woman but finally squatted. He took both her frail hands in his.

"Happy birthday Vera. Your music is my music. I'll play for you again any day." His voice carried clearly throughout the room. The two of them hugged as several people went looking for tissues.

"Time for lunch everyone." Jane called out. "Please help yourself. Mark will be playing again."

The conversation level in the sun-filled room went up as people got their food and found a table. Some went outside with their plates and enjoy the air, which was redolent with the fragrant smells of the flower gardens.

As the guests finished their lunches, Vito's various helpers cleared away dishes and took away the platters. The buffet was gradually cleared and a pile of small plates appeared with forks and napkins.

Mark got the signal from Jane and moved back to the piano. Again, he played some intro bars and gave another middle C to the assembled. But, this time, Vito strutted into the room pushing a trolley with a giant cake with three large candles at the top: 1- 0 – 0.

Cameras and iphones started clicking away as Mark played a jazzy rendition of Happy Birthday. The cake was covered in sparklers, which delighted the children. Vera looked at her son and daughter and reached a hand to both. Her family gathered around her as the cake was wheeled in and the sparklers gradually burned out.

Vera's daughter held onto her mother's hand. "Mum. You are the best mother we could possibly have. You took care of us. You hugged us whether we deserved it or not. Happy birthday mum."

Someone handed her a tissue. Vera smiled her thanks and held tightly to her daughter's hand. Her son sidled up and took her other hand.

"I love you. Always." Vera looked from one to the other and then at all her assembled family. Five generations. A reporter and photographer from the Boston Globe were recording the event for posterity.

"Do you have any idea how many tissues we went through today?" Jane was looking around the now empty room. "It never occurred to me to put boxes of tissues among the must-have supplies for a birthday party."

Mark, Lana, Danny and Ben were getting ready to leave. "That was unbelievably amazing Jane." Mark and Lana almost spoke in unison.

"I've never seen something like that before. Vera and her family were almost overwhelmed by the level of emotion and connection they felt." Lana had attended other birthday celebrations at the residence. But, this one had definitely been different.

"Your music and singing were a big part of that Mark. We all felt like you were channeling Sinatra." Lana had never connected some of the songs she knew with Old Blue Eyes, but now she knew. It had been quite an eye-opener to realize that many of the songs she loved had originally been performed before she was born.

Jane chimed in. "Kathy has warned me that you'll be doing more of this in the off-season for gardening. I'm really looking forward to it."

"I am too. This is in my bones. It's something I need to do." Mark's shoulders were slumping. "Lana. Danny. I need to go home now. It's been a long and wonderful day. But, I'm tired. My dad and I will get a cab."

Lana watched as Mark walked down the corridor with his father. She could see in his steps that he was tired.

"You okay, son?" Ben got Mark to sit in the shade while they waited for the cab. "I had no idea you could sing and play like that. You have a wonderful voice. Maybe you will have that career in music you dreamed of."

"I know Mom hoped I would follow in her footsteps. But it's so competitive these days." Mark combed his fingers through his hair.

"I can see your point. But know this. You have wonderful gifts in your playing and singing. It was clear that sharing those gifts today made a roomful of people very happy. I'm so proud of you. Mom would have been beyond proud if she'd been with us today." Ben put an arm around his son and gave him a hug as the cab pulled into the long laneway.

"I sometimes wonder if she can still see us. There was definitely a special energy in that room today." Mark climbed into the taxi.

"Do you write your own music?" The taxi had eased into the increasingly heavy mid-afternoon traffic.

"I've written some lyrics and set them to music. Once I'm more settled I hope to shop them around. Sell them if I can. I'm going to buy a keyboard in the next few weeks. I think I can be a songwriter."

"Do you think you'll make a career out of your job at Brentwood?"

"Right now I'm just glad to have a steady job doing something I really like. The environment at Brentwood is the best I've ever worked in. And it doesn't hurt that Lana works here too." Mark laid his head against the neck rest and closed his eyes.

Ben patted Mark's knee. "I'll just shut up and let you relax until we get you home."

JENNIFER SAT BACK AFTER PUTTING HER OFFICE PHONE DOWN. It was done. Her father had been moved to another wing of the residence where he would receive full-time nursing care.

Jennifer reached for the phone and called Ben's mobile. "Ben. Do you have any plans? I need a shoulder to lean on big time."

"Your father's been moved?"

"Yes. And he didn't do it quietly. He made such a fuss he had to be restrained. Can I come and pick you up? I have my car. Maybe we could go for a walk along the waterfront with Charlie."

"Sounds good. I'm at Mark's having a coffee. He put on an incredible show today. Had people crying in their teacups." Ben looked over at Mark, who was relaxing with his feet up.

"I'll be over within half an hour." Jennifer had already shut down her computer and was ready to leave.

As she crawled through the late afternoon traffic during a cloudburst, Jennifer thought about her father. His life was coming to an end but he was still fighting.

"Ben. Mark. Hi you two." Jennifer left her umbrella in the hall and stepped into the tidy apartment when Ben opened the door. "I hear it went really well today. Congratulations."

Mark grinned back at her and stood up. "It went great. We had a ball. Vera couldn't stop smiling. And then she cried a bit, which made everyone else start crying. It was so funny to see all these people dabbing at their eyes and blowing their noses at a party."

"You look tired."

"Yes. I'll admit it. But, I'm taking tomorrow off to make it a long weekend. I'll be fine. Please don't worry about me. My father's doing enough for both of you." Ben had gone back to the kitchen and was rummaging through Mark's fridge.

"Dad, I'm not hungry. I ate lots for lunch. I'm fine."

Jennifer had never seen this side of Ben. He was positively protective. Papa bear taking care of his young cub.

"Take him away, please. He's hovering over me like an old hen."

"I don't hover. I have never hovered in my life." Ben challenged Mark's comment with a sheepish smile. "All right. Maybe just once."

"Like right now, Dad." Mark shot back.

"Okay you two. Enough. C'mon Ben. You're coming with me." Jennifer chuckled at the two men nagging each other. They were definitely cut from the same cloth.

Ben picked his way through the heavy traffic. The rain had eased up to a light drizzle that would save a lot of gardeners their evening watering chores.

"I can't believe how fast he's gone downhill. Two weeks ago he was getting himself dressed every day. Was going out in his wheelchair for a couple of hours of pulling weeds. The residence doctor said he's having multiple small strokes. Each one seems to rob him of something. He can't stand up properly. Can barely hold a fork." Jennifer put her head down and finally let her feelings out. As she cried softly, Ben reached across to rub and massage her neck as he navigated her neighborhood.

"I didn't realize how much it would hurt to see him going this way. I know he's going to die soon. I hoped it wouldn't be like this." Jennifer looked up as they reached her driveway. She was glad she had this home to come back to. Lana had been right. Her home had a warm character and she really needed that right now.

They sat in the car waiting for another cloudburst to pass.

"When I was little, I used to crawl into bed with my mother and father on Sunday mornings before church. We got to sleep in a bit on Sunday. My dad would tickle me and make me laugh. I would make him kiss my teddy bear." Jennifer smiled as she remembered the dog-eared teddy that still had a spot in a bookcase somewhere.

"After church we'd go out for lunch at a restaurant. For months, we had to go to one that had grilled cheese sandwiches." Jennifer shook her head and smiled warmly at the memory. "I just got this thing about grilled cheese sandwiches. But I always gave the pickle to my father. To this day I do not like pickles."

As the rain began to let up, Ben dropped the keys into Jennifer's hand. "How about we make a run for the door?"

"I know you're not supposed to answer a question with a question, but how would you feel about moving in with me?" Jennifer knew she wanted Ben like this. Talking about her childhood memories. Sitting in the car together in the rain. And now going into the house together to make supper.

"I would feel like I was coming home. But are you sure this isn't part of your reaction to what's happening to your dad?" Ben put a finger under her chin and raised it to give her a light warm kiss. "You're too important to me to change our relationship for the wrong reason."

Jennifer shook her head. She felt a lightness she hadn't expected to feel given what was happening. It was true what they said. As one door closes another one opens. "It feels right Ben. It's not at all about my father. It really isn't. It just feels right. Let me get changed and we'll take Charlie out for a nice long walk. How long will it take you to pack up your stuff?"

"I think I could get most of it in a matter of minutes. We can go back for the rest next week sometime. I think this weekend's going to be pretty busy with Danny's party."

Charlie bounded out the front door and ran in happy circles around Ben's legs as Jennifer turned off the alarm.

"Hiya Charlie. Let's go out back and see if we can find Nemo." Charlie quickly checked a bush and left his calling card before dashing back to follow Ben inside.

"Help yourself to some lemonade. I'll be down in a minute." Jennifer called down. Ben headed for the kitchen, let Charlie out and then poured two glasses. Looking around the large airy kitchen, he noted the violets on the windowsill and the carousel of cooking utensils next to the stove. He studied the room in a new light. This was where he and Jennifer would be creating meals together and sharing them. He wouldn't have to leave and sleep alone. When he went somewhere, he would have this home to come back to. And the woman he was growing to love would be here for him.

Whatever else had happened in his jet-setting life was over now. He had a home and love in his life that he doubted he would ever want to part with again. He realized with a wry smile that he was finally becoming who he wanted to be when he grew up.

Jennifer came into the kitchen, walked straight over to him and wrapped him in the biggest hug should could muster. "You feel good. You smell good. And you look good. I am one happy woman in the feeling good department."

"There is one thing you need to know before I actually move in with you."

"Please tell me you don't have a lover stashed away somewhere." Jennifer looked up into the sparkling blue eyes of this man she was coming to care a great deal about.

"I love you Jennifer Barrett." Ben wrapped her into his arms and leaned his head against hers.

"I love you too Ben Powell." Jennifer felt cherished.

Chapter 17

"Happy birthday, Danny!" Lana whispered lightly into her sleeping son's ear and put her hand on his small shoulder. Danny's eyes fluttered open and then suddenly grew wide and alert.

"It's my birthday! I'm five years old now!" He bounded to his feet and jumped up and down on his Spider-Man bedspread. Lana stood beside the bed and held out her arms. Danny launched himself at her and wrapped his arms and legs around her. "Yahoo! It's my birthday!"

"Happy birthday to my big fine son." Lana planted a loud kiss on Danny's cheek and made big smacking noises.

"Ewww. Mommm." Danny wriggled out of her arms and ran off towards the bathroom, slamming the door behind him.

Lana smiled, made up his bed and did a quick tidy up. No use fussing over tidiness today, not with half a dozen boys descending on them in a few hours.

Down in the kitchen, Lana had already decorated Danny's chair with some streamers and a helium-filled Spider-Man balloon. She'd kept breakfast simple, really just a snack, knowing Danny was too excited to eat properly. She called Mark.

"Hi you. It's me. You don't have to wait until ten to come over." Lana could hear the smile in Mark's voice.

"Danny being a bit of a handful this morning?"

"Not yet but it's a long morning. I could use some help. I'm really not Super Mom. We can come pick you up. There's no traffic. Could be there in ten minutes or so."

"I'm ready any time. I've got Danny's gift wrapped and the card signed." He'd wrapped the gift the day he bought it.

"See you in fifteen minutes then." Lana looked up at the clock.

It was just a few minutes after eight.

"We're going to pick up Mark and bring him back here to help decorate." Lana smiled when she saw Danny had spied the balloon.

"Cool balloon, Mom. Thanks!" Danny pulled the string down to peer and poke at the colorful balloon. As soon as he let the string go it popped back up near the ceiling. After he'd done it at least four times, Lana suggested he get something to eat so they could go get Mark.

"Can I bring the balloon with me?"

"Only if you promise not to let it loose in the van. You have to hold on to it the whole time."

Danny promised and carefully untied the balloon.

"Cool balloon there, big guy." Mark climbed into the front seat of the van and looked back to admire the shiny Spider-Man. "Happy birthday." He held up a hand for a high five.

Arriving back at Lana's, Mark was quickly put to work with a fresh cup of coffee for fortification.

Jennifer and Ben arrived through the back gate and added their gifts to the table where Mark had put his. They all sipped on hot coffee as they set about transforming the back yard into party central.

An hour later, Ben, Mark and Danny stopped to inspect their work. "Okay. I think that's it men." Ben looked around. Everything appeared to be in place. The fence was festooned with balloons and streamers. There were easily three dozen balloons. More than enough for Danny and his friends to pop through the afternoon. Most of the toys were piled off to one side to leave plenty of room for running around. The small lawn was freshly mowed and raked.

Lana and Jennifer emerged laden with plates, cutlery and paper cups.

"Well. Look at this! I don't think this back yard has ever looked so neat. Am I in the right place?" Lana was genuinely pleased with the way the yard looked. She savored the moment, knowing it wouldn't last long. "You men have outdone yourselves. I'm impressed."

Jennifer smiled over at Ben, who made a slight bow in her direction.

"As of today, Danny is an honorary Powell. Only a Powell could have done such a fine job."

"The Fitzpatrick's are no slouches either, right Danny?" Lana threw up her chin and fisted her hands on her hips. "I'll have you know Ben Powell, that my Danny Fitzpatrick here can clean a yard with the best of them."

"He just did." Ben grinned and put his arm around Mark as they all burst out laughing.

"P minus twenty and counting." Lana smiled and set Mark to filling a cooler with a variety of drinks and water bottles. Jennifer finished cutting up raw vegetables for everyone to snack on. Danny and Ben made up the loot bags. Lana set out all the fixings for their hot dogs. The salads would come out last.

"I think we're ready wouldn't you say?" Lana glanced up at the kitchen clock and saw she had enough time to freshen up before her pint-sized guests arrived.

The tranquility of Lana's back yard was soon shattered with the sound of half a dozen young boys racing around. In less than an hour, one had fallen and a bandaid was duly dispensed. In under two hours almost every balloon had been burst.

By three o'clock it was time to bring out the cake and open Danny's gifts. The organized games had all been played before and after lunch. The hot dogs were history. They had barely dented the two large salads. But everyone had room for cake and ice cream.

Mark had taken all the gifts and put them in a pile at one end of the picnic table. Danny's chair with the balloon was there but he and his friends were standing crowded around the gifts. It didn't look like anyone was going to sit down until it was time for the cake.

Jennifer carefully uncrated the cake while Lana brought out the five sparklers and put them in an arch around one of Spider-Man's hands. "It'll look like he's got a lightning bolt in his hand."

"Do you really think these kids will notice?" Jennifer figured they'd have a minute or two at most to get some photos before the kids set in to demolish the cake.

"I guess not. Maybe we should take a picture here before we bring it out?" Lana turned on her digital camera and snapped two shots. "We have proof of cake. Let's go."

Jennifer held the door open for Lana to bring out the cake. The two women started singing happy birthday. Everyone quickly joined in while Mark and Ben took pictures of the happy group. Once the sparklers had died out, the serious work of cutting the cake and dishing out the ice cream began in earnest. As the caked was passed around, the sound level went down noticeably. It didn't last long.

"Open my gift Danny. It's the long one with the blue ribbon."

"Open mine first. It's the big one with the birthday balloons on it."

Danny covered his eyes and reached out in front of him. When he touched the first gift he opened his eyes, picked it up and gave it a shake. Then his fingers tore into the paper until the box emerged.

"Cool! A construction set. Thanks Braydon. It's super." Danny didn't even open the box before he covered his eyes and picked out another one. Within minutes, he was surrounded by ripped paper and an assortment of boy toys.

Ben solemnly handed his gift to Danny and watched his face light up. "My very own copy of the Spider-Man spelling game. This is the best birthday ever! Thanks Ben."

Next up was the talking garbage truck from Jennifer. It seemed Danny was the first one in his group of friends to get one. Lana silently apologized to the parents who would now be begged to buy one.

Mark handed Danny his gaily wrapped present. Danny carefully opened the Spider-Man gift wrap. He wanted to keep it. When he opened the plain box inside he was quiet. Then he gasped. "Oh Mark. Wow guys. Look at this. My very own Spider-Man baseball shirt!"

He pulled the official jersey out of the box and held it up for everyone to see. He put it on over his t-shirt and grinned. It was at least two sizes too big for him.

"One last gift Danny." Lana gave the cue to Ben who opened the shed door and rolled out a gleaming new bicycle.

"You got me a bike! Mom, wow, thanks!!" Danny ran to his mother, gave her a quick hug and then ran to the bicycle. He ran his fingers over the shiny handlebars and then got on as Ben held it for him. Jennifer snapped a couple of quick pictures as Ben helped him keep his balance.

As the last child left the yard with his loot bag, Jennifer shoved away a pile of wrapping paper and plopped down in a chair. "Let's see. There were seven kids including Danny. We were four adults. Are you as exhausted as I am?" The yard now looked as if a swarm of locusts had gone through. Toys old and new were strewn everywhere. The bicycle was leaning up against the shed. Plates with half-eaten cake in puddles of ice cream littered the picnic table. She swore she saw a half-eaten hot dog perched on a bush.

"Next year I may think of something else. I'm whacked." Lana cleared another chair. "Anyone want an adult drink?"

Ben appeared to have taken the whole afternoon in stride. He knew how to pace himself. He offered to bring out some wine and a couple of glasses. "Want a beer while I'm there Mark?"

"No thanks. I'm going to take Danny out to test drive that bike for awhile. Give you ladies a break. Enjoy. I'll have one later."

Lana and Jennifer smiled gratefully as Ben went off to play butler while Mark helped Danny adjust his new bike helmet and get the bike out the gate. Ben soon emerged with a bottle of chilled Chardonnay and two glasses. "I'll be back in a minute with my beer."

Jennifer waited until he'd gone back in the house. "Ben has moved in with me." Her smile radiated her happiness to Lana. "I didn't want to say anything earlier while you had the party on your mind."

"Oh Jennifer. That's wonderful! That's the best news I've had this week!" Lana held up her glass. "Here's to my wonderful friend. I hope you two will be very happy." As they clinked their glasses, Ben came out with his beer.

"Congratulations Ben. Jennifer told me you two are living in sin." Lana and Ben clinked glass and bottle. "Does Mark know?" Ben took one long pull of his beer and put it down on the table.

"No. But I better tell him right now. He hates being the last to know. I'll be back. Don't touch that beer." Ben strolled out the side gate to find Mark and Danny.

"Hey men. How's the bike riding lesson going?" Danny was still quite wobbly but Mark had one hand at the base of the seat and walked alongside him.

"We've decided to skip the training wheels stage and go right to riding it for real." Mark helped Danny turn the bike around to head back towards his father.

"I bet you'll be riding on your own by tomorrow Danny. You look like you're almost there now." Ben patted Danny's helmet. "Mark figured it out quickly too. You've got a good teacher."

The three went back to the house. Danny's birthday cake sugar fix was wearing off. He seemed almost glad when Ben asked if they could go back in. Once the bike and helmet were safely put away, Danny made a beeline for the talking garbage truck. Mark got a beer and the two men joined the ladies.

"Mark. Jen and I have some news to share. Jen has invited me to move in with her and I've accepted. As Lana put it, we want to live in sin." Ben was standing behind Jennifer with a hand draped over her shoulder.

"I'm the last to find out again?" Mark looked between them all.

"Only by a few minutes, I promise. Jennifer told Lana maybe five minutes ago."

"It's okay, Dad. Just teasing." Mark broke into a broad grin. "I'm really happy for you. What a surprise. Didn't take you two long at all." Mark went over and gave her a hug. "You'll be like my stepmother. Is there a conflict of interest with you being my social worker?"

Jennifer had been thinking long and hard about it since talking to John. "If you still need a social worker, it would be best if we find someone else. I could be your health advocate if the need ever arose. Does that make sense?"

Mark nodded. "Yes, it makes a lot of sense. We're all pretty certain the depression was caused primarily by the situation my mother and I were in. I'm a mature adult now. I've developed better coping skills. And I'm really glad you and my dad are an item. You've been a real team since you met." He smiled at both of them and then at Lana. "Time to clean up? I'm actually getting hungry again."

"You're always hungry. Almost a bottomless pit!" Lana hadn't had to deal with an adult male appetite in a few years. "How about we work on the leftovers? There's still plenty of potato salad and I've got some burgers we could barbeque."

Jen and Ben looked at each other. "We're going to get going and let you folks have some down time. How about we help with the clean-up first though?" Ben stood up and started gathering up the plates and cups to bring to the sink. Jennifer followed with another armload while Mark started cleaning up from the gift opening.

LANA AND MARK LOOKED AROUND. Almost all evidence of the party had been cleaned up.

"Wow. My dad and Jennifer. I'm happy for them. I didn't realize it had gotten so serious so quickly. I knew they'd hit it off really well but it's not even three months yet."

"My father and mother moved in together almost from their first date. They loved to tell the story of how my dad went to a housewarming party at my mother's new apartment. He went over and never left. He gave up his apartment not even three months later. They were married for almost thirty years before the accident." Lana took some containers out of the fridge.

Danny wandered into the kitchen. "I'm hungry. When are we going to eat?"

"How about we start the barbeque and get those burgers going?" Mark put his arm around Danny's small shoulder. "So what'd you think of your party?"

"It was the best." Danny was still wearing his Spidey jersey.

Lana figured he would sleep in it as long as she let him.

After a relaxed dinner, Danny faded fast. His next bike riding lesson would have to wait until morning. He was even too tired to focus on the spelling game. Lana got him bathed and into bed so Mark could say goodnight to him.

"What a day. I survived my first boy's birthday party." Lana and Mark walked into the living room.

"Make that we. You had help." Mark sank gratefully onto the couch and stretched out his long legs.

"We survived. Quite well, too. Although I'm glad tomorrow is Sunday. You going to stay around and help Danny learn to ride? Please? I'll make it worth your while." Lana plopped into her big armchair and propped her feet up on the couch's armrest near Mark's head. He reached back to rub a foot.

"Oh don't stop. That feels so good." Lana almost purred with pleasure. "I haven't had a foot rub in years."

"So what exactly will you do to make it worth my while?" Mark pressed his thumb around the arch of her foot and was rewarded with a happy moan.

"Let me think on it. I could offer you food. I know that works." Lana stretched and offered up her other foot for treatment. "Or, I could take us to a movie. That might be the only way to get Danny to give up the bicycle once he gets going with it. You might thank me for that."

"You're talking. I'm listening. Food's good. Movie's good too. Promise me both and I'll consider it." Mark turned on his stomach and propped himself up. "Give me a toe. I'm going to suck on your toe. Maybe eat it."

Lana giggled as Mark easily grabbed a foot and pinned it down with one hand. He stuck his chin forward and planted a smacking kiss on her big toe.

"I think I should have a shower before—" Lana broke off as Mark pulled her toe into his mouth and clamped his teeth on it.

"I'm not letting go until you kiss me."

Lana sat forward but was stopped short by her imprisoned toe. Laughing she reached forward and grabbed Mark's ear and gave it a little pull. As he let go, she jumped out of her chair and dove at him on the couch, tickling him mercilessly in the ribs and stomach. He writhed and squirmed until he was able to turn onto his back. Then he turned the tables. With arms strengthened by weeks of outdoor labor, he neatly clamped her arms to her sides and sat her on the edge of the couch.

"How about we go up and see about making it worth my while now?" He sat forward and kissed her lightly on each cheek and then more firmly on her mouth.

"Oh," she breathed in their mingled scents. "I think that's a wonderful idea."

Chapter 18

After stopping by Ben's borrowed condo for his clothes, Jennifer quickly cleared space in her spare closet for Ben's initial deposit. She'd rearrange the closet in the master bedroom another day and give him a permanent spot. But, for now, he had a place to hang up his jackets and shirts. She was impressed with their quality. Clearly European made, with crisp detailing and high thread counts. She adjusted one jacket on its hanger and saw that it was pure silk. There a soft gleam to it that made her think it would go just fine with her little black dress some evening.

"This jacket is worth a week's pay." Jennifer looked up at Ben as he handed her another to hang.

"I got that to wear when I was interviewing various heads of state in their palaces. They cost very little where I was buying." Ben ran his hand appreciatively down the soft wool. "You'll find when I start bringing things out of storage I have quite a wardrobe. I needed clothes for city, slums, mountains, ships, hot and cold climates. You name it, I had something for every contingency. The tailors in some places had never made clothing for a man my height. They'd get quite excited and call in their relatives and friends to see the giant. My interpreters got used to it."

"I don't know about you but I would like a long, warm bath." Jennifer hung up the last of the shirts and closed the closet door. "It's been a wonderful day. And wonderful to have you here to talk about it."

"Room for two in that tub of yours?" Ben reached out to stroke his fingers through Jennifer's hair.

"Let's go find out." Jennifer reached up to take his hand and led him towards their bedroom.

"I'm going to call and see about renting a boat for the July fourth weekend." Ben sipped the last of his coffee. They had awakened to a cloudless sky. "Let's see if Mark, Lana and Danny can come along. What do you think?"

"Sounds wonderful." Jennifer eyed the area of the garden she planned to deal with next. "I'll help pay for it."

"Oh no you won't. You've been feeding me. This is my treat. No arguments."

Ben went off to make some calls while Jennifer cleaned up from breakfast. *He has slipped into my life so easily,* she mused. *Three months ago I didn't know him as anything but a name in Mark's file and a face on television. And here he is, so full of life.* She arched her neck and smiled as she remembered waking up to find him beside her. Setting a plate to drain, she dried her hands and looked around. *There's a new man in this house. And he fits right in.*

"We're all set. I've found one I think you'll love. It sleeps up to eight and has a state-of-the art galley." Ben closed his phone as he came back to the kitchen.

"Let me call Lana." Jennifer took the phone out of Ben's hands and entered the number. She smiled as she connected. "Do you, Mark and Danny have any plans yet for the July fourth weekend? Ben checked and there's a sailboat available for a weekend rental if you'd like to join us. It sleeps up to eight and there's a good-sized galley. We could watch the fireworks from the harbor."

Jennifer was thrilled at the thought of spending an entire weekend on the water, trolling up and down the coast with Ben. If Mark, Lana and Danny could join them it would mark the first major time together for all of them as a newly-formed family.

"Are you serious?" Lana sounded stunned. "I've never spent a weekend sailing in my entire life. That's something rich people do. Danny will be beyond excited and I know Mark loves sailing. He told me he went with his dad several times as a child. What a wonderful surprise."

The two women chatted about what to wear and what they would bring in for the on-board meals. As soon as they hung up, Lana called Mark.

"Hi you. Jennifer just called to invite the three of us to spend the weekend sailing with her and your dad. Are you up for it?" Lana knew his answer.

"Are you serious?"

"That's exactly what I said!" Lana laughed happily.

"Wow. Can you imagine how excited Danny will be? He'll have to leave the new bike for a couple of days but I bet this will trump the bicycle big time." Mark set down a shovel and shook off his work gloves one by one as he juggled the phone. "I'm very definitely up for it. When, where?"

"I wanted to check with you before I got all the details. Isn't this amazing? What a fourth of July weekend. We'll see the fireworks from the harbor!" Lana felt like a kid herself. "They must rent out child-sized lifejackets right? If not, I'll go buy one today."

"Let's check with my dad. I'm sure they rent everything we need. I'm almost finished for today. Where are you?" Mark was picking up gardening tools to load into the small trailer behind the tractor mower.

Lana walked briskly down the hallway, smiling to patients as she spoke on her mobile. "I'm on my way to get Vera organized for an early dinner. I should be finished in about twenty minutes or so. See you in the parking lot?"

"I'll be there. How about I spring for pizza?" Mark figured it wouldn't hurt to offer food in exchange for spending more time with Lana and Danny.

"No need. I have a supper already planned that can be on the table in minutes." Lana knew the food card was a sure ticket to get Mark to come over. "Danny needs more bicycle riding lessons and I need some time to get the housework under control. You can have him until his bedtime."

"And after?"

"Can't be a late night. We both have to work tomorrow."

"Won't be late. But it will be good. I promise." Mark grinned his best grin at the phone.

Lana laughed and shook her head. "You are so bad."

"I know. And you love it."

"Hɪ Vᴇʀᴀ. Aʟʟ ʀᴇᴄᴏᴠᴇʀᴇᴅ ꜰʀᴏᴍ ʏᴏᴜʀ ʙɪʀᴛʜᴅᴀʏ ᴘᴀʀᴛʏ?" Lana walked into the centenarian's cheerful room. It was still full of flower arrangements and birthday cards. The tiara had pride of place in the center of her low dresser, while a photograph of her wearing it was already in a frame next to it. The Boston Globe article had also been cut out and laminated and was propped on a shelf above the dresser. It included the group photo with over thirty of Vera's descendents.

"That was a wonderful party wasn't it? I had no idea you had such a large family!" Lana maneuvered Vera's wheelchair next to the bed, locked the wheels and then helped her to sit up.

"Perfect." Vera had scrunched up her face and punched the words out. "Best day in life." "Alright. I will come in front of you and pull you up. Just lean towards me and let me lift you. Are you ready?" When Vera nodded, Lana bent her own knees a bit and hoisted the tiny woman forward and then turned them both and let her down gently into the wheelchair.

"There. All set. Do you need anything before I bring you to the dining room? Maybe a sweater for later?" Lana picked up a pretty coral sweater off the back of an armchair and draped it on Vera's lap. She smiled as she saw her stroke it. It had been a gift from one of the children or grandchildren.

"Off we go then. I smelled something heavenly when I went past the kitchen. I have a strong suspicion you're going to enjoy whatever it is that Vito has cooked up for everyone tonight." Lana slowed her gait so her patient could look around and see everything.

"I'm having dinner with Mark, the fellow who played for you at your party on Thursday. I'll share a secret with you. He's my boyfriend. He's wonderful and he loves my Danny so much."

"Marry?" Vera cocked up her head and turned it so she could see Lana's face.

"I think so Vera." Lana smiled warmly as she pictured Mark with Danny and his talking garbage truck. "If he doesn't ask me I will just have to ask him. We Fitzpatrick's are not shy."

"Idea good." Vera smiled like a co-conspirator as Lana wheeled her into the sunny dining area that was redolent with the aroma of some savory sauce. After settling Vera in with her usual dinner mates, Lana said goodbye and wished them a good evening.

"So, what's the plan? I need a shower before I do much of anything. I was really grubbing today digging out and moving some Blue Chip junipers." Mark climbed into the van after brushing his coveralls. This time, he had a change of shirts, underwear and socks with him. "They'll make excellent ground cover along the edges of the staff parking lot and encourage people not to take shortcuts off the paths. No point in putting a lot of flowers over there. No-one sticks around long enough to justify the cost. And they'll be a good balance for the azaleas. Just look at those colors!" As they rounded a corner, a bright riot of vibrant pink blooms greeted them. Even from a distance, they could see the bees navigating among the fragrant flowers.

Lana drove down the long laneway bordered with colorful plants, benches and planters and pulled slowly into the street. She wanted to get home and relax herself.

"How about you grab a shower while I get Danny and supper organized. It'll give me a few minutes to collect my wits. Then I'll have a short bath while you play with Danny. Maybe another lesson on his bike before supper and maybe after too?"

Lana loved being able to climb into the bathtub even for five or ten minutes and just soak for a bit. It helped her transition from work to home. It was great that Danny was old enough that she could get him settled with a game or movie for awhile and have some free time for herself. With Mark, she didn't have to worry in the least that Danny was getting into trouble.

"I'm sure Danny and I can figure out something to do for half an hour. But remember, we men will need some serious food to keep that bike moving." Mark looked at his hands and nails. "How did they get so dirty? I was wearing gloves."

"It's a man thing I'm sure." Lana laughed and patted Mark's lap. "There goes my electricity bill."

"You have to let me start chipping in for food and gas."

"We'll talk about it. Those Red Sox tickets earned you a few showers and at least another steak." Lana knew full well how much the three tickets had set him back.

"When are we going to tell Danny about the fourth of July weekend?"

Lana considered the timing. "If I tell him too close to his bedtime we'll have trouble getting him to sleep. How about we tell him during supper?" Lana didn't even realize she was sharing Mark in the decision.

"He'll be worn down enough by the bike lesson before and the one coming after supper that it shouldn't keep him from sleeping. He's going to be so excited. He's never been on a boat of any kind. I know he loves to watch them in the harbor."

BEN TOOK JENNIFER'S HAND as they walked along the street with Charlie on their after dinner stroll. The light was beginning to fade and fireflies could now be seen flitting about in hopes of finding a mate.

Ben had arranged for the remainder of his belongings to be shipped to her garage where they would be sorted and given to the good will or kept.

"Penny for your thoughts?" Jennifer looked up at Ben's pensive face in the warm evening light.

"I was just thinking that my belongings and clothes will give you a pretty good idea of the globe-trotting lifestyle I led until the past few months. I can't figure out now how I did it for so long. No wonder Heather gave up on me."

"I don't think she gave up on you. More like she gave you up. To your work. Sounds like you were married to that career."

"You're absolutely right there. It really was a marriage. It lasted over thirty years. In some ways, it was an abusive yet addictive marriage. I often hated what I saw and heard and yet I couldn't tear myself away, even when it destroyed my real family." They stopped as Charlie indulged in a long nasal read of a bush.

"What do you want to do with yourself now, other than to cater to my every whim?" Jennifer lightened the tone.

"I'm not one hundred percent sure yet to be honest. I think I have a memoir in me. I was asked by a few publishers over the years but didn't stop long enough to put anything down. Now I could." Ben put his free hand on the back of Jennifer's neck and massaged it absent-mindedly.

"You could have my old bedroom to set up as an office. It has the best light and overlooks the back yard." Jennifer was already thinking about selling off the bedroom set or giving it away and helping Ben re-decorate and refurnish the sunny room. "There's a walk-in closet you could use for supplies and off-season clothes."

Jennifer waved over a neighbor to introduce Ben. "Hi Gerry. The new porch looks super. I'd like to introduce you to my friend Ben." Both men shook hands. "Ben and I are living in sin. Make sure Ellen knows. It will save me having to tell everybody at the book club next week."

Gerry grinned and rolled his eyes. "Finally, I heard some gossip one step ahead of my lovely wife and before the rest of the neighborhood. Thanks Jennifer. Ellen will be so pleased to be the bearer of the latest news. She's a bit competitive in the gossip department but don't tell her I said so."

"You and Ellen will have to come over for dinner some evening so we can all get to know each other better. Ellen and Gerry have been neighbors for, what, thirty years now?" They calculated at least thirty-three. "Gerry helped my father a lot before he moved to the residence."

"How is he?"

Jennifer brought him up to date. "There's no point in visiting him. He wouldn't recognize you. And he's losing his power to communicate so there's no real conversation."

"Sorry to hear that Jennifer. I'm glad I had that last visit with him."
Gerry knew Art had gone downhill but didn't realize how far.

"Ben Powell. Of course. Mr. News. What are you up to? Haven't seen you on the evening news lately. Of course, I'm sometimes asleep in my chair before it comes on."

"Just before I met Jennifer I decided to retire from journalism. After I met her, I knew I'd made the right decision." Ben smiled at Jennifer and squeezed her hand. "We were just talking about me setting up a little office so I can write my memoirs."

"Well, I would be first in line to buy any book you write Ben. You must have a thousand stories to tell."

"That I do Gerry." Charlie made it clear it was time to move on. They all agreed that the ladies would organize something and tell the men where to be and at what time.

"Are you a beer man Gerry?"

"I am."

"I'll take care of it."

"We're going on a sailboat and sleep on it. Wow. How cool is that?" Danny was bathed and in bed as he and Mark shared a few quiet moments. "Will I get to drive it?"

"I'm sure you will. My dad is a good sailor. He'll show you how to steer the boat. He showed me when I was about your age." Mark smoothed back Danny's damp hair and watched the boy's eyelids droop. "Good night Danny boy."

Mark padded softly out of the room and nudged the door almost shut behind him.

"You have an amazing son Ms. Fitzpatrick." Mark walked into the kitchen where Lana was setting out tea for both of them.

"Why thank you. I thinking he's turning into a fine boy if I do say so myself. Thanks for getting him organized for bed. I feel like I'm out of a job when you're around. He only wants you."

"Gives you a break though right?"

"Bedtime and when he first wakes up are precious times of the day.

Another year or so I'm told he'll be all independent and won't want mom interfering. I'm grabbing it while I can. But for you, I'll share." Lana pointed to the door. They took their tea outside to watch the last light.

"Danny is so excited about the boat. It was good of your father to think of us and plan this outing." Lana was still trying to come to grips with the long weekend ahead. She'd never dreamed of such a weekend, let alone one that included Mark.

"As I'm getting to know him better I realize he's a really good man at heart. There was a time when I thought he was selfish and uncaring but I see now that it was more about his career. For years he was totally driven and competitive in a very competitive market. And then the PTSD. It seems to have been the wake-up call he needed to get his priorities straight."

"I never knew your father when he was like that. I do like what I know of him now though."

"I do too."

"I really enjoyed the concert you put on for Vera's birthday. You have a wonderful voice and you play beautifully." Lana sipped at her tea. "Being Irish, I've always enjoyed good music. I could listen to you for hours."

"Buy me a piano and I'll sing for you for hours." Mark smiled and stretched his legs out. "I'm going to do a few after-dinner concerts over the summer and fall. We'll be together then, but with an audience of course."

"I'll just have to pretend you're singing to me and me alone."

"I'll be sure to have at least one song that's for you and you alone. We'll pick it together each time so you'll know which one is for you."

"That's a very romantic idea. I like it." Lana went over and sat on Mark's lap and put her arms around him.

"When do you figure we should move in together and make it permanent?" Lana looked into Mark's eyes. In the twilight they were dark sapphire blue. "When's your lease up?"

"I can break it. I would consider the penalty worth paying to be a full-time part of your life and Danny's."

"Then break it," she said as she stood to lead him up to their bed.

Chapter 19

"When do I get to meet your beau?" Carol had decided it was beyond time to meet Ben Powell in person and size him up as a suitable suitor for her friend.

"He's more than a beau now. He's my partner. I asked him to move in." Jennifer smiled at the surprise on Carol's face. "Like you said, at our age, we don't have time to waste."

"But so soon? You barely know him!" Carol dropped her yoga gear beside the nearest empty chair. She checked her watch. The class ahead still had ten minutes to go. They could hear the wind-down starting. Sitting on the chair, she casually crossed her legs and turned towards Jennifer.

"I think over two months is long enough. I seem to recall you've invited your beaus to move in after two dates." Jennifer wouldn't let Carol demean her relationship with Ben.

"Well, I never." Carol uncrossed her legs, sat up and sputtered.

"Actually, you did. Several times. Ben and I have a loving and warm relationship." Jennifer needed Carol to hear and understand that. "Why don't we see about going to a restaurant. When is Michel in town?"

"He gets in Wednesday afternoon. We could meet up with you somewhere around six or seven?"

"Let me check with Ben but that sounds good. Let's say seven o'clock." It felt so different to make plans involving two people now instead of just one. Another happy adjustment.

Jennifer walked in the door just as Ben wrapped up a phone conversation.

"It's all confirmed. We can pick up the boat at nine o'clock Saturday morning." Ben clicked off the portable, put it on the charger and walked over to Jen. Wrapping his arms around her he nuzzled her neck noisily. "Better get enough of you before the weekend since we'll have to be quiet on the boat."

Jennifer laughed and kissed him lightly. "Would it be okay with you if we went out for dinner on Wednesday evening? My friend Carol wants to meet you and check you out. That tickles." Jennifer squirmed right and left but Ben had a strong hold on her. "Please Ben. I'm so ticklish."

"Wednesday night? I'll have to check with my scheduling boss, which is now you." Ben kissed her neck and nuzzled some more. "Are we available Wednesday?"

"Yes we are. Stop please!"

"On one condition."

"What is it? Anything!" Jennifer squirmed. Charlie danced around them happily, wanting to be part of any action.

"Kiss me like you mean it." Ben loosened his arms and turned Jennifer around to face him.

"You rogue. You took advantage of me." Jennifer stood on her tiptoes, cupped her hands to his cheeks and kissed him squarely on the mouth. She loved the warmth of his lips. The light scent of his aftershave made her think of Old Spice and sailing off with him into a golden sunset. As his arms reached around to wrap her into his embrace, she felt him deepen the kiss. Charlie went to lie by the door.

THE STORAGE COMPANY DELIVERED AT THE CRACK OF DAWN. Jennifer had just started working in the garden when the truck pulled up. She opened the garage door as the two men began to unload. Ben arrived and handed her a mug of coffee. They stood watching the truck empty.

"That's it Mr. Powell. Thirty boxes, including five full-height wardrobe boxes. When you're finished checking them, please sign here and they're all yours." Ben checked that there was no damage to the boxes before signing the electronic pad.

"Time for Christmas. Some of these boxes haven't been opened in at least six or seven years." Jennifer had cleared her father's tidy work bench at the back of the garage so they could sort Ben's belongings.

First up was a box full of the bestsellers of ten years or so ago. "We have to check these. Some of them are autographed."

"You know John Grisham?" Jennifer spied one of the author's numerous bestsellers and flicked open the cover. "To Ben. Thanks for telling the stories that need to be told."

"Met him a couple of times through Heather. Nice guy. Very down to earth. We should keep that in case I need to raise money to fund my sailing habit. I'm sure a signed Grisham is worth something." Ben had opened another box of memorabilia. "Wow. Forgot I had this." It was a Patek Philippe white gold watch. The sleek wristwatch rested regally in its box.

"I bought this duty free after a trip to Geneva to do a feature on the Red Cross's rehabilitation camps in Afghanistan. Put it away and forgot about it. This is a definite keeper." Ben took the watch out of its box and then put it back in. "No. It is not a keeper. I don't need a five thousand dollar watch now. Know any charities that could auction it off to raise funds? I have a feeling it's more watch than Mark would want."

"How about the Red Cross? You must still have some contacts. And with all the hurricanes and tornados I'm sure they could use some of what you are about to shed." Jennifer looked in the box and drew out a soft buttery yellow cashmere sweater. "This one stays for sure."

By the time they gave up some four hours later, the keeper pile sat at one end of the counter. A couple dozen boxes lined the garage wall, ready to be given away.

"You weren't kidding when you said you had a wardrobe item for every possible occasion." Jennifer held up a sturdy knapsack to Ben to store on a suspended ledge of the garage. It joined a pair of walking poles, an arctic parka and the one remaining travelling camera case Ben had elected to keep.

"I'll have to do some online research on the best places to dispose of some of these things. I'll email some former colleagues and let them know what equipment is up for sale. This stuff is way too good for eBay."

"How about we take a break and take Charlie for a walk? I've eaten enough dust for one day." Ben brushed off his arms after stepping off the ladder.

"Are you saying my garage is dusty?" Jennifer had cleaned it up quite a bit to get ready for Ben's boxes.

"Just on that shelf m'dear."

"Well it's your garage now too m'dear. And you're much taller than me. So guess who gets to dust the top shelf?" Jennifer grinned and mentally congratulated herself on having won that round.

"Guess I walked into that one didn't I?"

"You sure did."

"So where are we meeting Carol and her date for dinner?"

"I've made reservations at the place we went to on our first date."

"You mean you don't want to keep it just for us? The place we go back to every year for our anniversary?"

"Are you serious Ben? I can change the reservation."

"I'm not sure if I'm serious. I must be getting sentimental in my old age."

"You're not old." Jennifer chuckled. She could see by the sparkle in Ben's eyes that he was teasing. She loved being teased by him.

"The restaurant is fine. I'm looking forward to meeting Carol. She sounds like quite a character."

"She definitely is that." Jennifer could hardly wait to see what Carol would be wearing for this dinner out. She'd probably need an armed guard just for the jewelry. She did love to dress up.

"The one thing we need to buy is non-skid deck shoes. I already have mine. The renter stipulated that we can't wear shoes that have been worn on the street. Ben ran down a shortlist of things Mark,

Lana and Danny needed to know before they boarded the sailboat. "It's going to be cooler on the water, especially outside the inner harbor, so bring a warm jacket, a pair of gloves, full-length slacks and socks. Once we're outside the harbor it won't be bikini weather."

"Got it dad. Danny expects you to teach him to be a sailor the way you did with me. Can you remember that far back?"

"I'm not that old and neither are you. Careful. If you pin old age on me it will poke you right back." Ben grinned into the phone. "Just for that, you're in charge of the beer. And I will want several. And they'd better be premium brand too."

Mark laughed out loud. "I was planning on supplying the beer anyway."

"Well just be sure to bring lots. That salt air builds up a thirst in a hurry." Ben signed off. It still amazed him how close the bond had become between himself and Mark. The more time they spent together, the more he liked, no loved, his son. As Ben finalized his mental and written preparations for the sailing weekend, he realized it was the first major family event he had planned and organized in at least twenty years. And, he realized he was enjoying every minute and tiny detail of it. It felt good to be doing something that would bring happiness to these people he had come to love and cherish. He shut down his laptop and went off in search of Jennifer to see if she was interested in some wild and woolly sex before they went out for dinner.

Chapter 20

Jennifer and Ben arrived at the restaurant ahead of Carol and were seated almost immediately. She had opted to wear the little black dress again. She figured the classic look would stand up to whatever Paris runway look Carol would doubtless be sporting. Moments later, her assessment was confirmed. Jennifer tapped Ben's arm and pointed to the door. Carol was about to make her entrance.

Jennifer smiled as Carol swanned into the room in towering high heels. Her pure white ensemble of shoes, pants and blouse was in stark contrast to almost every patron in the restaurant and even the interior itself. She set the look off with ice-white diamonds. And lots of them. She glittered as she crossed the room to their table.

"Here we go. I hope you're ready for this." Jennifer grinned. "This'll be fun to watch I'm sure."

As Carol reached them, Jennifer noticed her handsome escort coming up behind her. He was as tall as her despite her heels and looked every bit the professional. Ben stood up as Carol was introduced. He shook her hand. He then shook hands with Michel Martin.

"Bonjour Michel. Bienvenue à Boston. C'est une de mes villes préférées du monde."

"Merci Ben. It's a great city for sure. I really enjoy coming here."

They ordered drinks and started to look over the menu. Jennifer gazed over at Ben.

"I didn't realize you speak French." It was a quiet aside, not meant to be heard by the others.

"I was based in Paris for a couple of years. And many of the countries I reported from in West Africa were all French-speaking." Ben kept his voice down as well. The sound level in the restaurant was high enough not to carry his voice further than her.

As their drinks arrived, Ben proposed a toast. "Here's to good friends and good friendships. Et bon appétit."

"I'll second that." Michel joined them in clinking glasses lightly as the conversation volume in the restaurant increased.

"So Michel. Jennifer tells me you're a corporate pilot. Who with?" Ben smiled over at Michel and took a slow sip of his martini.

"I'm with an aviation group that flies corporate jets for a variety of companies. Right now I'm flying VIPs for an outfit called the Genus Group. They're based out of Montreal but have offices all over North America."

"What do they do?" Ben was used to making easy conversation. He was a professional at getting people to open up about their work, their lives and themselves. And he knew a script when he heard one. That, plus Michel hadn't responded with even one sentence in French. He kept an easy smile on his face.

"They're an engineering firm. I haven't really checked them out. But they all come on board with laptops and drawings and stay huddled over them during the flights."

"What are you flying these days?"

"Challengers mostly."

"I had to take a few flights in a small passenger jet around Europe. Can't think of what it was. Boeing something or other I think." He remained deliberately vague.

"Probably a Boeing 717. It's one of their smallest passenger jets."

"You ever fly one?"

"I've always flown executive aircraft. Haven't flown for an airline."

"How long have you been at it?" Ben wanted to keep the conversational focus on Michel. He knew from long experience that it would only be a matter of time before he tripped up.

"Going on twenty years now." Michel was looking past Ben.

"So you must have flown some hours on Jetstars?"

"No. Can't say that I have."

"That was a fine plane. The network bosses had access to one. I caught a flight home with one of them from London. Talk about travelling in the lap of luxury. Non-stop all the way."

"Never been in one myself."

"Probably pretty much the same as the Challenger. About a dozen passengers, a little kitchen and a lavatory."

"That would be about the same, yes." Michel looked down at the table. Ben had learned what he needed. The man was a fraud.

The conversation stalled briefly when a waitress arrived to take their orders. Jennifer and Carol had been engrossed in conversation about a movie they both wanted to see. Men talking about airplanes held little appeal for either of them.

"Do you get to Boston often?" Ben kept his questions neutral and non-threatening. He didn't want to alert this Michel to his suspicions. He'd be checking him out through his networks within the next few hours.

"I'm usually here every week. The guys I'm flying in are negotiating a building project. I guess it's getting pretty close now."

The two couples tucked into their dinners as the conversation shifted to Carol and Michel.

"So how did you two meet?" Jennifer had ordered the planked salmon again. If she and Ben bought a barbeque they could grill their own.

"Michel called me at the office. Said he'd seen one of my adverts online. He came to the office, we talked about what he was looking for, it turned into dinner and here we are." Carol beamed a bright smile at her beau. He beamed one right back.

"What attracted you to Boston? I've never been to Montreal but I understand it's quite a cosmopolitan city." Jennifer savored a plump morsel of asparagus , unaware that Ben was mentally storing every piece of information she was eliciting from Michel.

"Boston has a vibe I really like. After my wife and I split up, I just wanted to go somewhere new and start again."

"And he met me. I've brought a whole new vibe to your life haven't I cher?" Carol liked to be the center of attention. It played right into Ben's little inquisition.

"Oui, ma chère. You have made me want to make Boston my home for sure." Michel put a hand over Carol's. A hand that glittered without about ten carats of diamonds on her tennis bracelet and at least another two on her dinner ring.

"What area of Boston are you hoping to buy into?" Jennifer was unwittingly feeding Ben's interest.

"I'd love to have a harbor view of course. Who wouldn't? I want to be fairly near the airport. Being in the harbor area would take care of that. Carol has shown me a few places that might do." Michel was giving out more and more information.

"Carol. Did you show him the place you showed me?"

"Yes, but Michel is looking for something a bit larger."

"Are you selling?" Michel chimed in.

"I live in my father's home. I was raised there." Jennifer smiled across at Ben. "Make that we live in my father's home. He's in a nursing home now. And no, I'm not selling."

The talk turned to other topics.

"What are your plans for the long weekend?" Michel directed the question to Jennifer.

"Actually, Ben has rented a sailboat for a four-day cruise. What about you two?"

"I won't be here that weekend." Michel sent his regrets across the table to Carol. "It's Canada Day weekend. None of my clients are flying."

"Too bad. You'll miss a major fireworks display over Boston."

"We'll have the same over Montreal. July first is our big weekend. Fireworks and all."

As dinner ended, the two women excused themselves to visit the ladies' room. Ben pulled out his smart phone as the two women came back to the table.

"Hold it there ladies. Let me get a shot of the two most lovely women in the room." He held up his phone and the first photo was done. He nabbed a passing waitress. "Would you mind taking a picture of the four of us please?"

It happened so quickly, Michel didn't have a chance to protest.

"That was fun." The four of them were out on the street. "We should do it again sometime." Jennifer sensed that Ben wanted to get going. Yet it was still early. She knew he wasn't tired. Something was up but she didn't want to say anything in front of the other couple.

"You seemed in a bit of a hurry to get going." Jennifer couldn't say he'd been rude as they said their goodbyes. But he certainly didn't linger to chat.

"I'll explain shortly." Ben didn't say anything until they were back at her car and inside it with the doors and windows shut. "Michel is a fraud. He's not a pilot."

"How do you know?" Jennifer had found Michel perfectly charming and quite handsome. But, where Carol was concerned, that had spelled trouble before.

"I told him I had flown non-stop from London to Boston in a Jetstar. Any pilot with twenty years flying executive jets would have known a Jetstar never had the range to fly that distance non-stop. We had to refuel in Iceland." Ben never relied on one piece of evidence. "Then I said the Jetstar and the Challenger were probably pretty similar. Maximum of twelve passengers. Neither of those jets were designed for twelve passengers. Both were designed for eight to ten passengers plus the flight crew of two; a pilot and co-pilot."

"Couldn't they squeeze in two more?" Jennifer asked.

"No. There are very strict regulations about maximum capacity and payload. I learned a lot about that from talking to pilots while sitting on crates in overloaded cargo planes."

"So what are you going to do?" Jennifer felt a little chill around her neck. Carol didn't need this again.

"I've got his photo on my phone. I'll send it to a buddy of mine in the NYPD. I'd lay bets that Michel, or whatever his real name is, is in a criminal database somewhere."

"Do you think we should warn Carol?" Jennifer thought she already knew the answer.

"Not just yet. For one thing, I don't think Carol would believe us. For another, we don't want to spook him and send him running. He'd just go find another mark. Guys like him often don't get caught. They steal enough to fund their lifestyle but not so much that the woman will call the police."

"I know. I've seen that happen with some of my clients. They fall for the smooth charm and what they think is a sincere person who cares about them. Take a lonely elderly woman or man and a friendly face and next thing you know, money or jewelry is missing and a bank account's been emptied." Jennifer shook her head. "Carol puts on a brash front but underneath I think she's afraid of growing old alone. She's the perfect target for someone like Michel to prey on. She'd be too embarrassed to tell anyone. How long do you think he'll stick around?"

"Not sure. I don't like the fact that he's only here during the week and never on weekends. That doesn't ring true at all. Executive pilots are often away from home on weekends because the bosses want to fly somewhere to play golf or they have a weekend home in Florida. I think he may be after more than her jewels."

"How about we have a glass of wine in the yard and let Charlie run around for awhile?"

"Let me just go upload the photo and send out a couple of queries. Give me five minutes." Ben dropped a kiss on her head and headed for his computer.

Jennifer looked around her kitchen in a daze. She found it hard to believe Carol had been taken in so easily. Then she corrected herself. It had happened before. But this time she felt a frisson of fear for her friend. Brent had been a hanger-on. This Michel was a calculating con artist. Who knew what he might be capable of if he felt threatened.

"How long do you think it will take to get some feedback on your queries?" Jennifer brought out two glasses as Ben uncorked a Chablis.

"Should have something within twenty-four hours. The guy I contacted checks his email regularly, even when he's off duty. I'll probably hear back from him later tonight or tomorrow morning."

"Is there anything else we can do?"

"Take this wine out on the patio and try to put this in perspective while we wait for some news." Ben put his hand on Jennifer's shoulder and guided her towards the door.

Chapter 21

"How would you like to do some shopping later and grab a bite to eat at the same time? There's a few things we need for our sailing weekend with Ben and Aunt Jennifer." Lana carried Danny's knapsack to the van so he could protect his latest artistic masterpiece from the sudden rain shower.

"Can Mark come too?" There was a recognizable Spider-Man in the childish drawing.

"He's gone home to shower and change. We'll be picking him up in an hour after we go home. I need to change and freshen up." She closed the sliding door as Danny did up his seatbelt. He was already fishing around in the pouch behind her seat for the bag of raisins and nuts she kept there as a snack. More than once it had carried them through a heavy Boston rush hour.

"I told Lisa and the others about going sailing this weekend. I have to tell everyone all about it next week. They made me promise." Lana smiled as Danny spelled out his homework assignment.

"I'm bringing my camera. We can scan some pictures into my computer and print them out for you to bring with you on Tuesday. How would that be?"

"That would be great, Mom. I'm supposed to find out the name of the boat, how big it is and how tall the sails are."

"I'm sure Ben will have all that information for you. He knows his way around sailboats."

The traffic seemed lighter, as if some people had booked off early for the holiday weekend. They were home in less time than usual, leaving Lana some precious extra time to actually have a quick tub. "How about you put the things we need to bring on Saturday on the dining room table while I get ready. Do you remember what we need?" Lana liked to challenge Danny's memory. He was getting quite good at remembering longer lists. It had become a game they both enjoyed.

"I need to have clean pyjamas, two pairs of underwear, two pairs of socks, my Spider-Man jersey and some games." Danny split off to his room as Lana walked into hers and kicked off her shoes. Stripping down, she turned on the water for her tub and removed her make-up. My time to freshen, she thought as she poured some lavender bath oil into the steaming stream of water.

"I CAN'T BELIEVE THEY HAD SPIDER-MAN SHOES he can wear on the boat." Lana had to remind Danny he couldn't wear the shoes in the street. He had reluctantly let them be boxed and put in a bag, which he now clutched closely.

"They have Spider-Man everything Lana. Trust me. I'm a big fan. Always have been since I was a kid. He was my hero long before Tobey Maguire gave him a 21st century face." Mark remembered his dog-eared Spider-Man comic books. Danny was dancing ahead of them in the mall. "It wasn't until I got my depression under control that I realized what an influence he was on me."

"Why do you say that?" Lana knew only what she'd seen in one movie. It hadn't really engaged her critical thinking. To her it was just an action flick.

"Spider-Man was a reject. He was different. Nobody could really relate to him except his aunt and uncle. When my mother got sick, all my friends disappeared. I can't blame them. I couldn't relate to them any more than they could relate to me. My life revolved around my mother and her care. I didn't have any great powers but I had a lot of responsibilities."

"Are you talking about that line 'with great powers there must also come great responsibility'?" Lana remembered that line. It had struck her that as a single mother, she too had a great responsibility.

"Yes. When I got depressed I lost whatever emotional power I

202

had left. But the responsibilities wouldn't go away, at least not 'til my mother died. Spider-Man was a good influence."

Lana linked her arm through Mark's as they followed Danny towards the door to the parking lot. "I seem to recall in Spider-Man 2 that he raised his mask just enough to give Mary Jane a good kiss. Thank you for removing your mask Mark. I wouldn't have you any other way than the person you are now. The person you have become." Lana squeezed his hand. Together they gathered in Danny and headed out into the sunshine and the steamy parking lot.

"I'm GOING TO SEE MY FATHER BEFORE WE LEAVE for the weekend. Will you come with me?" Jennifer handed Ben a plate to dry as they tidied up after their back yard supper. "It'll be another hour or so before they settle him down for the night. It'll be a quick visit."

"Sure. Let's go. Can we bring Charlie?" Ben adored the dog. The feeling was mutual if the pile of toys being delivered to Ben's feet was any indication.

"The ward he's in is different from the ambulatory ward. I'm not sure he'd be welcome. It's a hospital wing." Jennifer wondered how they would find him this evening. He'd been barely coherent when she'd seen him after Danny's birthday party.

"Let's go and see my honorary father-in-law then." Ben put the tea towel over a chair to dry. "Charlie, we'll be back to take you out for a last walk. Promise."

BEN HELD JENNIFER'S HAND CLOSELY as they entered her father's room. She was shocked to see that he was now hooked up to a monitoring machine. The readouts showed his heart rate was thready and his blood pressure very low. The frail figure in the bed had shrunken in on itself. She barely recognized him. She turned in to Ben's arms as he enfolded her close.

"Your father is comfortable. He is in no pain." The nurse reassured them both when she came in to check a few minutes after their arrival.

"How long does he have?" Jennifer felt a hollowness she hadn't felt since talking to the officers who came to tell her about the plane crash. She felt as if she was talking from the bottom of a well. The words closed in around her head and threatened to suffocate her.

"We can't say for sure. He could be in this state for a few days or a few weeks. There is no way to predict." The nurse checked the monitors, straightened the sheets slightly and looked at Ben as if to ask, is she all right?

He shook his head almost imperceptibly and the nurse left the room.

A few minutes later, a young chaplain arrived. "Mrs. Barrett, I'm Jared McRae. Could we go to the lounge and chat?"

Ben led Jennifer out into the hall and toward a spacious lounge that overlooked the back gardens of the Manor. The three found themselves a secluded corner and sat down.

"I'm aware that your father won't be with us much longer. Is there anything I can do to help?" Jared looked from one to the other.

"I don't think so. He's gone downhill so fast. It's a bit of a shock." Jennifer held onto Ben's hand tightly and stared out at the gardens. She hadn't seen them very often in the twilight. It was a beautiful sight. One her father would never see again. "He was just so vital. You never knew the man he was before his mind and body were stolen away."

"Ben, you've seen my little greenhouse at the end of the garden. He built that. He laid the paths that go through the gardens. Carried in every stone himself. He taught me how to ride a bicycle the way Mark is teaching Danny. He held my hand when I had nightmares while my mother went and made hot chocolate. He carried me into the hospital in his arms when I broke my leg when I was ten."

Jennifer turned her eyes away from the garden to look at the two men. "He came and got me and took me home the day my husband and daughter were killed. My mother and father were probably the only reason I was able to get through the horrible weeks and months that followed. The man in that bed is not the father I've always known and loved. It's his shell but it's not him."

Her eyes were dry. "I'll be all right Jared. Thank you for your concern. Everyone here has been wonderful to my father. Really made his last years the best they could be. We're going away for the weekend with family." As she said the word, she squeezed Ben's hand again. "I've left my numbers in case anyone needs to reach me."

"Your phone may not work where we're going. I'll leave my satellite phone number at the nursing station." Ben stood and offered his hand to Jennifer.

They all rose and shook hands. Jennifer and Ben went back to the room. She picked up her father's limp hand. It was cool and lifeless. His skin felt like dry parchment and she saw the bluish tinge of his nails that told her his oxygen levels weren't good. She bent over to kiss his forehead and smooth back the silver hair. She whispered in his ear, gave him another kiss, turned and walked with Ben out the door.

"We can postpone the plans for this weekend." They were nearing the parking lot. Another rain shower was building. They hadn't spoken since they had left her father's room. It was a comfortable silence. Jennifer hadn't felt the need to talk.

"You heard what the nurse said." Jennifer smoothed an imaginary stray hair. "It could be days or weeks. My father wouldn't want us to change our plans. He liked Danny. He wouldn't want us to cancel his first sailing trip. Let's go ahead. I'll be fine."

"Let's get home, get Charlie and go for a walk. The shower should pass by the time we get back."

"Can I borrow your car and Danny for a few hours?" Mark waited until they had finished clearing away the supper dishes.

"Sure. What's up?"

"It's a guy thing. For the weekend. Just something I want to get to make the trip more special for Danny's first sailing trip."

"Aww. That's so nice. You're so good to him Mark. You seem to know instinctively what he likes and how to make him listen. I'm so happy we all found each other." Lana was already planning what to do with this sudden spare time. Manicure for sure. Pedicure as well. Oh, and a facial.

Mark watched Danny buckle himself in before putting the van in reverse and backing out into the street.

"Danny boy. You can't say a word to your mom about what we are about to do. Promise?" The boy was sitting up front with Mark. It was a rare treat as his mother always insisted he sit behind her.

"Promise. What are we going to do Mark?" The sailing weekend was already a huge event in his mind.

"This is a real man thing Danny. And you must keep the secret." Mark wasn't sure how to start. "You know when we talked about kissing? How I like kissing your mom?"

"Yeah, I remember. You said we have to do it 'because'."

"Danny. I kissed your mom because I love her and I love you. I want to marry your mother and adopt you as my son. What would you think of that?"

"You'd be my father? My real forever dad?" Danny punched his arms up in the air. "I could call you dad and we'd go to baseball games and you'd come pick me up at school every day?"

"Yes. All that and much more."

"Wow. Yes. Please. I really, really want you to be my dad even if you kiss my mom all the time. It's okay."

"So I have your permission to ask your mother to marry me?"

"Yes. Can I call you dad yet?"

"Not yet. This is a huge surprise. Can you wait until after I ask her?"

"Yes. Wow. Where are we going?"

"We are going to buy your mum a sparkler."

Danny sat back, a puzzled look on his face. "You mean like what I had on my birthday cake?"

"No. It's a girl sparkler. We're going to buy her a diamond ring." Mark grinned at him. "We talked about kissing your mum to make her happy just because."

"Yes." Danny listened solemnly.

"Well, someday when you want to get a girl to marry you, you have to kiss properly and then you have to buy her a sparkly diamond. It'll make her all happy and mushy inside. When I give the ring to your mom watch what happens."

Danny mulled over all this new information. "Can we get an ice cream after we buy the ring?"

"You bet."

"I'D SAY WE'RE ALL SET FOR TOMORROW." Ben surveyed the small pile of items on the dining room table, echoing a similar inventorying taking place minutes away in Lana's dining room. Danny was long gone to bed. Charlie had been out for his last walk. Jennifer and Ben and Lana and Mark were separately getting ready for their last sleep before they headed out on their sailing adventure. The weather forecast was perfect for the entire fourth of July weekend.

"I don't know about you but I would love to just sit out back and have a glass of wine before bed. How about you?" Ben was so pleased with the way things were going. Especially the weather. After seeing how much Jennifer had been affected by seeing her father the way he was, he wanted to make everything as good as it could be to give her a wonderful memory to return to in the days or weeks ahead.

He didn't believe for a minute that Art would survive more than a few days. He'd seen many an injured man in the field and recognized the signs of a body that was shutting down vital organs. He knew she recognized it too, even if she couldn't openly admit it. He wanted this weekend to be a special time she would cherish even as she grieved the loss of her father.

"Let's do it. We can finish the Chablis from last night. Maybe open a Pinot Grigio if we feel the need for a second glass."

"I'm on it. Go get changed into something comfortable and I'll meet you on the deck.. I'm going to check my email one more time to see if anything has come about Michel." Ben winked at her as he took out two glasses before trotting down the stairs to the little basement fridge to bring up a Pinot.

Jennifer saw the wink. Her heart swelled with love just in that small act. *What a wonderful man I've found. He really gets me,* she thought. As she went up to their bedroom she remembered back to the hospital and how he'd said just the right things at the right time. He'd respected her feelings and emotions and made it clear he was there for her all the way. She opened a drawer and drew out a filmy caftan she rarely wore. It was pure hand-painted silk from China. A Chinese garden with winding paths, birds trailing flowering branches and lovely pagodas was portrayed in soft shimmering colors. She slipped the confection on, luxuriating in its soft smoothness. No-one could see into her back yard. She fairly floated down to the kitchen and the door to the garden.

Ben had poured the last of the Chablis into their glasses and was sitting at the patio table when she came out. She immediately sensed his tension.

"Who is he?"

"He's a con artist with a rap sheet that stretches from here to Chicago. He's only been charged twice but there have been calls and messages to NYPD from ten states. He's smart. He doesn't stick around long. He goes by several name variations but his real name is Michael Demercado." Ben cast his mind back to the email. "He's not violent. His cover story is pretty well always the same. He's a corporate jet pilot, he's broken up with his wife and he's in the market for a high-end condo within striking distance of the airport. He preys on single female real estate agents."

"How does he find out if they're single?" Jennifer was somewhat mystified about the workings of the criminal mind.

"He probably Googles them. Real estate agents rely on being highly visible on the Internet. There's probably more than enough information about them online because of their work, their community involvement and their industry profile. I'd bet it's easily accessible to anyone with basic research skills."

"Then you'd think he'd have done more research about the kind of jet he's supposed to be flying." Jennifer sipped her wine and looked up into the cloudless starry night.

"He probably got lazy. Or maybe he'd never planned to meet up with Carol's friends. I wonder if he tried to get out of our dinner date. Be interesting to check with Carol after this is over."

"So how do we make it be over?" Jennifer wanted this man out of her friend's life before he stole something and before he could injure her pride and self-esteem any further.

"After we get back, I'll get in touch with a buddy in the FBI. With all this guy's interstate activity, the NYPD alerted them a few years ago. There's probably someone who's been trying to track him enough to build a case."

"Do you think he'll stick around that long?"

"He said he wouldn't be around over the long weekend. I'm not sure what to make of that but we have to assume he has a plan that will keep him around at least a few more days. Long enough to get the FBI onside to assign someone to track him down."

Ben poured them both another glass of wine. Dozens of fireflies were flickering above the bushes and in the trees. "Did you know that fireflies use their light to find mates?" In some species, only the male can light up. In others, the males light up while the females wait in bushes and then they light up to invite the brightest male over."

He warmed up to his little story. "Can you imagine if they ever saw each other in daylight? They are ugly grubs. I used to catch them in bottles at night and watch them glow on and off. Then, in the morning, I'd look in and they'd be these ugly grey blobs at the bottom of the jar."

"Ben. You were doing fine romantically right up to the females waiting in the bush part." Jennifer sipped the smooth Italian wine and watched the glowing bugs flitting about. "I'd like to think the males and the females just spark from each other. Like us. That's much more romantic don't you agree?"

"Yes but I'm a guy and we like bugs and grubs and yechy stuff."

Jennifer laughed out loud, as her wineglass wobbled in her hand.

"You sound just like Mark. Lana told me he got Danny to wash his hands properly by telling him that when he digs in the dirt he gets worm poop on his hands. If he doesn't wash right he actually eats it."

"That's my boy." Ben grinned in the dark.

Leaving aside Carol's conundrum, they talked about their weekend trip.

"What if your father passes away over the weekend? We need a plan for that." Ben was holding Jennifer's hand across the table.

"All the arrangements have been made with the funeral home. Brentwood has instructions to call them once they have a signed death certificate. Everything can be put in motion without me." Jennifer had known this day would come. "We won't be more than a day's travel away. We can be back here faster than some people who would have to fly back."

"True. I just want you to be comfortable in the event something does happen."

"I won't be comfortable but I just can't sit there day and night. I know there's nothing I can do and nowhere I can be that will change anything." Jennifer finished her glass and stood up. "Tomorrow is a big day. C'mon big Ben. Time for bed."

Chapter 22

"Rise and shine Danny. Time to go sailing!" Lana opened the curtains as Danny quickly went from sound asleep to wide awake.

"Yippeee!" Danny ran to the bathroom. Lana heard a flush about one second before he was back in his bedroom and grabbing the clothes they'd put out the night before. "How long before we leave mom?"

"We'll leave in about an hour, after breakfast and packing up. The weather is going to be perfect with a good wind I think." She helped him straighten up his bed, keeping back his favorite pillow with the Spider-Man pillowcase to bring along.

Lana called Mark. "I'm going to pick you up first, then we'll swing by to pick up Jennifer and Ben." They arranged to meet and Lana hung up. She looked around to see that the kitchen was all back together after their whirlwind breakfast. Time to get this wagon train on the move, she thought, as she moved their overnight bags to the door and got out a jacket for each of them.

"All set Danny?" Lana moved them out the door with their bags, set the alarm and the first part of the adventure was officially on.

"Wow. That's a big sailboat." Danny grabbed Ben's hand as they set out in front of the others down the quay. He ran a little and skipped as he tried to keep up with Ben's long strides. "How long is it? What's its name?"

"It's thirty-six feet from stem to stern. And her name – boats are female – is Shelagh's Repose. We'll all have plenty of room to stretch our legs on this lady." Ben was pleased he'd been able to rent such a fine boat over the long holiday weekend. The weather forecast was almost perfect. Maybe some showers here and there but nothing major. As they arrived at the gangplank, Ben unlocked the metal gate. "Hold on to the railing on each side Danny and follow me," he ordered.

"What do you call the thing the sail is on? The big pole." Danny was looking way up.

"It's called the main mast. The mast on this boat is fifty-five feet tall. It's probably taller than your house." Ben knew all the specs for the boat.

"Wait a second there men. I need to take a picture for Danny's report for day care next week." Lana pulled out her camera as Ben scooped Danny up in his arms and dutifully posed. "That's it. Smile!"

"Who's taking care of Charlie?" Lana and Jennifer followed with overnight bags and food. The men would be going back to the van for a second load that included their bedding.

"My neighbors Ellen and Gerry. They've been my back-up for many things in the past few years. Actually, I'm inviting them over for dinner soon. You should come and meet them." Jennifer walked up the gangplank.

"I'm pretty sure I did last summer." Lana did the same. "She's in your book club right?"

"The one and the same. I'd forgotten. I'll let you know when we have a date set." Jennifer went back for a bag of groceries.

When everyone was on board the first order of business was to change into their deck shoes. Their street shoes would be stowed away except when they got off to explore.

"Look at the size of the galley. This is huge." Jennifer looked around in awe at the state-of-the-art kitchen, dining and living room area. The fully-appointed kitchen had gleaming counters with natural light pouring in from no less than two ports above them plus two more on each side. Even with tinting the room was flooded in light. A long table with padded cushions would seat them all more than comfortably.

"I don't know what you paid for this dad but I can stand straight up." Mark glanced out the port holes and then looked back inside.

"Look at all the wood detailing. It's teak right? This is a piece of art."

"It sure is." Ben tossed his duffel into the aft bedroom. "Not only that, you and I will both fit the beds on this model. I made sure of it. Not going to wreck our weekend in beds that aren't long enough."

After they had put their bags and supplies away, Ben called them together at the table as Lana snapped more photos of the sleek interior and the people in it.

"I want to spend just a couple of minutes setting down some basic rules. Even though this looks like a floating hotel, being on a boat like this is way different from being at home. There are some things we have to do differently. First off is the bathroom, or the head as it's called." Ben was the commander giving orders to his crew. "There are five of us and one head. Everything goes into a tank. Only human waste goes into the head. Everything else goes in the trash bin and we bag it out."

"Why is it called a head?" Danny looked confused.

"Back before any of us were born, boats didn't have bathrooms. When sailors needed to go, they went to the front of the boat. It was called the head of the boat. There was an opening and everything went into the water. It was a way to keep the ship clean. The word just stuck." Ben's answer seemed to satisfy Danny.

"The other thing you need to know is that the water heater only holds five gallons. We have seventy-five gallons of fresh water on board. So only use as much water as you absolutely need. No long showers."

"We'll spend a couple of hours in the inner harbor to get a feel for the boat. Then I've charted a course on the GPS to go down to the Plymouth Bay area. There's a good wind today so we can take time to explore the Stellmen Bank for awhile. Should be some great whale watching."

"Whales? We're going to see real live whales?" Danny's eyes went wide with surprise. "Mom. You have to take pictures. Lots of them!"

"Danny, stick close to me or Mark and wear your life vest whenever you're on the deck. Got it?"

Danny nodded eagerly. He was already suited up in his vest with his Red Sox cap pulled tight on his head. He gazed around at their boat and all the other boats in the quay. There was plenty of action, with the holiday boaters out in force. Gulls squawked loudly overhead as they dipped and swooped among the boats, looking for food. Others stood on the quay, their keening cries warning others to stay off their territory. Gaily dressed couples and families clambered onto boats of all size and types, sending the shrill gulls flapping away. Danny kept looking around him as his mother took more pictures.

"Time to bring in the lines and stow them. Mark you release the stern lines. Lana you get the ones in the bow. We'll motor out into the bay before we raise the sails." Ben checked that all the gauges were working and confirmed that the GPS was programmed and ready to go.

Down in the galley, Jennifer finished unpacking the food and putting it in the fridge and the locking cupboards. Everything had to be stowed away before they left the slip so nothing would fall once they were in motion. Even the counters had lips on them so plates and cutlery wouldn't slide away. She was impressed with the design of the interior, noting that her bedroom and Lana and Mark's were at opposite ends. She had never expected to have such privacy on a boat.

"Everything locked down there?" Ben called down.

"I'm done here." Jennifer finished hanging up some clothes, stowed her bag and went up to join him in the cockpit.

Ben had started the diesel engine to let it warm up for a few minutes before they finally cast off. A last line was holding them to the slip. Mark waited for the signal to cast it off. Lana and Danny sat on the bench in the stern watching all the waterfront activity.

Ben gave a last look at the gauges, revved the engine a couple of times to check it was running smoothly and gave Mark the order to cast off. He slipped off the mooring rope and nimbly jumped onto the foredeck as Ben geared up the engine.

"We're off!" Ben stood tall as he navigated them away from the quay. Jennifer stood beside him with an arm around his waist. Mark sat down with Lana and Danny. He touched her hand and motioned towards his father. "I done good didn't I?"

"What do you mean you done good?"

"I introduced them. Jennifer was visiting her father. My father was visiting me. We met each other going up to the main building and I introduced them."

"I remember seeing you all in the dining room that day and thinking what a lovely couple they would make." Lana smiled up at Mark and stroked his arm lovingly. "And they most certainly do. Good job."

In less than an hour Ben was ready for the sails to be raised. He'd spent time telling them what would be done, where they each should be and what they could expect once the wind filled the main sail. The sleek craft was designed to be handled completely by one person. Having a couple of extra hands available was a bonus. Ben could stay in the cockpit and unfurl the sail remotely while maintaining their course.

"Danny. C'mon into the cockpit." Ben was ready to show the boy some of the gauges and features as they tacked into the wind to fill the sails. They all watched as the mainsail rose, flapping noisily in the brisk wind. Ben edged the boat around slightly and was rewarded with a final snap as the mainsail caught the wind and filled in tautly. Next they unfurled the spinnaker. The smaller aft sail would enhance their speed by catching air movement off the mainsail.

The keel underneath the boat would convert the wind energy into the forward motion that would keep them moving towards whatever target they chose. At this point, they were heading towards Spectacle Island. Once they left the harbor the winds would be much stronger.

Danny peppered Ben with questions. "How old is this boat? What happens if you run out of wind and gas?" "Are you gonna buy this boat Ben?" "Where do I sleep?" Even as he was asking questions, he waved to passing boats. People waved back at him, which prompted them all to wave greetings.

Lana watched Ben and Danny with a big smirk on her face. All yours Ben, all yours, she thought and turned back to her conversation with Jennifer.

Ben called Mark over to gain whatever adult advantage was possible.

"Danny's wondering where he will sleep. Can you take him down to look around? Please?" Ben was pleading. Mark just grinned.

"C'mon Danny. Let's check out the sleeping arrangements." Danny jumped off the captain's chair and headed down the stairs ahead of Mark. "You owe me dad. Big time."

"You can take off your life jacket Danny." Mark helped him unbuckle the bright yellow and red jacket. "See the long cushions for the table? They're made so you can put two of them together to make a bed."

"Where are you sleeping?"

Mark was alone with Danny. No help from his mother who was on the deck chatting with Jennifer. "I will be sleeping in the same bed as your mother."

"You can sleep out here with me if you want."

"Thanks for the offer, Danny." Mark grinned. "But, dads usually sleep with moms. Since I'm going to be your dad, I should probably sleep with her. You can climb in with us in the morning if you want."

Jennifer heard the last bit as she came into the galley area to organize lunch. She smiled warmly but said nothing about hearing Mark say he was going to be Danny's father. *Not up to me to start any rumors,* she thought.

"Danny. Can you help me get our lunch ready please? We're going to eat on Spectacle Island in a few minutes. "Mark, I think you're needed on deck."

They moored at Spectacle Island after landing one of the last available slips. After over two hours of cruising around the harbor in the wind and fresh air they were all famished. Jennifer and Lana had made sandwiches, with some vegetables and chips. Simple and easy so they could enjoy every minute.

"Is this a good spot?" Mark stood with his legs akimbo and his hands on his hips, like an explorer staking out new territory. They had come ashore and now stood looking at the quay below. From this hill, they would have some privacy while still being able to keep an eye on the boat. Endless views of pale blue sky, dancing darker blue water and this island of green in the midst of it all provided a sunny vista as they got ready to eat.

"This is lovely. Perfect." Lana set down her pack beside Jennifer's. Ben put down the picnic kit and stretched.

"How're you doing?" Jennifer noticed Ben massaging his neck.

"I'm doing fine. But feel free to rub my neck." He smiled tenderly as Jennifer reached up to give him a little neck massage.

"I'm hungry." Danny stood in front of the four adults, two of whom towered over him.

Plates and platters were quickly produced. Soon they were all chowing down while gulls hovered and squawked nearby.

"How do you like working at Brentwood Mark? I don't think I've had a chance to ask really." Jennifer bit into her sandwich, which exploded with flavors of ham, gouda, herbs and grainy mustard. "Great sandwich Lana."

"The people are great, both staff and residents. The property is fabulous. It's beautiful already but still has so much more potential. And, of course, I can play the piano. Kathy insists I keep in practice, says it's part of my job description." Mark smiled as he looked out over the water. "Vera's family made a donation to thank us for the wonderful party. Her son took me aside and gave me an envelope with a hundred dollars in it. I didn't know what to say. First time I've been paid to sing."

"You earned it." Lana patted his thigh and offered him some celery. "It was such a professional concert. And I love your voice. You can sing to me any time."

"Me too Mark. I like Mack the Knife." After hearing it several times Danny could sing along with most of the words.

Ben was working on his second sandwich. "You ladies know how to feed a hungry man. No namby pamby little party sandwiches. You have to work to get your mouth around these puppies. When's the next concert? I'd like to be there too and bring Jennifer."

"I've offered to do one every two weeks for about an hour after dinner on Thursdays. In exchange, Kathy is going to let me take Friday afternoon off. I haven't worked for anyone like her before."

"I've enjoyed chatting with her from time to time. She seems like a very competent manager who gets out and really interacts with the staff and patients." Jennifer had met more than one residence director who could spend an entire day behind their desk without even emerging for lunch. Kathy Hunter wasn't like that.

"Let's get out to the Stellwagen Bank and see some whales. There should be lots of them at this time of year. It's a perfect feeding ground." Ben grinned as Danny twirled around with delight. He winked at Jennifer. He hadn't felt so happily jazzed himself in a few years.

No-one rushed as they packed up and made their way back to the boat, which was bobbing gently in its slip. The strong sun was still high overhead. Even with the harbor wind they could feel the heat as they prepared to cast off again.

They made their way towards the sandy banks some twenty-five miles from Boston harbor. On this sunny holiday weekend they weren't alone. Numerous motor boats, sail boats and even a few yachts had left the harbor to explore the marine nature sanctuary.

"Danny, watch the horizon for a spout of water. It's like water coming out of a hose if you stick it straight up in the air. When you see a spout, it's a whale coming to the surface to get fresh air before diving again." Danny was standing beside Ben in the cockpit and peering all around him.

"I've only seen whales in picture books and on the computer. How big are they?"

"There are many different kinds. If we're lucky, we'll see some that are bigger than this sailboat." Ben scanned the water for both boats and whales. There was a fair bit of marine traffic.

"Wow." For once Danny was speechless.

"The females bring their calves here to feed on sea lance. That's a kind of eel that likes to burrow in the sand. There's also plankton, a kind of grass, and fish that whales like. We're going fairly slowly to be sure not to hit anything and to be able to turn if a whale comes up too close to the boat. So, you keep a sharp eye out."

They hadn't gone far into the bank when they were rewarded not once but twice in quick succession. A huge humpback whale breeched off the port bow not two hundred feet in front of them. It was followed only seconds later by a smaller whale breeching. The mother and her calf appeared oblivious to the boat sailing towards them, disappearing in a splash of water and foam.

"Wow! Ever cool. That whale was bigger than our van."

"And that was just the baby Danny. The mother whale was at least as long as this sailboat."

"Look. What are those?" Danny pointed excitedly at a pod of bottlenose dolphins chasing their wake and diving in and out of the white-capped waves.

"Those are dolphins. They're very friendly with people. They've been known to help injured divers stay above the water." Ben admired the silvery gray creatures swimming alongside them. "I interviewed a diver once who was attacked by a tiger shark off Australia. The dolphins chased the shark away by butting their heads into it."

"How did they know what to do?"

"You Danny, are a budding journalist. You always ask a follow-up question. And it's a good one too." Ben angled the sailboat away from a small speedboat with its engine off.

"Dolphins are very intelligent. And they seem to like humans. Those dolphins must have realized the diver was in trouble and came to help."

As the sun slowly transited the sky towards the western horizon, they saw several species of whales. Mark had gone through the cupboards below and surfaced with a book that was full of photos and descriptions of the many species to be found on the Bank and down the coast towards Cape Cod.

"I read somewhere there are about one hundred and thirty different kinds of whales, birds and reptiles that feed on the Bank." Mark had done a bit of research after learning where Ben planned to go. "If we're lucky we'll see a Leatherback turtle. Those things can get huge."

"How huge?"

"The size of a trash can lid."

Danny's eyes widened. "We have turtles at my day care. I can hold three of them in my hand at one time."

"You'd have to find a Leatherback that was pretty young to be able to hold it in your hand."

Jennifer watched the two men feeding Danny's mind with all this new and interesting information. He was soaking it in. She had a feeling he would be making quite a report to the kids at day care come Tuesday. She sat back and gazed out over the water. She didn't feel like talking and was happy to be left alone with her thoughts.

She thought back to her father lying in the bed hooked up to the monitors. *He wouldn't know if I was there,* she reasoned. *He's being well cared for. There's nothing more I can do at this point. Perhaps I should have stayed though.* She remembered the days before her mother died. Her father had sat by her side all day until Jennifer came by after work. Only then would he leave to get something to eat in the hospital cafeteria. At the end though, neither of them was in her room when she passed away. Jennifer had gone to work. She had to practically order him to go home to get some sleep. *Now he's the one who's alone.*

She chided herself for becoming maudlin on such a beautiful day. Her father had over eighty years of life, much of it with good health and a strong mind. It was time to let him go. She stood up, straightened her shoulders and planted a smile on her face.

"Who wants something to drink?"

"I'll take one of those fine beers Mark brought on board." Ben angled his face around so Jennifer could kiss his cheek.

"Lana, care for a glass of wine?" Jennifer ducked down to the lower deck where Lana was curled up with a book on the cushioned bench.

"Sure, if you're having one."

"Red or white?"

"Whatever you're having will be fine."

As afternoon turned into early evening, Ben brought them into the protected waters of Plymouth Bay. With the wind behind them all the way the full trip had taken less time than he'd originally calculated. They still had a few hours of sunlight.

"How are you enjoying the cruise so far madam?" Ben was navigating them towards an area of the bay he had visited many years ago. It was sheltered from the cool ocean winds and would offer them a quiet and private place to moor for the night.

"It's magical. Truly magical. I've never done this before. We did the odd bit of day sailing with friends but never a whole long weekend like this. It's so special." Jennifer leaned into Ben as he put one arm around her to hold her close. "How are you holding up? It's been a long day."

"Let's say I'm looking forward to a quiet evening." He took a good pull of his beer and set it down in the holder. "It takes more energy than you realize to keep the boat under control, even with all the technological support. Sailing has changed a lot in the past forty years but it still takes some strength and stamina."

"Why so serious?" Jennifer looked at him quizzically. There was a look playing across his face she couldn't read.

"How would you feel about making this a regular event? I'm seriously thinking about buying a boat." Ben prepared to bring down the mainsail. They were nearing their mooring area. "This is in my blood. I had forgotten just how much I love being on the water. Can't believe I spent at least half my career in the mountains and desert."

"What did you have in mind?" Jennifer couldn't fathom doing this almost every weekend. It was outside of any experience she'd ever had. It felt downright decadent.

"I'm thinking of something big enough to get us to the Bahamas or even down to Barbados, St. Lucia or the British Virgin Islands. We could take off for a couple of months during the colder weather and keep our bones warm."

"Can you afford it? Can we afford it?" Jennifer was thinking of her modest cushion of savings. It didn't include buying a yacht and sailing off through the Caribbean for weeks at a time.

"I know we're not married yet. But, you should know you have found an extremely eligible bachelor. One who can take care of you very comfortably for the rest of your life. One who hasn't even begun to spend his retirement savings."

"Not married yet?" Jennifer abruptly ignored the money situation. "Are you planning to ask me?"

"I'm seriously thinking about it. But only if you'll agree to let me spoil you silly." Ben teased.

"How about we work on some dinner first? I'd like to explore this idea further but not on an empty stomach." Jennifer went down to the galley. Lana followed and soon the two women were happily chopping vegetables and meat for a stir fry. The cool air and brisk breezes had left them all looking forward to something warm and comforting. Lana had brought pre-cooked rice along to warm up in the microwave.

Ben cracked open another beer and sat at the counter. "I am no longer driving. My weekend has begun."

"Well, you can't just sit here and not work." Jennifer pushed across a cutting board, knife and some peppers and onions. "Can you cut these up please?"

"No rest for the weary. You are a slave driver, woman." He pulled the board in front of him and set to work. "I was thinking we could picnic over by Plymouth Rock tomorrow. Have a look around. What do you think?"

Jennifer grinned at him. "I haven't been there since I was a little girl. Have you ever been Lana?"

"No. Between my studies and having Danny, we never had time to travel much. My parents ran their own store so we didn't get much in the way of vacations when I was little either."

Mark and Danny came down from the deck, drawn by the tantalizing smells from the galley.

"What's for dinner, Mom? How long before it's ready?"

"We're having chicken teriyaki, stir-fried vegetables and rice. It'll be ready in about twenty minutes."

"I'm hungry now."

Ben pushed across some strips of green and red pepper. "Here Danny, tuck into some of these."

"Could I have a carrot too?"

"Please." Lana pulled out a carrot and handed it across.

"Please and thank you." Danny carried his little stash of food over to the couch and turned on the television.

"Let's see what DVDs there are." Mark opened a drawer and found several children's films. "Danny, did you ever see the movie Up?" He showed him the case.

"Nope. Haven't seen that yet."

"May I have a look at the case please Mark?" Lana was very careful about the movies she'd let Danny watch. There would be no Spider-Man 3 in her home for some years to come.

"Oh, I remember hearing about this one. Danny was still too young when it first came out. It opened the Cannes Film Festival. Apparently it's the first animated film to ever open the festival." Lana handed the case back to Mark. "Maybe we could all watch it together over dinner. A dinner and a movie night. I seem to recall promising you that a couple of days ago Mark. Remember?" The two of them grinned at each other and winked.

Jennifer was frying up onions, garlic and ginger and missed the exchange. Ben was hunched over the cutting board and missed it too.

"Man, that smells good. Makes me think back to a little restaurant I used to haunt on this one island in Japan. It was downstairs in my hotel. About eleven o'clock every day the whole building would start smelling just as it does in here. The only thing missing is the fish smell."

A few minutes later, they were all seated at the roomy table. The ladies were enjoying some wine while the men washed their food down with beer. Jennifer and Ben looked around the table and then at each other.

Mark had popped the movie in and was in charge of the remote. "Hey look, Dad. That's you in about fifteen years! He even sounds like you." Everyone laughed and chuckled as Ed Asner's gravelly voice filled the room. The silver-haired senior in the movie did bear a faint resemblance to Ben. But it was the voice that was really similar.

"I'll never be that short."

"Bet you'd look great in a bow tie." Jennifer scooped up a forkful of the teriyaki chicken and raised her eyebrows towards Ben. "Your voice really is similar."

"Let's just eat and watch the movie." Ben smiled as he said it. "I've been a long-time fan of Asner. It's a real compliment to be told I sound like him."

They finished eating about half-way through the movie and started cleaning up, leaving Danny as an audience of one. Ben and Mark took over the dishes while Lana and Jennifer put things away and organized tea and dessert.

"How about we take everything onto the deck and watch the sun set?" The adults left Danny to watch the end of the movie with a date square nearby.

"This is heavenly Lana. What a treat." Ben forked up a crumbly mouthful of his square. "Look at that western sky."

"I really appreciate this whole weekend adventure." Jennifer gazed up at the orange and gold colors that flecked the twilight sky. A few stars were visible. Soon there would be millions.

"Humans are so small and insignificant in the greater scheme of things. My mother used to tell me the stars are lights to help guide our souls to heaven. I'm sure she's waiting up there for my dad to join her. Hope he won't be a nagging angel though." Jennifer chuckled.

224

"I'm glad we could all be together. You warm enough?" Ben felt Jennifer shiver just a bit. "I could bring you a sweater. I'm getting a bit cool. Maybe time to bring out the jackets. Anybody else?" Ben put his mug down and went below. When he came back, Jennifer was telling Mark and Lana about her friend Carol's predicament.

"She's just way too trusting around men. Always has been since I've known her. But this time I think she's in way over her head. I'm worried something's going to happen before the police can get him. What do you think Ben?"

"I'm not sure. We don't know enough yet to know what he wants or what he's planning. But it's pretty clear he plans to relieve Carol of some of those diamonds she was splashing around the other evening. He kept looking at them as if he was trying to appraise them. It was pretty obvious."

"I have to admit I didn't notice a thing." Jennifer realized her own radar must have been turned off because she was with Ben and Carol. It never occurred to her to think anything unusual was happening.

"I don't know about you folks but the bed down there looks pretty inviting and I've had a long day." Ben finished his tea, double-checked the night running lights were all on and said goodnight. Jennifer followed him, leaving Lana and Mark to enjoy the starry night.

"You ready to go to bed yet?" Lana had pulled a blanket over a sleeping Danny. He'd almost made it to the end of the movie but not quite. She and Mark now had most of the boat to themselves.

"I think all the sun, wind and fresh air has done me in. Bed is sounding pretty good."

"Me too. I'll race you." The two walked through to their bedroom, turning off lights along the way. As they snuggled into the roomy bed, the boat rolled gently on the soft swells. Soon all were sound asleep.

Chapter 23

After a leisurely breakfast that included juice, sausage, eggs and toast, Ben and Mark cleared up while Jennifer and Lana organized their picnic lunch.

"I warned you they would eat us out of house and home." Jennifer pulled out a container of tuna salad she'd made up at home. She put it together with a bag of fresh vegetables, an asiago cheese dip she'd found at her favorite deli and some pita bread.

Lana was in charge of the snack food. She tucked some trail mix and juice containers into the cooler. "It's so cute to see the way they both eat the same way, they have the same grin, they even sound a bit alike. It's so obvious they're father and son."

"And they both have really good temperaments, especially when it comes to Danny." Jennifer had seen the way both men had gone soft on the boy. She looked over to where Ben and Mark were giving Danny the clean dishes to put away. He was just the right height to re-stock the under counter cupboards.

"This is so relaxing. I haven't had a vacation in years. There always seems to be so much to do at home. With a full-time job I never seem to have time to get everything done, let alone read a book." Lana added some napkins and a bag of grapes to their stores. "I didn't realize how much I needed a complete change of scenery like this."

"I feel the same way. Between my work, visiting my father almost every day, taking care of my house and going to my yoga and exercise classes, the week is full. Plus, with my book club, I want to read some every day. Being in that club makes me discipline myself to do something for me and my mind." The two women looked around. The galley was spotless, the bags packed. They were ready to go.

"Okay folks. Let the adventure begin." Ben went up to the cockpit to get the boat under way. He checked the marine weather forecast for the area. There was zero possibility of precipitation anywhere near them. They'd be spending the day in Plymouth Harbor. There would be no sailing. They could motor to a slip near the town.

"Anyone want a mug of coffee before we get going?" Jennifer called up from the galley.

"That is a fine idea my dear. I still have a good five to ten minutes of things to do before we get under way. Fresh coffee sounds great. Thanks."

While Jennifer organized coffee for four, Lana and Mark talked to Danny about where they were going and what they would see.

"First, we're going to see Plymouth Rock. Have you ever heard of it Danny?"

"We watched a film at day care one day about the Mayflower. I saw this rock stuck in the sand. What's so important about a rock?" He climbed onto Mark's lap.

"Hundreds of years ago there were a lot of people who were not happy about where they lived. Some couldn't find work . They didn't have enough food for their children. They decided to cross the Atlantic Ocean and make a new life for themselves and their families. Remember all day yesterday on the water?"

Danny nodded.

"You were pretty tired last night weren't you? Well, these people were in a small, cramped ship for over sixty-six days, some of them weeks longer. You'll see, when we go on the Mayflower II, many of the adults couldn't even stand up straight."

Lana smiled as Mark warmed up to the story. She could see Danny was listening closely. No sign of squirming.

"The Mayflower was about twice the size of this sailboat, but it carried over one hundred and thirty people. Do you know how many people that is?"

Danny shook his head.

"Think about everyone at your day care. Then think about the people from two day cares all living on a boat even the size of this one. Do you get the idea?"

Danny's eyes widened. "Where did they sleep?"

"Anywhere they could. The Mayflower was made for cargo. There were almost no beds or bunks."

"Did the kids have toys and stuff?"

"Maybe one each. But there was no PlayStation back then. No television. No movies. No refrigerators."

"But why is a rock so important?"

"When the Pilgrims reached America they wanted to remember the day and the place the ship landed. This huge rock was near where they landed. They had named their landing spot and new settlement Plymouth. So, they called the rock the Plymouth Rock."

"Why did they call it Plymouth?"

"A lot of names in the United States come from the names of villages, towns and cities in England. Plymouth's the name of a town in England. One of the early leaders had explored this area and called it New Plymouth." Mark looked over at Lana. She smiled and said nothing. His high school history knowledge was better than hers. He had to be running out of things to say though. How do you make a rock important to a five-year-old? The thought had just crossed her mind when Danny pushed again for an answer.

"I still don't understand why a rock is so important we need to see it."

"Do you ever visit the place where your father is buried?"

"Yes. My mom takes me. It makes her cry."

"Why do you go and see your father's grave?"

"So we won't forget him?" Danny tilted up his head to look in Mark's eyes.

"Yes. Same thing for the Pilgrims and for all Americans. We don't want to forget where we came from and the hardship people went through to settle America so we could be here today."

Danny looked out over the water. "I think I understand now. When we see the rock it helps us remember."

"You got it Danny. You got it." Mark put his hand on Danny's shoulder and gave it a warm squeeze.

Ben had navigated them between and around the dozens of moored watercraft to get to the town wharf. The trip across the bay hadn't taken long. In less than half an hour they were moored at the municipal wharf. They looked around as they carried the cooler and some folding cloth chairs off the quay.

"Looks like a lot of other people had the same idea." Ben surveyed the busy waterfront. "Let's walk over to the Mayflower II and see if there's a line-up. I had no idea it would be this zooey."

"Well, we've come this far. We have to show Danny the ship." Jennifer wasn't used to all the people and noise. She realized her mind was preoccupied with her father. "Oh Ben. Maybe I should have stayed back with my father."

"You say the word and we'll leave." Ben put his hand in the small of her back to guide her along the quay. "But, a year from now your father won't be with us. If we go back now all you'll remember is how he died. Or, you can set that aside and try to enjoy this weekend. Then, you'll have this to remember a year from now."

"It's true. I have to let him go and keep living my life and my future." Jennifer put her arm around Ben's waist and together they joined the throngs of tourists.

Mark, Lana and Danny held hands as they made their way along the waterfront street. Families with babies and strollers were out in numbers, with children running around all over. The freshly-painted ship stood tall at its mooring. When they reached it, they were able to walk right onto the gangplank.

Jennifer approached a woman about her age clothed in a period outfit. "I'm curious. How long does it take to get dressed in your costume?"

The woman smiled but stayed in character as one of the Pilgrim women. "On the voyage we had very few opportunities to change our clothes or clean them. Fresh water was very scarce. And there were so many of us we had no privacy either. It was such a relief to reach America and be off the ship at last."

They chatted for a few more minutes. Jennifer found it amusing to talk to someone as if she were back in the sixteen hundreds. It really helped take her mind off her father. As she strolled off to explore the ship, she looked up into the rigging, trying to imagine sailors climbing swaying ropes to bring in the sails as a storm approached.

"I'm glad I wasn't a sailor back then." Ben came up behind her carrying his digital camera. "That mast is at least as tall as the mast on Shelagh's Repose. Did you see the paddle boat out touring the harbor?"

"I saw it as we were coming in. It doesn't really fit in with the history of this area. But neither do the yachts moored out there. There's a few million in sailing toys in the bay."

"What do you think of it all? First impressions." Ben rested his hands on Jennifer's shoulders as she leaned back into his light embrace.

"It's a picturesque area I must say. All the small buildings with the little shops. It seems very cozy. And yet, when you turn around and look out into the harbor and the ocean it's such a vast vista, with boats everywhere you look."

"Think you'd like to see more harbors like this?"

"If they're anywhere near as neat and pretty as this it could be fun to explore."

"Marry me Jennifer and let's explore together." Ben slowly turned her around to face him. He put a finger under her chin and tilted her head up until they could look each other in the eyes. "Please say yes."

Despite the surprise of it, Jennifer knew he wasn't teasing.

"Yes." Jennifer's warm smile and shimmering eyes bathed the word in soft tenderness. "You sure know how to give a girl some special memories."

Ben wrapped his arms around her. They stood wordlessly watching the harbor activity for several minutes before moving to explore the ship further.

"MOM, MARK. LOOK AT THIS." Danny had found a large woven basket on the deck. "I could hide in here." He was about to climb in when a woman in period dress walked up to them. She was smiling but it was clear she didn't want Danny to get in.

"I'm sure the children aboard the Mayflower played and hid in baskets just like this." Lana intercepted him. "But, if you don't mind, how about you just look at and touch this basket Danny." Lana took his hand and pointed way up above him. "Look up there. Know what that is?"

She was pointing at a large platform around the top of the mast. "It's called a crows nest. Sailors would climb up there to see if they could see land yet or to see if other ships were coming."

"I wouldn't climb up there. That looks pretty scary." He pulled his mother towards an opening that led to the lower deck. "What's that?"

"Oh my. That's the cooking stove." Lana looked at the brick enclosure. "I can't imagine having to cook with something like this or in this space. It must have been really hot and smoky."

Mark stepped into the cramped space. He couldn't stand up to his full height.

"I can't begin to imagine over a hundred and thirty people on this ship. It must have been so uncomfortable. And for over two months." Mark looked around. "I just saw the sleeping areas. They must have been sleeping three or four to a bunk."

After a few more minutes touring the boat and talking to the people in costume, the five modern day sailors wandered over to visit the gift shops. Danny immediately made a beeline for a counter with toys, books and souvenirs.

As they looked over the children's display, Mark reached out and picked up a colorful book. "Danny, check this out. It's a treasure hunt."

Danny reached for the book and looked at the cover. "A real treasure hunt? What treasure?"

"Have a look."

Danny handed the book back to Mark. "Can you explain it to me?"

"It's kinda like your Spider-Man spelling game. You have to find the letters that spell out the clues to where the treasure is hidden."

"Can I get it, Mom? Can I?"

Lana approved the purchase as Danny clutched his latest treasure. He was learning to read in a fun and entertaining way.

After visiting the canopy where a piece of the Plymouth Rock was on display, the little group gathered to find a spot to spread out and eat their lunch. They strolled back towards the harbor where they had seen some benches and grassy areas that would be good for their picnic. Ben and Jennifer lagged behind the others to decide when to tell their news.

"How about tonight over dinner?" Jennifer wanted to keep the secret between them just a little while longer.

Ben was in complete agreement. "I won't tell if you don't."

"We can open one of those lovely Pinot Grigio's I brought along and propose a toast. Sound good?"

"Sounds perfect. Let's go eat."

"As always, you have your priorities straight." Jennifer hugged his arm and grinned up at him. "Food first, middle and last."

"Is there any other way?"

Jennifer and Ben caught up to the others just as they reached a shaded spot to set up for their picnic. She opened up a bright blanket for them to sit on as Lana and Mark brought out dishes, cutlery and food. Within minutes they were enjoying their finger foods and pita and tuna wraps, even as gulls swooped around crying out and looking for handouts.

After lunch, they spent a couple more hours exploring the area. They had quickly learned that Pilgrim Memorial State Park isn't much larger than the two monuments that stand on it. By mid-afternoon they had seen all they wanted to see and headed back to the boat to sail around the harbor until it was time to moor for the day.

As they reached Shelagh's Repose, Ben looked out over the harbor. "We'll need to motor out well beyond the busiest perimeter of small craft. There's a brisk breeze. I want to be well clear of the inner harbor before raising the sails." He waited for Mark and Lana to get into position.

"Ready to cast off." Ben nodded to Mark who deftly released the line and jumped on board. "You're getting pretty adept at this. Might make a sailor out of you yet."

"Got the right teacher I guess." Mark grinned and leaned against the cockpit. He followed his father's gaze out over the water. "You seem pretty comfortable with all this. You going to take it up regularly?"

"More than that. I'm thinking of buying a boat like this to live on down south a few months of the year."

"What would one of these things set you back?" Mark gazed around the boat. "This looks like top quality."

"I'm not sure but I have a very comfortable portfolio for retirement. I spent many years of my life all expenses paid plus a very handsome salary. The share I didn't give you and Mom sat and grew and grew. I was surprised a few weeks ago when I sat down with my financial advisor. I hadn't looked at the total in a few years. And those years were a bull market and a half."

"There's no bull market now though. Didn't you lose a bundle the past few years?"

"I lost some. But the capital is well preserved. I could easily afford this."

"That's right. Spend my inheritance." Mark grinned at his father. "But seriously, I can't think of a better way for you to spend it. Jennifer has the house. You have the boat. They're probably worth about the same. Does she want to go along?"

"I'm not supposed to say anything yet but I've asked her to marry me. She said yes and it was contingent on sailing off to explore other harbors together. She's definitely on board."

"You mean I actually found out something before anyone else?" Mark slapped his dad on the back and then hugged him. "I won't say a word I promise. Way to go, Dad!"

Down in the galley, Lana and Jennifer had put away the lunch leftovers and were organizing for supper. Lana had brought some roast pork with gravy they were going to heat up in the galley's oven.

Between them they were putting together a salad while Danny sat with his treasure hunt book and started to work through the clues.

"Just a few more minutes Danny and I'll come and help you."

"Go ahead Lana. Everything is under control here.

I'm going up and join Ben and Mark and just relax for half an hour or so before we launch supper. We're in no rush."

All was quiet on the boat for the next hour. Jennifer, Ben and Mark chatted as Ben navigated them near the mouth of harbor. Many craft had headed back to the marina. The water was more open and the clear sky was still bright and sunny.

Lana and Danny quietly explored for treasure hunt clues. Every few minutes they'd work one out and Danny would let out a loud whoop. Mark looked down after the first cheer. He stayed back to give Lana time alone with her son.

After mooring in a calm area of the bay, Lana and Jennifer completed the dinner preparations. It was dusk when they finished eating. A plate with a few crumbs on it in the middle of the table was the only remaining evidence of one of Lana's cheesecakes. Ben offered everyone a refill of their wine.

"I want to propose a special toast." He drew out the word propose. Jennifer grinned and happily passed her glass across. When all the glasses were topped up and Danny had some apple juice, Ben stood up, raised his glass and turned to Jennifer.

"I would ask you to raise your glasses to the future Mrs. Powell. Jennifer has graciously accepted my offer of marriage."

Jennifer beamed as they all reached around to clink glasses. Both Lana and Mark jumped up in unison and went to hug them.

"You two are great together. Congratulations!" Lana threw her arms around Jennifer's sturdy shoulders. "This is so exciting. I'm really happy for you both."

Mark hugged his dad and then kept a hand on his father's arms. "I'm really happy for you dad." He winked at his father and then turned to Jennifer to give her a warm hug. "Welcome to the family,

Mom. May I call you that?"

Jennifer felt tears welling up. "Oh yes please. It may not look like it at this moment but that would make me feel very, very happy." She dabbed at her eyes, overwhelmed by emotions she had held at bay for a very long five years and a very long and happy afternoon.

They spent the rest of the evening talking about Ben's idea of buying his own sailboat and travelling with Jennifer a few months of the year.

"We'd be happy to take Charlie over while you're away." Lana got a confirming nod from Mark. "Danny loves him and we have a fair-sized yard." Lana had been thinking about getting a pet. Charlie was already their test pet. "We'd take him for walks every day."

BEN AND MARK LET THE WOMEN GET THEMSELVES ORGANIZED FOR BED FIRST. Danny was sound asleep on one of the long couch cushions. The bathroom mirror light was on to guide their way. The two women pulled out their pyjamas and chatted quietly. After finishing their nighttime ablutions they returned to the deck.

Ben and Mark then had their turn and emerged moments later in polo loungers and tee shirts as the evening air bathed them in its silkiness.

"I'm heading down to bed Jennifer. You with me?" Ben finished the last of his wine, stood up and offered his hand to her. She took it and the two of them descended the steps together. After a few minutes of muffled conversation, all was quiet below.

LANA AND MARK STOOD BY THE COCKPIT looking up at an inky black sky, which was now full of stars. Neither of them knew any of the constellations but they were awed by what they could see.

"I've never seen the sky like this in the city. There's too much light." Mark put his arm around Lana and cuddled her in close. "Makes me feel very, very small to be standing on this boat, in an ocean this large on a planet this big."

"Me too." Lana shivered a bit. "This is so surreal. I never imagined

I'd be standing on a sailboat moored out on the water looking up at millions of stars. It was never even on a wish list."

Mark turned Lana to face him. "You deserve to have a wish list Lana. You and Danny. We need to work on that." He hugged her in close and then tipped her chin up to kiss her warmly and then more deeply. Lana reached her arms around his shoulders and molded her body into his.

"You're first on my wish list." Lana wriggled up against Mark.

"I think we could work on that right now," Mark took her hand and led her to their bedroom as the stars twinkled on in the night.

Lana wakened first. At this hour, with the sun barely peeking above the horizon and almost no wind yet, the air coming through the open porthole was cool and fresh. She stretched like a contented cat and rolled on her side to look at Mark. The wind and sun had lightened his already fair hair and she was sure she saw some freckles that hadn't been there before. She leaned in and gently kissed his eyelids. At the touch, Mark moved and reached out an arm to encircle her.

"How did you sleep?" Lana planted light kisses around Mark's face.

"I slept very well thank you." Mark pushed a hand through his hair and stretched as Lana leaned back to look at him. "May need a nap this afternoon though. How about you?"

Lana sat up as Mark pulled himself to sit up against the wall. Once he was settled, she came in for a cuddle. They could see a couple of gulls angling over the boat. "I slept well. It's so soothing sleeping on the water next to you."

"Any idea what time it is?"

"Probably around six. We're all early risers. How about I get a pot of coffee going?" Lana sat up and planted a kiss on his nose. He reached for her hand and pulled her down for a morning kiss.

"You look beautiful out here with the sun on your hair. And there's a glow in your cheeks. All this fresh air is obviously good for you." Mark combed his fingers through her hair and rubbed her neck.

Lana moved to the edge of the bed and stood up part way. The head space in the bedroom was nowhere near full height. "You'll say anything to get your cuppa."

Within minutes, the aroma of fresh-brewed coffee was wafting over the boat. Mark was already in the galley when Ben emerged from the larger bedroom, finger combing his hair with one hand and rubbing the sleep out of his eyes with the other.

"I smell coffee. Elixir of the gods. And you are the goddess." Ben accepted two steaming mugs from Lana and took them back to where Jennifer was doing some morning stretches.

"Danny's still asleep." Mark savored the hot brew and watched the boy who would be his son.

"He was up late and it was a long day. I think we still have a few minutes before he wakes up. Coffee doesn't seem to trigger him." They both went up the steps to greet the sun that had now cleared the horizon and was dappling the water with glittering sparks of light. It wasn't long before they heard noises from below. Danny was awake and ready for a new day.

"Morning, Mom. Morning, Mark." Danny bounded up the steps with a mug of juice in one hand and his Red Sox cap in the other. "What's for breakfast?"

"How about you go get a granola bar to munch on until the rest of us are ready for breakfast." Lana was in no hurry to rush her morning let alone anyone else's. "You can have an apple too. You know where they are."

Danny went back down for his snack.

"How about I set him up with a movie and pour us some more coffee?"

"Sounds like a fine idea." Lana handed her mug over. She leaned on the railing and lifted her face to the early morning breezes. The sky promised another sunny day.

"It's quite an experience having him around other people for an entire night and day. We've never done this before." Lana took the full mug from Mark's hand when he passed it to her, enjoying the rich smell of the coffee mixed with the fresh salty air. It was all new to her and Danny.

Lana finished the last of the coffee just as Danny returned.

"Mom. We need to have breakfast soon. The granola bar is gone." Danny had waited patiently. It was later than his usual breakfast time.

"Danny. Before we have breakfast, what do you say we bring out the surprise we got the other night. You know. The special surprise. It's in my knapsack. And ask my dad and Jennifer to come up too." Mark winked at him.

Danny flashed a brilliant smile and dashed off.

"Excuse me just a minute?" Mark went down the steps.

Lana was still trying to figure out what was going on when all four of them came up onto the deck. Danny was now grinning from ear to ear. Ben and Jennifer looked a bit puzzled.

"Lana, can you sit down over here please?" Mark pointed to the bench in the stern next to the cockpit. Lana sat down, uncertain what Danny and Mark were up to. "What is it Mark?" She gazed questioningly at him.

Mark knelt down on one knee in front of her as Ben and Jennifer held each other's hands. "Lana Fitzpatrick, will you do me the honor of becoming my wife? I asked Danny for your hand in marriage. He has given me permission to ask you."

"You asked Danny?" Mirth welled up in Lana and she laughed. "You asked Danny if you could marry me? Is that what your man trip was about the other night?" Lana was impressed. She knew they had formed a close bond but hadn't realized how far it went.

"Actually, no. Our man trip was about this." He brought out a small velvet box, opened one of her hands and placed the box lightly in it. "Open it."

Lana stared at the ring box before opening it. She stared up at Mark who still was above her even as he kneeled. "Is this what I think it is?"

"Just open it Lana."

Lana slowly opened the box and gasped. "Oh my. It is so perfect." She stared at the white gold band set with six small but perfectly matched pavé diamonds. "I've never seen anything so beautiful."

"Each diamond is for your family: Your parents, Tim, Danny, myself and you. We're all part of your life, past, present and future. Danny figured it out when we were at the store."

"He didn't say a word. That's a huge secret to keep. How did you get him to not say anything?"

"Must have been that ice cream cone, right Danny?" Mark grinned.

"Right." Danny beamed at them both.

Lana gave the ring to Mark and held out her hand. As she watched him slip the delicate ring on her finger she felt her eyes brimming with unbidden tears. This man she loved had asked Danny if he could be his father. She looked up at Danny as the tears started to fall.

"She's crying just like you said she would Mark." Danny stepped forward into his mother's outstretched arms.

"I'm not crying. I'm just leaking a bit." Lana sniffled loudly as Jennifer produced a tissue.

Lana gazed at Mark through her tears. "I think I've loved you since the minute I first set eyes on you. I want you to be part of my life for the rest of my life. I hope you want me as much as I want you."

"I do Lana. With all my heart. And you too Danny." Mark hugged them as Jennifer and Ben started to clap. Ben gave his loudest whistle and punched the air with his arm. "Woohoo!"

Ben and Mark shooed the women away and took over the galley. "We'll make a real Powell breakfast for you ladies while proving we are handy in the kitchen."

Mark rummaged through the fridge and handed out eggs, bread, jam and milk. Then he looked into the cupboards and found brown sugar. "How about we make French toast dad?"

"Let's do it. Any bacon or sausages in there?" Ben located a large mixing bowl and set to breaking eggs into it one after the other. "Any cinnamon?"

Jennifer and Lana looked on at the production in the galley. Jennifer shook her head. There would be quite a clean-up to do after they were finished. *But, it's worth it to see those two going all domestic.* She smiled at Lana and went off to get dressed. Lana did the same.

"What's the plan for today?" Mark set a pan of bacon on to cook on one burner and brought out another for frying the egg-coated bread. Ben rummaged in the drawers for cutlery and put some dishes in the oven to warm up.

"I was thinking we could go to the pirate museum at Provincetown. It's a bit of a hike but we could be back here for the night. What do you think Danny?. There's real pirate treasure and old weapons."

"Cool." Danny sat at the counter watching the two men. "Can I help steer the boat today?"

"Sure thing Danny." Ben gave him the cutlery to bring to the table.

"That sounds like fun for everyone. I'm sure there's a bit of buccaneer in all of us." Mark flipped a piece of French toast and turned the bacon. "You'll have to show me how to plot our course. I'd like to know more about this sailing business."

As the boat filled with the aromas of fresh coffee, bacon and French toast, Jennifer stood out on the deck and thought about her father. He'd never been a sailor but she felt he would have enjoyed this. He loved being out in the fresh air and in nature. And he would have liked Ben. The one time they met they didn't get to talk much. In another time and place it would have been different she was sure.

She listened as the men talked and clattered below. Waking up beside Ben, she remembered with a thrill that they were going to be married. *Funny,* she thought, *three months ago I was telling Carol I might never remarry. Now look where I am. Standing on this beautiful sailboat, my future husband down in the galley cooking breakfast with my future stepson and my future daughter-in-law and grandson watching them. Oh Dad, I wish you could know how much my life has changed for the better these last few months. I know you were worried about me. You won't have to worry about me any more. I'll be just fine.* She sent up a quiet prayer for him.

"Time to eat. All gather please." Mark tapped the tongs on the side of the bacon pan.

Danny ran to the bathroom sink and rinsed his hands without being asked. Lana said nothing about the lack of soap. They were on water rations.

Jennifer stepped down from the deck and smiled at the happy commotion. *This is my new family,* she realized with a feeling of bliss. She caught Ben looking at her and smiled back at him. "Thank you", she mouthed to him.

Ben handed Danny a plate with French toast, bacon and some strawberries. "Bit of brown sugar on the toast?"

"We're going to see real pirate treasure Aunt Jennifer." Danny nodded as Ben sprinkled a bit of sugar over the toast. "Mom, you need to take pictures of me with the treasure."

"Now I need to take pictures for you?" Lana laughed. "You really learned that lesson about the difference between needing and wanting didn't you?"

"Yep I did." Danny grinned.

Ben and Mark were poring over the navigation charts when a call came in on Ben's satellite phone. He'd given the number to only one contact: Brentwood Manor. Jennifer quickly stepped up to the cockpit. She knew what the call meant.

"When did he pass away?" Ben listened. "I see. Let me pass you to his daughter."

Ben gently handed the phone to Jennifer.

"This is Jennifer Barrett. Hello Kerry. Thank you for calling me." Jennifer listened as Kerry told her that her father had passed away quietly early that morning. She spoke to the nurse for a couple of minutes and then passed the phone back to Ben.

"He's gone. Around seven o'clock this morning. I remember I was standing by the railing thinking about him. I told him how great my life is now. And about my new family. I told him not to worry about me. That I'd be fine." Jennifer felt the tears welling up. "He must have heard me. Kerry said he just sighed quietly and was gone. The light over his head glowed brightly for a couple of seconds. It really startled her."

"What do you want to do now?" Ben reached out and stroked her arm. "Shall we head back?"

"No. My father is gone. I said my good-bye to him this morning. I feel in my heart that he's at peace now and knows that I'm going to be fine." Jennifer made her decision. "I want us to take Danny to see the pirate treasure."

"How about we do that and then go back to Boston tonight instead of staying on the boat overnight?"

"Okay. If it's not too long a day for you."

"Let's see what we can manage. I can at least get us closer to Boston than Plymouth by tonight." Ben set up the GPS and prepared to get them under way.

"I'm so sorry Jennifer. You okay?" Lana was all concern for her future mother-in-law when Mark told her about her father's death. "We can go back."

"No Lana. My father has passed on. I want to remember this trip and Danny's excitement a year from now. I want happy memories to mix with my loss." Jennifer laid her hand on Lana's arm. "Danny is so excited. I'm fine. I really am."

Danny was indeed thrilled by the pirate museum. But, after less than hour looking at dusty muskets, pistols, pieces of eight and a cannon with treasure still trapped inside it, they were ready to leave. Jennifer was relieved. She wanted to go home, get Charlie and nest away from the others for awhile. She felt emotionally drained. Her father was gone. And she hadn't been there.

"Do you think we can make Boston by tonight?"

"I think so. We have a strong tailwind. I'm pretty confident we'll make it before dark." Ben got them organized and under way as soon as they were back on board. "I'll stay up here. If you can bring me a sandwich or something we'll head back non-stop. The motor is gassed up in case."

Jennifer made a sandwich for Ben and brought it up to him.

"I'm going to lie down for awhile just to be by myself if you don't mind."

"Do whatever you need to do, Jennifer. I've got the helm." Ben gave her a hug and watched her go down the steps.

Jennifer lay down in the roomy bed. Sunlight streamed in the window overhead. The sailboat was skimming over the waves in a gentle wave motion that lulled her. She thought about death and life and about the circle of life. Clutching a pillow to her, she cried quietly for the strong man who had been her father. Then she slept.

They arrived at the marina in Boston shortly after the dinner hour. Ben had put all his skills to use to race the boat back. They were a full day early but when he explained the situation, the rental brokers offered to contact the owners about a fee reduction. Ben asked them to see if the owners might be interested in selling.

They all bundled quietly into Lana's van for the drive home. Danny was already asleep and had to be carried by Mark. Even loading the van didn't disturb the boy's slumber.

When Jennifer and Ben were dropped home, Jennifer walked into the house, put down her things and slumped into a chair. "I never imagined I would feel like this. He had a long, long life. He accomplished so much. So why do I feel so sad?"

"Partly because you're a loving daughter. And partly because you have been caring for him all these years and now he's gone. Your life is changing." Ben went around to turn on more lights. He called Gerry to tell them they were back but asked him to keep Charlie until morning.

"Thank you. I thought I wanted to see Charlie tonight but I think I'd rather just have quiet time with you. I can't imagine being completely alone in this house tonight. I'm so glad you're here."

"We've had quite a weekend haven't we? We got ourselves engaged. Mark and Lana are engaged. But now your father has left us." Ben walked over to Jennifer and squatted in front of her. "What would you like to do with the rest of the evening, sweetie?"

Jennifer stood up. "Just hold me for awhile. Just hold me."

Ben gathered her in his arms and quietly rocked Jennifer until her crying subsided. Then he led her up to their bed.

Chapter 24

The memorial service for Jennifer's father was small. The little chapel adjacent to the funeral home was more than large enough to accommodate the two dozen or so mourners. Jennifer had thought about foregoing a service but, out of respect for her father and his faith, had asked the Brentwood chaplain to conduct a small service.

After it was over, they all moved to another room where sandwiches and refreshments had been set out. Carol stayed close by her friend.

"You've been through so much. You know I'm here for you." Carol had dressed head to toe in black. She was the only one who had.

"Thanks, Carol. I knew it was coming but it's still difficult to absorb. He was a big part of my life these past few years. I'll certainly have a lot of free time on my hands."

"I'm sure Ben will have some ideas of how to help you spend that time." She saw Ben headed towards them. "Wait'll you hear what happened over the Independence Day weekend. One of my top condo listings was staged by an art thief."

"What do you mean staged?" Jennifer tried to think.

"Some guy managed to convince the doorman that he had been hired by me to stage the condo. He had my business card and his own phony one. The doorman thought he'd seen him before and let him into the unit."

"What did he take? Where were the owners?" Ben was listening attentively.

"The owners are in Europe for a few weeks. I was the one supposed to keep an eye on the place." Carol looked at them both with unaccustomed uncertainty in her eyes. "About an hour after he arrived, a truck pulled up at the back service entrance. The two men told the doorman they were from the staging service and were there to pick up some items for storage. He let them in."

Carol fingered a diamond stud in her ear. "Long story short. They took a dozen very valuable paintings and some very rare ceramic art. The paintings alone are worth close to half a million. One item, a unique hand-crafted and painted vase by a Quebec artist, was worth about ten thousand. There were several more like it. All museum quality. We don't know what else is missing. The owners are on their way back now. Should be here tomorrow."

"Has this happened before?" Jennifer knew she and Ben were thinking the same thing. Michel had said he wouldn't be in Boston that weekend because he was planning the hit on the condo.

"Actually, a couple of my listings have been broken into the past few months." Carol did a mental count and realized this was the fifth break and enter in as many weeks. "The others were simple. Jewelry stolen, a couple of tablets, cameras, that sort of thing."

"Security cameras catch anything?"

"A tall male. Nothing to identify the face."

"You working with the police?"

"They called me after the third break-in. I was the listing agent for each property. They questioned me pretty closely but it became apparent I had nothing to do with any of them. Now of course, with my business card being used, they're taking interest in me all over again."

"Where's Michel these days?" Jennifer tried to make the question sound innocent. It worked.

"He called this morning from Detroit to say he'll be back here later this week or early next week. His company's new client has more western trips than eastern."

"So you haven't seen him for a few days?"

"Haven't seen him since the day after we had dinner together with you two."

Jennifer said goodbye to a couple of neighbors and turned back to

Jennifer. "There's something Ben needs to tell you. I suggest you turn off your phone for awhile."

Carol saw the serious look on both their faces and turned it off without comment.

"Let's go sit down." Jennifer led her friend over to a couch at the back of the chapel. "Ben, you take over with Carol. I have to chat with a couple of people but as soon as they're gone I'll be back." Apart from Lana and Mark, there were only a few people left and they were almost finished their coffees.

"What's up Ben?" Carol looked decidedly uneasy.

Ben decided candor was best. "Carol. Michel is a con artist with a long history of preying on pretty single real estate agents. He's known to law enforcement in ten states. There's an FBI file on him." Ben watched Carol's shocked reaction as she absorbed what he was saying.

"How did you find this out? What made you suspicious? You've only met him once." Carol's eyes were wide. She kept shaking her head.

"Well, for one, he can't speak French. For another, he's not a pilot. I threw out some inaccurate comments about jets. He should have known it but he never corrected me. After dinner that night I emailed a buddy in the NYPD and he filled me in. I've been meaning to get in touch with a contact in the FBI but I've been busy helping Jennifer since her father died."

Jennifer walked back to them after the last guest left. Mark and Lana had gone to pick up Danny and take the rest of the day off.

"Is anything missing from your condo that you know of?" Jennifer could see the very troubled look on her friend's face. *This cannot be easy,* she thought, as Carol pulled out the business card of the police detective she had seen. She passed it to Ben, who immediately called the detective to arrange to meet at Carol's condo.

"I keep my jewelry in a couple of boxes in my bedroom. Michel would have seen them but not the most valuable ones. I keep those hidden. I haven't noticed anything specific other than that I seem to have misplaced a couple of pieces. Oh wait." Carol hung her head dejectedly. "That night after we had dinner together we went home. Michel poured us each a glass of brandy. And then another. We both got tipsy. I remember taking off my dinner ring so it wouldn't catch on anything. I haven't seen it since, not that I was looking for it though."

"Let's get over to your place You can check around before the detective arrives."

"I can't believe I fell for his scam."

"You were not alone. You have a lot of company." Jennifer gathered up the few sympathy cards that had been left and the white lily flower arrangement she had ordered. Its fragrance had filled the chapel, reminding her of her home and her parents. They were both gone now. *If there's a heaven*, she mused, *I hope there's a big year-round garden for Dad to dig in.*

Ben retrieved her father's urn and together they went out to her car with Carol following quietly behind them.

When they walked into Carol's condo, with its sweeping vista view of Boston Harbor, they both had the same reaction. It looked like a magazine spread for an architectural digest.

"How about I put on a pot of coffee and then I'll get my jewelry boxes." Carol led them to the kitchen area. They sat at the counter as she measured out the water and coffee.

"Jennifer, the next time I date a man I want you along as my chaperone. I seem to need one." Carol brought out four mugs and put them on the counter. "I'm sure Detective Guzzo will want coffee. He seemed to be living on it when we met at his precinct."

While the coffee brewed, Carol went back to her bedroom and brought out the two large wood jewelry boxes one at a time. She went back once more. Suddenly, there was a cry from her room.

Jennifer ran towards the sound. "Carol. Are you all right?" She found Carol sitting on the edge of her large bed holding an empty shoe box.

"The bastard. He got my best pieces. I kept them hidden among my many shoe boxes. I never told him or showed him. He must have gone through each box when I was in the shower or out in the great room. That bloody bastard."

Returning to the living room, Carol pulled out her tablet and set it on the counter. After pouring coffee, she started to itemize what had been taken. "He got my Denver diamond."

"Your Denver diamond?" Jennifer had never heard of it.

"Remember when I went to Denver to the real estate convention two years ago?"

Jennifer nodded and sipped her coffee.

"I bought a princess cut diamond ring. Over five carats. Top grade. That rock set me back fifty thousand. It was my reward to myself for grossing over twenty million in sales that year."

"What else did he get?" Ben was just starting to do the math on what Michel had made off with. It sounded like he might be planning to retire to a secluded island somewhere. They needed to move fast.

By the time Detective Guzzo arrived, Carol had finished the list and two cups of coffee. They calculated he had stolen well over a quarter of a million in jewelry, both loose and set. He had probably walked out with them distributed around his pockets. Fortunately, Carol had taken out supplemental insurance for her collection.

"Detective Guzzo. Meet my friend Jennifer Powell and her fiancé Ben Powell." They shook hands all around.

"Ben Powell. Used to watch you on the news. You retired?"

"Yes. Getting ready to write my memoirs."

"From what I'm hearing, you may be able to add a new chapter on catching one of the most elusive con artists we've seen. Let me get out my recorder so you can tell me what you know."

Almost an hour later, Detective Guzzo wrapped up. He had more than enough to call in the FBI. Demercado had called from Detroit, which gave them a new lead to follow. Carol had given him some items that might have his DNA on them. Ben had given him a copy of the very clear photo of Demercado from the restaurant.

"The DNA may not do us much good. He was in the condo as a potential buyer. We would expect to find his DNA there. I'm going off shift soon but before I do I'm going to get this out to the FBI and Interpol. So far, Demercado has been travelling within the continental United States but I agree with you Ben, he may be planning a retirement trip. For that he'll need a passport. With this photo and his various names and aliases, we can put him on the no fly list. Next time he turns up for a commercial flight, the FBI will be notified and he'll be arrested on the spot by airport security. He won't know what hit him."

"Remember Ms. Brock. If he calls, keep it really light and easy. Try to get his travel plans. I'll get a court order so we can monitor his phone and email. We're going to go by the book on collecting evidence. He's not going to get away on my watch."

Shortly after he left, Jennifer and Ben said their goodbyes. They were all exhausted but very relieved. Carol had already had the locks changed. Michel or Michael or whoever he was today would not be able to waltz back into her condo.

"Thank you so much you two. I owe you big time. How about an extravagant dinner out when he's behind bars?"

"You're on. Maybe we will order that Dom Perignon 1996 eh Ben?" Jennifer winked.

"When that bastard is caught, we'll order a case of the stuff." Carol hugged them both.

"Check the price m'dear. Check the price." Jennifer chuckled as she and Ben headed out the door together.

"What do you think? How's she holding up?" Ben didn't know Carol very well but he realized she'd taken quite a hit over her latest boyfriend.

"I think this is probably the biggest wake-up call she's ever had. Her last boy toy was just a hanger-on. He didn't actually steal from her. This Demercado guy is in a different league. He plotted and planned and he used her. And, he has plenty of experience. As bright as she is, she didn't stand a chance."

"I have to agree with you there. He did his homework all right."

"But not enough to fool you. You cracked this case Sir Ben. Maybe you should think of a new calling in your journalistic retirement. Maybe that investigative bent you've developed could be turned to other uses." Jennifer handed him the keys to her car. "But for now, let's go home."

THREE DAYS LATER, CAROL CALLED JENNIFER. "He called me. The police know exactly where he is! His smart phone has a built-in GPS. For a guy who's supposed to know about navigation aids, he's pretty dumb." Carol was driving and talking into the phone on its dash mount. "The FBI are involved. Right now, the Detroit police are tracking his movements with the GPS. He's already been to a couple of known fences. He's probably cashed in half my jewelry by now. They've also traced some expensive shipments from Boston to Florida using one of his aliases. Probably a few of the paintings left town. And one more thing. He has a wife. That's why he was never around on weekends."

Jennifer listened closely as Carol brought her up to date. They'd all been concerned about the silence the first few days. Carol had tried to reach him after the police wiretap was set up but it kept going to message. There had been fears he might have left the country before his name and aliases were added to the no fly list.

"Oh yes. The things I gave them that might have his DNA? Bingo. Apparently the FBI had started collating evidence from various crimes and suspected they were dealing with the same person under different names. He's been doing this for over twenty years. It's been his lifelong career. They have DNA evidence from numerous heists. He will be convicted on multiple, multiple counts."

"Sounds like he wanted to retire. One last big con. Ben will be so glad. By the way, the night we all met for dinner, did Michel try to get out of it?"

Sitting at a red light, Carol stared at her phone. "Yes he did. Why do you ask?"

"Ben figures he probably tried to isolate his marks from their friends and family so he couldn't be questioned too closely. And to keep from being photographed."

"The sneaky bastard. He told me he was tired and didn't think he could last the evening. I told him to go have a shower and a nap. Then he poured us both a glass of wine and tried to get me to have more so we'd get a bit sloppy and couldn't go." Carol eased the car forward but she had both hands in a furious grip on the steering wheel. "I'd better get off the phone. Traffic is heavy. But this is a great development. Talk to you when I hear more."

"Why don't you come over for supper? Lana, Mark and Danny are on their way."

"I'd like that. Thanks. I was just going back to the office to do paper work but it can wait until tomorrow. Can I bring something?"

"No, just you. Lana is bringing a new dessert she wants to try out on us. And we have all the ingredients for supper in front of us. C'mon over."

"I'm turning as we speak."

Lana arrived with a large cake plate, followed by Mark and Danny who were both wearing Red Sox caps and jerseys. Charlie greeted their arrival with his personal dance of joy. Danny ran out into the back yard with him.

Ben offered Mark a beer and opened one for himself after pouring a couple of glasses of wine for the ladies.

Jennifer brought them all up to date on the hunt for Carol's con man.

"She's on her way over to join us for supper. The police are tracking his whereabouts."

Carol appeared at the front door in less than half an hour and gratefully accepted a glass of wine from Ben. They all retired to the patio to watch Danny and Charlie and chat.

"Have you folks set any dates for your weddings?" Carol stretched her legs and had a sip of her wine.

The four looked at each other. Jennifer spoke first.

"With everything that's been happening, Ben and I haven't given it much thought. Living in sin is fun."

Lana looked at her engagement ring and then grinned at Mark. "I haven't really come to grips with being engaged to this big oaf.

He proposed so prettily though. Guess I should make an honest man out of him soon. A spring wedding would be lovely."

"How about we ask if we can get married at Brentwood?" Mark reached over and took Lana's hand in his and winked. "I know a garden bed that would set off your coloring really well for wedding photos."

As they discussed wedding plans, Jennifer and Ben served up the cold supper of chicken, ham and salads on the patio. They all tucked in hungrily and were almost finished when Carol's phone rang.

"Hello Detective Guzzo. What's the news?" She listened briefly, smiled and looked around at them nodding her head. "This is wonderful. You sure moved fast. What's next?"

She closed down the phone and grinned like the Cheshire Cat. "They got him. Not only have they arrested him, this afternoon a whole squad of plainclothes officers were sent out to visit the traceable locations. He had a real racket going. They've found several of the stolen paintings, figurines and, thank you very much, most of my listed jewelry and jewels. He's denying everything of course but it's a solid case. The ownership of the stolen items is itemized and registered. They can't say they fell off the back of a truck." Carol was beaming.

"My dimwit beau was simply an anachronism. Apart from using the same story line for twenty years, he didn't keep up with the technology or his jets. He bought a smart phone without checking what it could do. He never pushed beyond his high school French from a few years in Canada when he was a kid. He counted on his good looks and smooth talk to charm his way through."

She shook her head ruefully. "I'll be the first to admit that his schtick worked. He reeled me in but good. Points for that. Would you believe he's actually trying to use his fingerprints as his alibi? He's told them, of course they would find his prints because he had officially visited the units as a potential buyer. He offered me as his proof. The man has balls, you have to give him that. When they linked him to heists in several other cities, all for listed properties going back several years, his story couldn't stand up. Apparently even his lawyer knew the game was up."

"I don't have any Dom Perignon but Ben, bring us up a bottle of Pinot. Carol, you may need to cab home or stay in the spare bedroom. I think this calls for a little celebration." Jennifer was thrilled at this news. How many women had the man conned. Given all the years he'd been running it, it had to be at least a hundred. And now, thanks to Ben's radar, he was shut down and would go to prison.

"Carol, you said something about a celebratory dinner when this was over? Let's get your jewels back and then we can celebrate. By the way, what the heck were you thinking buying a fifty thousand dollar diamond? Don't you have better things to do with your money?"

"I got carried away." Carol looked at them with new eyes. "When I see you all and the joy in your lives, I'm starting to wonder where my priorities have been lately. I used to think it was all about the fancy car, the million dollar condo, the next boy toy in my bed." She hung her head. "I needed this wake-up call. I've been a bitch to my kids for years. I have no idea if they even want me in their lives beyond the next check. Do you think there's any hope for me?" She looked so forlorn Jennifer felt immediate sympathy.

"They're your children. You've never abused them and you have supported them. Give them a chance and they'll be back. I'm sure of it."

Carol sighed mightily and stood up. "I think I have a lot of fence mending to do with my children, if they'll let me. I've only had two glasses of wine. I'm okay to drive home now. Thank you Jennifer for being the friend I've needed. Maybe not the one you deserved though. Once this is done we will have a celebratory dinner. Mark and Lana, you must come too. And Danny." She gathered up her purse.

"Jennifer, thank you. If it hadn't been for Ben, I don't know what would have happened."

"He would have left you to prey on the next agent." Jennifer walked her to the front door. Ben came up behind her and put his hands on her shoulders.

"As we say in my line of work, stay safe Carol."

"Stay safe and stay smart. Thank you again Ben."

They watched as Carol got into her car and backed out into the street.

"Think she's learned her lesson?" Ben massaged Jennifer's shoulders as they stood at the door.

"I think she's learned several." Jennifer sighed with pleasure as Ben kneaded the muscles. "Let's go back to the young people. After they leave I'm going for a bath."

"Care to share?" He playfully tickled her waist.

Going back out to the patio, Lana smiled up at them. "Mark has a great idea. Want to make it a double wedding?" Lana could imagine her new mother- and father-in-law being married the same day as she and Mark. "It would cut the planning and work in half."

"A double wedding. I think it's a wonderful idea if you don't mind having to share the spotlight." Jennifer knew Lana would steal the show no matter what she wore.

"We want it very simple and intimate. Just close friends and family. It will save everyone giving up two Saturdays. Ben what do you think?"

Ben laughed. "Count me in. One rehearsal. One speech. One day stuck in a suit. Works for me. How about you, son?"

Mark looked at these three people who were now his family and glanced back to his son Danny who was playing with Charlie. "I think it would be a great idea. Hope Danny can handle all the rings."

"So Mark." Jennifer smiled at her about to be son-in-law. "How would you feel about being a groom, a best man and the wedding singer?"

Now, read an excerpt from *New Beginnings,* the exciting sequel to *Winds of Change*

Chapter One

"DAMN. I DON'T HAVE TIME FOR THIS." Carol Brock stared down at her electric-blue BMW in dismay and growing anger. She'd been completely boxed in by a SUV on one side and a glossy black pickup on the other. Not a chance she could get in either the driver or passenger doors. *I'm supposed to show a house in thirty minutes, half way across town. I don't need this.* Then she saw her driver's side mirror and gasped. It was dangling on a couple of wires.

"What the hell?" Taking out her phone, she pressed on the camera app and started shooting. "Think you can get away with this? Think again."

She snapped the scene, the vehicles, and their license plates and sent the photos to someone she knew in the Boston Police, with the message: "Guzzo, you're my witness. I'm having the pickup towed out so I can get in my car."

As she called for roadside assistance, Carol stamped her feet to try and warm them. It was another cold, wet, gray November day. Gone were the sweet smells and vibrant colors of early fall. While her soft leather boots were beautiful and comfortable to walk in, they were not meant to stand around in. *I should call the Fowlers and let them know I'll be a bit late*, she thought and keyed in another number. *I can blame it on the traffic.*

The tow truck arrived. Within a few minutes, the driver had hitched up the gleaming black pickup and was pulling it onto the truck bed when a loud voice yelled over the grinding whine of the hydraulics.

"Whoa. Wait a minute. What do you think you're doing? Stop."

Carol turned to see a very tall, well-dressed man running across the parking lot. She stood her ground and watched his approach, with a smirk on her glossed lips. *Great eye candy, but boy, does he look angry. I might enjoy venting on such a magnificent male. If you're going to have a good mad on, might as well be mad at someone good looking.*

As he drew up beside her, Carol looked up into molten hazel eyes that were flashing with anger. She felt a small frisson of fear but brushed it aside. She already had a business card in her hand. Before he could say a word, she held it out to him.

"You ripped off my side mirror. Here's my card. I'd appreciate yours if you have one. You owe me for the mirror." She could almost feel the heat of his anger and swallowed a bit nervously. But adrenaline was coursing through her veins. Her emerald green eyes stared straight into his.

"My God, woman." He looked at her card. "*Carol Brock, real estate agent.* Well, you're a real piece of work, Ms. Brock, let me tell you. What gives you the right to move my truck? I could have you charged with theft."

"Go ahead and try. I've already sent photos to the police. I can prove you boxed me in and ripped off my mirror. I'm sure I can have you charged with something too."

"Well, I'll be damned. You don't miss a beat. Photos to the police already."

Carol watched in amazement as the flashing fire of anger was completely extinguished and replaced with mirth. She was sure the color of his eyes had changed in an instant. Now the brazen man was smiling and laughing at her. Her temper seethed as she fixed him with a look that only a mother could muster.

"I hardly think this is anything to laugh about." Her voice dripped with disdain as she fixed him with a steely gaze. "I have a full day ahead. You've thrown my entire schedule off, and you've damaged my car. I'm going to lose valuable time getting it fixed."

"Okay, Ms. Brock, mea culpa. I did park badly, but I didn't realize I'd damaged your car. Now I see that I have, and I'm making you late for your next appointment. Can't argue with you on any of those points. My name is Devin, Devin Elliott." He held out his hand, which now held a business card.

Carol took the card but refused the offer of a handshake. She couldn't argue with him. She swallowed her temper reluctantly.

"Devin Elliott, the architect." Carol knew the name. Anyone in Boston real estate circles knew Elliott and Co., Restoration Specialists. "Well then, at least I know you can afford to pay for the mirror. That honking big truck of yours was a pretty obvious clue, too. The mirror will cost at least eight hundred dollars. It's articulated, electronic, and heated." She looked at her phone. "Damn. I really am going to be late. I need to get going."

"Excuse me?" They both looked over as the tow truck driver leaned his head out of his window. "Where do you want the pickup, sir?"

"Just put it over there, please." Devin pointed towards the entrance of the lot and then turned back to Carol. "What do you say we get the tow truck to take your car to your dealership? I'll drive you to your next appointment if they don't have a loaner for you."

Carol snorted and put a hand up to smooth her coppery auburn waves. "I do not need a ride, and I am perfectly capable of handling this situation. You've been quite enough help already." She pulled up to her full height. Even with towering heels she couldn't look him straight in the eye. She thrust her chin up stubbornly.

He smiled down at her. "After seeing you in action just now, I'm quite convinced you can take care of just about anyone or anything. But I don't think your day will get any better driving around with your side mirror hanging off." Devin continued his delicate negotiations. "You'll just get stopped by the police, ticketed, and pulled off the road. Then you'll be calling for the tow guy again. He's already here. Why not take advantage of it and save some of that valuable time you just mentioned? Plus, we can get the estimate, and I can pay for it right then and there."

His small jab of sarcasm was not lost on her, but he did have a good point. "Oh, all right. I accept your offer." The driver agreed to switch the vehicles.

Devin walked over to the tow truck. Reaching into his pocket, he took out a thick wad of bills, peeled off a twenty, and handed it up to the surprised driver. "Thanks for taking care of this." He walked back to where Carol was stamping her feet again.

"This way, madam." He opened the passenger door of the pickup. "I still don't know how I managed to rip off your mirror without feeling or hearing anything. And I can't see any damage to my truck."

As they got in and buckled up, he turned the key in the ignition. The truck cab was immediately rocked with Aerosmith at a decibel level normally reserved for a concert hall. Devin winced and quickly turned it off. "Guess I know why now." He grinned sheepishly.

"Thanks for turning it off." Carol wasn't ready for loud music or conversation. "Just drive, please. I need to call my client, re-schedule our meeting, and probably several more."

After programming his GPS, Devin pulled into the steady stream of traffic and headed towards Carol's dealership.

She made a number of quick calls to rearrange her schedule and confirm a loaner. After making a couple of call-backs, she closed the phone and gazed around her, somewhat more confident about the day ahead. The truck smelled new but with another very faint scent. It wasn't a perfume smell. It was more a slight musk. It made her think of the horses and riding stables, where she'd spent many happy Saturdays as a teen. Looking at his expensive tailored clothes, she found it hard to imagine him mucking about in a stable. But then people probably wouldn't imagine it of her either.

"Devin, first an apology and then my thanks for your offer. I was seeing red when I couldn't get into the car. When I saw the mirror, I was totally pissed off." She looked over at her chauffeur, noting his chiselled jaw line and what she could only describe as sculpted ears. "I don't usually have such a wicked temper."

"Could've fooled me." Devin drawled out the statement while signalling a lane change. "From what I saw, you've had some practice I'd say."

"I've been told I have a few control issues." Carol pursed her lips and smiled faintly. "Okay, maybe more than a few." Being driven around by someone else was a whole new sensation. She always drove herself and almost never took a taxi. She felt herself relaxing even as she wondered how she was going to get everything done for today.

"Feel free to put Aerosmith back on. I'm pretty partial to *Dream On*."

"I'd rather talk to you. By the way, are you free for dinner tonight? It's the least I can do after throwing your whole day out of whack." Devin smiled and glanced sideways at her.

"Thanks for the invitation, but I have a class I don't want to miss this evening."

"Some other time, then. I'd like to make it up to you other than just paying for the mirror. You have lost valuable time. I know how I would feel."

"It's really not necessary." Carol felt her good angel warning her not to fall for yet another good-looking man. She wanted to swat her away but remembered her promise to herself. "I appreciate you taking me to the dealership and agreeing to pay for the mirror. That'll be fine."

"I'm crushed." Devin hung his head down in a gesture of dejection, but he was still smiling. "I don't often get turned down for dinner by beautiful women."

Carol smiled and looked again at his handsome profile. "There's a lot going on in my life right now. Let's leave it at that." She turned to look out the passenger window. Damn the good angel. She wouldn't shut up.

"I was only talking about a simple meal. No big deal." Devin shrugged and drove on in silence. He signaled his turn to the exit nearest the dealership.

Carol went to register for the mirror replacement. She wasn't surprised when the clerk estimated over a thousand dollars with the labor. What did surprise her was her reaction. *It's just a damn mirror,* she thought. *When did I start to need a car with thousand dollar mirrors?* She shook her head to clear it.

Carol watched as Devin pulled out a charge card and chatted with the parts clerk as she processed his payment. She smiled sardonically as the young woman blushed prettily when Devin complimented her on her earrings. *What a shameless flirt*, she thought. *Why do men like him feel this need to hit on every good-looking woman they see?* She let go an exasperated sigh and wandered into the showroom.

"It's all paid for." Devin came up behind her. "Carol, I really hope you'll reconsider my dinner invitation. I do feel badly about the damage."

She turned to face him, her face a neutral mask. Now that she'd put him in the player category, she really didn't want to bother with dinner no matter how handsome he might be. She knew his type. He was nothing but trouble. "As I said, it's really not necessary. It was nice meeting you, in an awkward kind of way. I'd better get going. Take care." Carol put out her hand. She was all business. After a quick handshake, she turned and walked back to the service area.

Carol plowed through the rest of her day with a zeal that surprised even her. Despite the morning debacle with her car, she managed three showings and helped two other clients put together offers of purchase. By six o'clock, she was primed for her yoga class, ready to call it a day.

"Have you heard of Devin Elliott, the architect who restores old heritage properties?" Carol stood next to her friend Jennifer and stretched gratefully as they finished their session. The tension had drained from her body even as her muscles received a powerful workout.

"Actually, I have. His firm handled one of the houses down the street from me. Brought the house back up to code, re-did a roofline, and found replicas of the antique windows to replace the originals. Everyone in the neighborhood was impressed. You met him?"

"In a manner of speaking. He parked too close beside me at the bank and tore my mirror off. I couldn't get into the Bimmer, so I had him towed out. He ended up driving me to the dealership. Long story short, he paid over a thousand dollars." Carol took a long drink from her water bottle.

"Sounds like he did the right thing all around. What did you think of him?"

"He asked me out for dinner, but I said no. My attractive-man-meter hit the top with a major whammy. But, I don't need another entanglement with a cute guy. I'm still trying to sort out the mess Michel left me in. My reputation took a huge hit when the con story and trial hit the news." Carol shook her head and took a deep, slow breath. "Several clients demanded I be taken off their listing."

"I remember that very well." Jennifer picked up her mat. "But Devin Elliott is well-known and respected."

"I know, but you know my track record with handsome charming men."

"So you attracted Lance the leech and Michel the con artist. You're a high-profile, successful professional who happens to be quite good-looking. It was probably just a matter of time until some criminal tried to profit from your contacts and clients. With social media, you're very visible. Maybe too visible?"

Carol loosened her pony tail and fluffed out her hair, preening just slightly at Jennifer's compliment. "That visibility is important to my work. Being a successful agent is all about networking and visibility. I suppose you're right about Devin being well-known and respected professionally. But he's still a flirt. He had the clerk at the dealership blushing. I'm not ready to get involved with a man with major magnetism, who clearly knows how to use it.

"Besides, I've gotten used to being alone this past year. There's no drama. Other than spending time, when I can, with Ash and Jim, I've pretty much kept to myself. A lot of people I thought were my friends disappeared after the art theft story broke."

"Well, you've still got Ben and I. Speaking of which, we've finally set a date for the double wedding. Lana didn't want to get married while she was pregnant. You need to keep next May twenty-fifth open.

We want you to be our witness."

"That's wonderful news!" Carol gave Jennifer a warm hug. "Let me book it in right now." Carol fished her tablet out of her bag and blocked off the full day and the day before. "My personal wedding gift to you—the day before the ceremony we get our hair done and have a manicure, pedicure, and facial. What do you say? My treat. Get you all primed for a wild wedding night with your husband." Carol cocked her eyebrows as a wicked grin played across her lips.

"That's no cheap gift, Carol. Are you sure?"

"It's my way of saying thanks for not calling me the matron of honor. I'm not ready to see myself as a matron, even if my kids are in their twenties."

"We thought witness was more contemporary." Jennifer chuckled. "And no, I could never see you as a matron. Many other things, but never a matron."

"And what other things would those be?"

"Sexy cougar, for one."

"A few months ago, yes, for sure. Now, no." Carol tossed her water bottle into a turquoise blue tote as they prepared to head back to Jennifer's for dinner. "Now I'm focusing on being a good mother. Jim and Ashley still aren't sure if I'm sincere about being interested in their lives. I got pretty wrapped up in my career and a parade of men during their later teen years."

"And got them both to college. They can depend on you a lot more than their deadbeat dad."

"That's for sure. Did I tell you he completely forgot to send even a check to Ash or Jim for their birthdays? I couldn't believe it. He has a wife. He has assistants and a private secretary. What does it take to put the date in your agenda?"

"What was his excuse?"

"Said he forgot. That with the new baby, he and Charlene don't have a routine. Yadda, yadda, yadda." As they strolled across the parking lot, Carol tried mightily to retain the Zen feeling from yoga. It was fizzling fast thinking of her ex.

"I almost feel sorry for Charlene. Gord hasn't changed his stripes one bit. He was like this during our entire marriage. Funny thing? When he was courting, he didn't forget anything. That razor-sharp lawyer mind retained it all. First date, first kiss, first roll in the hay. He remembered the day, date, time, and year. Forget something? Not Gordon Brock. Mind like a steel trap."

As they reached their cars, a bitter cold drizzle had started. "Let's go get some warm food and a glass of wine. Ben is organizing dinner."

"Sounds wonderful. I'll follow you." Carol threw her bag and mat into the back seat, got in, and started the loaner.

"WE'RE HOME." They came in through Jennifer's back patio door to the kitchen, which was redolent with fragrant aromas. A flurry of excited dog came scrabbling across the ceramic floor to greet them.

"Hey Charlie." Jennifer scratched the dog's ears before walking to the counter where Ben stood making a salad. "I thought we were having leftovers."

"Hi sweetie. Thought I'd surprise you with a Ben Powell special." He leaned down and planted a loud kiss on Jennifer's head. "Hi Carol. Let's get you two ladies a glass of wine. It's pretty cold and damp out there. I'm sure you need some fortification."

Ben poured each a generous glass as they took off their outer wear. Carol wandered over to the stove, lifted the lid off one pot, and rolled her eyes in ecstasy.

"Oh my. That smells absolutely heavenly."

"It's my Vietnamese green curry. The vegetables are about to go in. Have a seat, and we can talk while I prepare."

Carol and Jennifer sat at the kitchen table to keep Ben company and stay close to the aromatic smells. Looking into the dining room, Carol saw the table was set with a damask tablecloth, tall candles, water glasses, and shining cutlery. "This sure beats the heck out of going back to my condo to eat takeout at my kitchen counter."

"Carol had a little run-in with Devin Elliott this morning." Jennifer sipped her wine appreciatively. "He's the architect who oversaw the remodeling at Gerry and Ellen's old place."

"Run-in?" Ben drained the steamed vegetables and added them to the curry.

"I'll let Carol tell you. It gets better with the telling." Jennifer grinned devilishly. "We can embellish this to the point where he totaled the Bimmer. Just need to work on it a bit more. Over to you, Carol."

Carol filled him in with delight. "I have to admit, I was so totally pissed off at the situation I let him have it. I gave him the look, too."

"Not The Look?" Jennifer's eyes widened. "That poor man. I'm surprised he wasn't reduced to a smoldering puddle on the ground."

"No, he was actually laughing at me, which just made me angrier."

"He laughed at you? Poor guy." Ben rolled his eyes as a smile played around his lips.

"Then he admitted it was all his fault, that I was right, and he would pay for everything. Took the wind out of my temper sails. What a frustrating man." Carol smiled just slightly as she remembered being bested in the fair fight department.

"He asked her out for dinner, and she said no." Jennifer breathed in the fragrant scents in her kitchen. "She actually turned down one of the most eligible bachelors in Boston. I don't think he's ever been married. I seem to recall he was engaged."

"I remember now. His fiancée was found murdered. That was years ago. She was an up-and-coming lawyer." Carol said. "That must have been so heartbreaking for him."

"Okay ladies, let's move to the dining room. Dinner is ready."

Carol and Jennifer strolled, arm in arm, into the dining room and got comfortable as Ben served. Both men were forgotten as they tasted the silky green curry that was now swimming with tofu, broccoli, cauliflower, bamboo shoots, red pepper, celery, and baby corn on a bed of Jasmine rice. Ben produced a fine Pinot Grigio, and the three friends tucked in to their meal.

"Thanks so much for a very, very fine dinner, Ben." Carol slipped one arm into her leather jacket as Ben held it for her. "After the car issue this morning, I figured my whole day would go to hell in a hand basket. But it's turned out to be a great day, capped off by your sublime curry. I don't think I've ever tasted better. Would you consider catering a dinner party for me?"

"Don't think I want to get into catering, Carol. But thanks for the vote. I'm really into my memoir writing now. Cooking is a way for me to take a break and let my mind work on remembering some of my journalistic escapades over the past three decades."

Carol checked herself in the hall mirror, gave a little extra tilt to her hat, and hugged Jennifer and Ben. "Great evening, you two. Next time, it's my treat."

"What restaurant did you have in mind?" Jennifer smiled indulgently at the offer.

"Okay. Maybe, I could just order in at my place."

"Maybe, you could just come here again. Bring Ashley or Jim, the next time one or both are in town."

"Which would just confirm to both of them that I'm not much of a cook." Carol laughed merrily. "Thanks for your help there, Jen."

"We'll figure out some way to rehabilitate you as a mother figure." Jennifer was enjoying seeing Carol returning to her motherly ways. It was a far cry from the friend she had known even just a year ago.

"I sure need all the help I can get. Must tell you, today, when they gave me that thousand dollar plus estimate for a bloody side mirror, I found myself wondering why I even drive a car that expensive. Can you believe it? I'm actually questioning my—dare I say it— extravagant lifestyle. Tell me I'm sane and not going through a midlife crisis."

"Carol, what you're going through is a re-evaluation of what's important in life." Ben put a hand on her shoulder. "I went through it last year, big time. After decades of jet-setting around the world, chasing the latest headlines, I finally realized that knowing my son and being part of his life was way more important than making big bucks and trying to figure out where to spend them. If that's a midlife crisis, then we all need one. Right, Jennifer?"

She smiled and nodded. "Carol, what I see now is a woman who's facing her demons head-on and trying her very best to make amends to her daughter and son. You're absolutely sane, my friend. And I love you for it." Jennifer put her hands on Carol's shoulders. "You're doing what you need to do to get your kids back and get your life back. Just keep on."

It wasn't the wine, but Carol found her eyes welling with tears. These were her real friends. She was determined to get a real life back, including her wonderful daughter and son.

"Thank you, Jennifer, and you too, Ben. I don't know where I'd be without you two." Carol walked out to the loaner, shivering slightly in the damp, cold air.

While the car was warming up, she retrieved a text message from Ashley confirming her arrival time at the airport and smiled. *I'm so glad she's coming home for Thanksgiving. I need to think of something to make Christmas memorable this year,* she mused. *We need to build some new family traditions that get beyond splashing money around and eating in restaurants.*

As she drove home, she turned over different ideas. *Maybe I could book a ski holiday in Vermont. I don't ski but there must be other things I could do. Or a cruise. Never been on one of those.* Then it hit her. *About time I worked on some of my control issues,* she realized. *Maybe I should just ask Ash and Jim what they'd like to do for Christmas. They're both adults.*

She arrived home a few minutes later and texted her kids as she walked into the living room and turned up the lights. "Hi guys. Need to get a plan together for Christmas. What do you say we get out of Boston? Any ideas?"

There, I did it. I didn't go into control mode. Good girl, she thought, looking out over Boston's sparkling nightscape. *I'm sure there's hope for me yet.*

CPSIA information can be obtained at www.ICGtesting.com
Printed in the USA
LVOW100524080513

332721LV00002B/10/P